Black Quill Winner: Editors' Choice-Best Dark Genre Fiction Collection

The Haunted Heart
and Other Tales
by Jameson Currier

I0678417

Twelve stories of gay men and the memories that haunt them.

Jameson Currier modernizes the traditional ghost story with gay lovers, loners, activists, and addicts, blending history and contemporary issues of the gay community with the unexpected of the supernatural.

"Jameson Currier's *The Haunted Heart and Other Tales* expands upon the usual ghost story tropes by imbuing them with deep metaphorical resonance to the queer experience. Infused with flawed, three-dimensional characters, this first-rate collection strikes all the right chords in just the right places. Equal parts unnerving and heartrending, these chilling tales are testament to Currier's literary prowess and the profound humanity at the core of his writing. Gay, straight, twisted like a pretzel… his writing is simply not to be missed by any reader with a taste for good fiction."
    Vince Liaguno, *Dark Scribe Magazine*

"I am completely amazed by the range of ghost stories in this collection. These are awesome ghost stories, and the literary connections to gay life are deep and complex."
    Chad Helder, *Unspeakable Horror* and *The Pop-Up Book of Death*

"Currier's characters are sumptuous, his plots are freshly twisted and his prose magnificent. A perfectly chilling collection of tales from one of the modern masters of the genre. Powerful stuff, indeed."
    Jerry Wheeler, *Out in Print*

"Jameson Currier is a story teller who weaves his tale around you until you genuinely care about the characters. He has the ability to capture dialogue with an almost journalistic objectivity; this places you in the scene as an eavesdropper, making you part of the story. He is one of the few writers who can be equally literary, erotic, dramatic and damn funny, sometimes all in the same sentence. His collection of ghost stories, *The Haunted Heart*, allows him to showcase these abilities in original stories that are not intended to frighten so much as entertain. There are a multitude of ghosts here, not just the spirits of the dead that you would expect, but the ghosts of abusive relationships, bad decisions, personal flaws, and the ever-present ghost of AIDS that forever hovers in the lives of gay men."
    Sean Meriwether, author of *The Silent Hustler*

"Currier's writing is flawless and his knack for conveying emotion, with both the spoken words and thoughts of his characters, is unparalleled. Fans of the author have come to expect that his work isn't exactly light or escapist, which makes it all the more affecting."
    Chris Verleger, *Edge*

The Haunted Heart
and Other Tales

JAMESON CURRIER

Chelsea Station Editions
New York

Book design by Peachboy Distillery & Designs with assistance from John Malloy and Toby Johnson

Cover painting by Richard Taddei
Author photo by Jack Slomovits

Originally published by Lethe Press 2009

Published by Chelsea Station Editions
362 West 36th Street, Suite 2R
New York, NY 10018
www.chelseastationeditions.com
info@chelseastationeditions.com

ISBN: 978-0-9832851-9-9
Library of Congress Control Number: 2012948809

Some of the stories in this work were originally published, some in different versions, in the following: "The Woman in the Window" first appeared in *All Hallows, The Journal of the Ghost Story Society* and was reprinted in *Wilde Stories 2008: The Best of the Year's Gay Speculative Fiction*. "The Country House" first appeared in *Best Gay Romance*. "The Haunted Heart" first appeared in *CreamDrops Literary Journal*. "The Theater Bug" was reprinted in *Best Gay Stories 2010*. "Death in Amsterdam" was reprinted in *Wilde Stories 2010*. "Wait!" first appeared in *Velvet Mafia*. "The Man in the Mirror" first appeared in *Icarus*. "The Bloomsbury Nudes" first appeared in *Unspeakable Horror: From the Shadows of the Closet* and was reprinted in *Wilde Stories 2009: The Best of the Year's Gay Speculative Fiction*, and *Art from Art*.

CONTENTS

To the living and the lost

INTRODUCTION

When many of my freelance and book reviewing outlets disappeared in the wake of 9/11, I turned to idea of writing genre fiction—mystery, horror, science fiction, and fantasy short stories—the kind of stories I have enjoyed reading since I was a boy. I started by re-reading many of the anthologies that were still on my bookshelf—books that I had transported over the years from my parents' house in the South to my tiny Manhattan apartment because I cherished them—collections like *Alfred Hitchcock Presents Twelve Stories for Late at Night*, *Night in Funland and Other Stories*, and *Some Things Fierce and Fatal*.

Though I outlined ideas for a few science fiction and mystery stories, the first story I began to write was a ghost story about a haunted snow globe—a natural choice for me because a) I collected snow globes from around the world and it was an obvious place to start—write about something you know and love, and b) because I'd written a "sort of" ghost story years before—in the mid-1980s. I say "sort of" because that story, "Ghosts," which was included in my first collection of short stories, *Dancing on the Moon*, was an exploration of a young man who summons up the ghost of his recently departed lover as a way to overcome the grief of losing him to AIDS. At the time I wrote that story a close friend of mine had been diagnosed as HIV-positive (then, in those years, equivalent to a death sentence), and on our trips together to the library while he researched details on a famous British mathematician (he was a devoted Anglophile and at work on a play), I searched through books on myths and folklore for metaphors that reflected how I was feeling and discovered a Danish superstition about ghosts. "Ghosts," which incorporates that superstition (that ghosts cannot cross water), was also one of the first short stories I wrote about AIDS.

Because of the impact AIDS has had on my generation of gay men, a further exploration of ghost stories seemed a natural route for me to take as a writer. But by 2001, I was also trying to consciously move away from being labeled "only an AIDS writer"—by then, the cocktail drug therapy had changed the nature of the disease to become something more manageable—and I had, in fact, specifically written more romantic and erotic short stories in an attempt to keep up with the changing dynamics of popular culture and the gay community.

But I was still a haunted man. I had lost too many friends and lovers and coworkers to not write about AIDS. AIDS was always at the basis of my consciousness and my reason for writing, but in an effort to address other issues of importance to the gay community, I started by making lists.

My first list was of issues currently relevant to gay men—topics like substance abuse, gay marriage, serving in the military, domestic abuse in gay relationships, hate crimes, homophobia, and living outside of urban areas. Another list was of great ghost stories I had found on the Internet—works by M.R. James, Henry James, E.F. Benson, Edith Wharton, and Ambrose Bierce, to name a few. I wanted to read and study their structure and see if there was a way I could incorporate contemporary gay issues within the format of a traditional ghost story. And I also needed a more concrete set of rules on how and why ghosts appear and are used in fiction. And along the way I discovered I had to make a few of my own decisions about ghosts—did I believe in them and how did they fit in with my faith and contemporary religions? How did metaphysics incorporate a supernatural world? Was I a skeptic or a believer of the afterlife?

And then two things happened simultaneously. My computer broke down and the holidays arrived and I went to spend some time with my parents in north Georgia. And there, on the shelf of books I had read as a boy but had failed to carry northward, was *Famous Ghost Stories*, edited by Bennett Cerf. By the time I had finished reading "The Mezzotint" by M.R. James I had the idea for "The Woman in the Window," my tale about a haunted snow globe. I wrote my first draft in longhand in my boyhood bedroom on scraps of wrapping paper I had used for Christmas presents to my nephews and nieces.

The next ghost story did not come as easily, or, rather, it came as easily but I fretted over it because it was an AIDS story. "The Haunted Heart" poured out as fluidly as my haunted snow globe tale had once I discovered the facts about the gale of 1841 that had pounded Cape Cod and I had devised the way a deceased sea captain could haunt a contemporary gay couple.

As more ghost stories arrived—some spontaneously, some through many drafts over several years—each tale an attempt to be different than the one I had previously completed, I fretted over other concerns: Should I incorporate more horror into my ghost stories—both physical and psychological? How much fear and suspense should I include? How do I keep my gay characters grounded in reality? How do I avoid the stereotypes of gay villains? Should I keep these tales gay-positive? I've always been the sort of writer who wanted to present positive images of gay life even when characters are flawed and challenged—I'm of that generation of gay men who wanted to see ourselves reflected in our literature and entertainment as normal guys and accepted members of society—and I had always been troubled by the earlier depictions of evil gay antagonists in Hollywood movies and the gay villains of fiction. Conflict in my fiction had always arrived naturally, via relationships, illness, desires, and character personalities.

And as I wrote more questions arrived. What should my characters learn from a haunting? I have always written characters who reach a moment of insight where something is learned about themselves or of their world—how do I sustain this in a ghost story? How do I move between historical and contemporary scenes? How do I incorporate the back story of the ghosts and could I find a relevant gay back story to use? And did I want my ghosts to be malevolent spirits? M.R. James had noted that this was the first and foremost rule for telling a ghost story—there was no room for amiable spirits—but thankfully not every writer of ghost stories before and since has adhered to this dictum. Ghosts, in my opinion, operate on many levels—as haunters or protectors and sometimes as both, and once I had come to this conclusion it became an important principle for my own stories.

The results are the twelve ghost stories that follow in this collection, written, re-written, and polished over a period of eight years. I hope that they will entertain—that some may scare or cause anxiety, some will amuse, some will enlighten, some might raise your consciousness or trouble your subconscious, and some may leave you wondering how to handle your own haunted heart.

Jameson Currier
September 2009

The life of the dead is placed in the memory of the living.
—Cicero

THE WOMAN IN THE WINDOW

I'd started collecting the snow globes during a summer abroad in Europe before my senior year in college. I didn't have room in my backpack for the usual souvenirs—beer steins, ashtrays, paperweights in the shape of the Eiffel Tower or the Coliseum, so I picked up a plastic snow globe in Frankfurt because it was cheap and small and light, and then got another one at the train station in Munich, then another in Vienna, and a few more in Venice, Florence, and Rome. By the time I was at the airport to return home, I had a dozen that I carried safely on board the plane in a plastic shopping bag. After then, whenever I traveled, I continued to pick up a snow globe as a souvenir—sometimes by special design at a hotel or museum gift shop, other times hurriedly at the last minute as I was running to the airport gate to make a flight. By the time Allan and I set up house together I had collected more than two hundred snow globes and when we adopted our son Justin I began to bring them back as gifts for him. At eight, his own collection exceeded more than a hundred and included snow globes from as far away as Tokyo, where I had gone one year for an economics conference.

I'd picked up this particular snow globe during a road trip upstate—my uncle had passed away and I had braved the bad winter weather alone on a four-hour drive to attend the funeral and check up on my parents. Allan had stayed home with the two children—his own job in the city and the kids' school schedules made it too difficult to take the whole family for a midweek outing such as this. The services were somber and respectful, as they usually were in my family, and by the time I left my parents' house for the drive back to my home, the icy rain had turned to snow. The drive was slow and exhausting—I'd had to concentrate harder because of the slippery and icy patches, so I stopped at a village midway through the trip that Allan liked to shop at when we made the trip with the kids in the warmer, summer months. It was a cluster of gingerbread Victorian houses and shops and restaurants, a mix of retail outlets, craft stores, and antique shops, nestled in a small valley among the mountains. The kids particularly liked the more unusual stores—the kite shop, the chocolaterie, and the toy store filled with nearly every kind of stuffed animal imaginable. I'd only stopped at the village to fill up the gas tank and stretch, but decided to eat something at the coffee shop and afterward stopped in the store next door, an antique shop full of eccentric and unusual curiosities, which is where I found the snow globe.

It was made of glass, not plastic, like a few of my special ones were—the one I had picked up in Aspen, the one my sister had brought back from Manhattan, and the one Allan and I got on our first vacation together in Mexico. This snow globe featured a ceramic Queen Anne Victorian house designed like many found in this village, a set of stairs leading up to a large front porch and a blue-painted front door with a stained glass window. The trim of the bay windows and gingerbread latticework were also painted in the same soft blue color, but the wood of the upper floors was of a deeper tone, and the dark gabled roof and black shingling gave the house a strong silhouette. But it wasn't the house that I first noticed when I spotted the globe sitting on a table next to a stack of leather-bound books, but the flakes of snow stirring in the water; before I even reached out to pick it up and shake it, the snowflakes were swirling as if the globe contained its own storm.

I hesitated to purchase it. Allan disliked me bringing back glass-domed snow globes for the kids—the last one I had brought back from the Smithsonian had dropped and shattered in less than fifteen minutes back in the house and months later he was still finding little specs of glitter, which had been in the water, on the carpet. But I knew Justin would like it and so I bought it, and gave it to my son when I reached home, with a warning to be careful with it—he should find a permanent place for it and let it stay there and not keep picking it up. He took to it right away, calling it both "cool" and "spooky." I'd arrived back home close to his bedtime, and he ignored the TV to study the snow and the three-story painted house. He placed the globe on a lower shelf of the bookshelf in the dining room, where he could sit on the rug and stare at it, much to the displeasure of Allan, who always liked to think that that room of the house was off limits except for special occasions. But the box of chocolates I had also stopped to purchase for Allan, along with the small stuffed toy turtle I found for Claire, our five-year-old daughter, smoothed out my partner's cranky disposition.

"Tom, did you see the lady in the top window?" my son asked while Allan told me to get him upstairs and ready for bed. Justin was on his knees, his eyes close to the glass and from where I stood in the doorway the snowflakes swirled steadily inside as if cast by an enchanted spell.

"What lady?" I asked, leaning down over him. I vaguely remembered seeing something different about one of the upstairs windows when I had picked up the globe in the antique shop—a faint glow, as if there were a table lamp or candle inside the room.

"On the second floor," Justin said. "You can see her dress."

I looked at the upper floors of the house through the swirling snow and Justin tapped the glass globe lightly with a finger where he had seen the shape of the woman. At the end of a row of darkened windows there was one that was distinctly white, and in the background of the room was the silhouette of a woman's dress. "There's someone beside her, too," I said. Another small form was barely discernible, as if it were a child's head.

"Where?" Justin asked. He looked deeper into the water and the snow and the house. He sighed when he spotted the smaller figure, then said, "No, there's two kids. She's got two kids beside her. Maybe she's putting them to bed."

That was my cue to become a father myself, urging Justin to go upstairs to bed, but instead I looked into the snow to find the three figures. "What makes the snow move so fast?" Justin asked me.

"You must have hit it," I said.

Justin protested, saying he hadn't touched it at all. The snow was falling on its own. This was when I told him it was past his bedtime, and I followed him upstairs to his room, kissed him good-night, and checked on Claire in her bedroom. She was already asleep in one of her awkward, contorted positions, half on and half off the bed. I was the last to go to bed that night—I watched the late news and Leno's monologue, then made sure the front and back doors were locked, the security system was activated, and all the lights were off, and went upstairs. It had been Allan's idea to adopt children and move to the suburbs to better raise them, and at first our presence in the neighborhood had unsettled a few of our stodgier neighbors. We'd suffered through a period of egged cars and flattened mailboxes. But we weathered that as we often weathered the bad weather, though I'd always found it queer that I was more suspicious of everything living here, in middle-class America, than I had ever been on my own in a two-room tenement in the downtown gay ghetto.

In the bedroom, Allan was sleeping on his side, and I settled in around him and fell easily asleep. It wasn't much later—or seemed to be not much later—that I heard a noise downstairs. It sounded like the back door of the house opening and shutting—the particular sounding whumpf that door had. Our house was a typical kind of suburban ranch style—a long first floor leading to a staircase and a smaller second floor with bedrooms and baths. Next I heard the kitchen floor creak like it always does when there's too much weight passing on top of the floorboards. I lay still, trying to imagine if it could be one of the kids. Lately, they had become sound sleepers, not waking up during the night, and whenever they did, whenever they were scared or hungry or not feeling well, they came to our bedroom first, never going downstairs to the kitchen. When the idea occurred to me that we might be being robbed, I began to think of what kind of defense I might have upstairs to use against intruders—an industrial flashlight that I kept in the closet, a blow-dryer in the shape of a gun, the ceramic base of the lamp on the table beside the bed. I got up and easily found the flashlight on the closet floor, then went to the hallway to listen more closely.

The sound had stopped and I waited a minute before heading downstairs. I made my steps on the staircase heavy and noisy; in case there were intruders, my goal was not to surprise them but to make them flee. I walked heavily into the family room, where only a few minutes earlier I had been watching TV, and flipped on the overhead light, but found no one, and nothing was disturbed. Then I went into the kitchen to check the back door.

I found no one in the house, nor anything suspicious that might convince me that there had been intruders—the back door was safely locked, the sliding glass door which led to the outside patio was locked and closed, the house's security system was still on and armed. As I was turning out the downstairs lights to return upstairs, I stopped in to check on the status of the living room and dining room. No one was there, either, though when I entered the dining room I felt a sudden blast of cold air, as if a window was open. Outside there was a howling winter wind, and I rationalized a good strong gust must have hit the house and unsettled the back door, the kitchen floor, and the air in the dining room. I checked the windows but they were all securely closed and locked, and then I went back upstairs. As I was passing by Justin's room, I thought I heard him crying. I stopped and looked in—he was sleeping on his side but trying to say something in his sleep, which sounded like whining. He awoke just as I came toward him.

"You're okay," I said, reaching out to my son. "It must have been a bad dream."

"I saw a woman," he said. "She was trying to say something to me but she couldn't—she had holes in her face."

"It was just a bad dream," I said again.

I waited till Justin was calm and back asleep and then I checked on

Claire and went into my bedroom. Allan was sleeping in the same position Justin had been in and now he was mumbling something in his sleep. He awoke as I slipped into the bed.

"What is it?" I asked him.

He looked at me as if I had been in his dream, too. "Just a dream," he said. "I thought there was a woman in our room."

"A woman?" I asked him. "What kind of woman?"

"She had a strange face," Allan said. "Full of holes."

I didn't say anything about Justin having had the same dream. In fact, I was a little slow in connecting the two similar nightmares—by now I was relieved that there was no intruder in the house and tired and exhausted and thinking how I would feel the next day at work if I didn't get to sleep soon. I didn't even tell Allan that I had gotten up because I had suspected there was an intruder in the house. "It was just a dream," I said to him. "I have to get some sleep or it will be hell tomorrow."

In the morning I found Justin sitting on the floor of the dining room, looking at our newest snow globe again. "They're gone," he said when he saw me standing at the doorway watching him. "The lady and the two kids."

"It must have been the snow," I said. "Or maybe there was something stuck to the side of the house. Some of the old globes have dust in the water. Maybe it was just dust."

In the kitchen I found Allan in a particularly agitated mood. "I didn't sleep well last night," he said. "I kept having that same dream over and over."

I thought he was going to say something about the woman with the holes in her face, but he said, instead, "I kept trying to get to Justin and Claire and I couldn't. I couldn't seem to get to them, even though they were near me. They were frightened and I knew something was going to harm them." He sighed, and then yelled to Justin in the other room. "If you don't eat something right now, young man, I'm not going to put any cookies in your lunch bag."

I left Allan to find Claire in the den watching TV. She was half-dressed in her pajamas and school outfit and talking to the rag doll she had in her lap. Our morning routine was that I would get Claire ready and Allan would tend to Justin, our more hyperactive child. I would drop off Claire at kindergarten, a longer drive, and Allan would take Justin to the elementary school on the corner. Two kids, two cars, two parents—each with their own destination.

"Who are you talking to?" I asked Claire when I turned off the TV.

"Sally said she had a doll just like this," Claire said.

"Who's Sally?" I asked.

"Ben's sister," Claire answered.

"Who's Ben?"

Claire laughed as I lifted her off the floor and carried her in my arms out of the room. "He's Sally's brother!" she squealed.

On the drive to Claire's school she continued to talk to her imaginary friends. She was in the backseat of the car, bundled up in a puffy pink coat and ski cap and buckled into a car seat so I could see her through my rearview mirror.

"Where did you meet Ben and Sally?" I asked Claire.

She giggled again and said, "They're waiting for their mommie!"

"Their mommie?" I echoed from the front seat. "Where's their mommie?"

"She went to look for the other mommie!"

"Oh," I answered her, as if it all made sense.

At the school, Claire asked me if it was okay for Ben and Sally to wait in the car for their mommies. I tried not to show my annoyance—I thought this silliness had gone far enough, but I didn't want to scold Claire and send her off to school agitated. "Sure, they can wait," I said.

"They said it's safe in the car," Claire said while I was unbuckling her from the car seat and helping her to the ground. "They don't think the bogeymen will find them in the car."

"The bogeymen?"

"Yes," Claire said. "That's where their other mommie went—to find the bogeymen."

"That's enough, Claire," I finally said, and we walked together into the school building. "Don't worry about Ben and Sally," I said when we had reached the door of her classroom. I had had a change of heart about the imaginary friends—or, rather, I had stumbled into the mental conundrum of what exactly a parent should say to a child who had an imaginary friend. I thought that perhaps the gentler approach was a better one. "Don't try to eat the crayons," I said next, as if I had to find something parental to say.

"We're not coloring today," she said.

I kissed her on the top of the head, watched her enter the classroom, and then walked back to my car. For a moment I expected to find Ben and Sally seated and waiting for me, but by the time I reached the highway I had forgotten about my daughter's friends, thinking, instead, of the confrontations ahead in the office.

When I got home from work that evening, Justin was again in front of the new snow globe in the dining room.

"Somebody's on the steps," Justin said.

"What do you mean?" I asked him. My tone was short and annoyed. I had had a stressful day grappling with an analyst's report that had been released that morning, and it had affected my work schedule and meetings throughout the day—one person after the next complaining about the report.

"There's two guys on the steps that go up to the front door," he said. "They look like they're carrying guns or something."

I loosened my necktie and squatted beside my son, looking over his shoulder and into the glass globe. Sure enough, barely visible through the snow, there were two tiny figures waiting on the steps of the house and carrying something in their arms. "Looks like rakes," I said. "Or brooms. They were probably there yesterday and we just didn't see them."

"They weren't there yesterday," my son protested. "I know they weren't there yesterday."

I watched the swirling snow inside the globe. Neither of us had touched it and I felt the defensive pang of a parent confronted with something he knew he could not explain. "Go wash your hands," I said to my son. "Allan's ready for supper."

At the dinner table there was no further discussion about the globe, the two strange men, Claire's imaginary friends, the bogeymen, or the nightmare woman with holes in her head. Allan had turned on the TV that sat on the counter and the kids sat watching a program of funny home video clips. Tomorrow was Saturday and Allan was eager to find some activity to keep the kids occupied—we were in the lull between the end of the winter session of karate and ballet classes and the beginning of the spring ones.

"The weather's supposed to be lousy," I said. "We could take them to the movies."

Allan mentioned that he would check the movie schedules and then added he might take Justin to get new shoes—he was close to growing out of the new ones he had gotten a few months ago.

After dinner, Justin found me in the den reading the newspaper. "They're at the door," he yelled at me. "The two guys are at the door now."

"It must be a piece of dust that's floating around," I said.

"No, Tom, come check it out," he said. "They're there. At the door. And they both have guns."

The tone of his voice both alarmed and irritated me. "Justin, if you keep this up, I'm going to have to put it away."

He seemed to take note of my annoyance—finally, I acted and sounded like a parent, the kind of parent I never wanted to be. I remembered my father displaying the same behavior toward me when I was a kid and he didn't want to be disturbed. I tried to find a better way out of it and be a better father to my children. "Why don't you and Claire watch one of your videos?" I said to him.

My suggestion worked. Justin abandoned the snow globe and the kids watched *Monsters, Inc.* for the three-hundredth time, then Allan and I settled them into their beds upstairs. Again that night I stayed up later than Allan—watching the late news, the Leno monologue, and then the beginning of a behind-the-scenes documentary on the movie *Poltergeist* before I fell asleep on the couch in the den. I woke when I thought I heard the sound of shattering glass—it sounded as if the sliding glass door had fallen off its runners and shattered on the cement ground of the patio. I got up to check on it and heard again the distinctive squeak of the kitchen floor. My heart was rapidly beating in my chest as I approached the kitchen—we either had intruders or someone in the kitchen had hurt himself. I didn't bother to reach for any kind of weapon—I was not thinking that fast this evening— only reacting quickly to find the source of the disturbance. When I walked into the kitchen no one was there—the back door was locked, the sliding glass door was in place and perfectly fine, undamaged. It, too, was locked. I looked out the glass door to the patio, thinking I might see someone out there on the fringe of the lawn, but there was nothing except the bare, cold winter night—clumps of snow that had never melted surrounding the posts of our backyard fence. I checked the doors again, activated the security alarm, then went and turned the TV off, ready to go upstairs, thinking I must have heard something in the TV show or a commercial that had made its way into a dream I was having.

Before I went upstairs I stopped to check the living and dining rooms and, again, I felt a bitter blast of cold air surround me. I flipped on a lamp and leaned down and looked at the new snow globe on the lower shelf. There were no figures in front of the house but I noticed now that the pale blue front door—which had always been closed before—was open. On the second floor, where the night before I had seen the light in the window with three figures, the window and the room behind it were dark. But the snow continued to swirl inside the globe. I felt the sides of the bookcase, wondering if I might feel an undetected vibration of the house, but I sensed nothing except my own bafflement. I stopped looking and stretched my back, thinking I was just tired, and tried to shake the heavy concentration from my mind. I felt I was just imagining it all, so I turned off the light and went upstairs to bed.

But again it was a restless night for the family. This time Claire woke up crying, saying she had seen a woman with an ugly face. Allan settled her down, only for her to wake up a few minutes later and crawl into our bed between us. This time I fell into my own version of the nightmare. I dreamed that I saw two men breaking into the house—not our house, but the house in the snow globe. They had entered through the pale blue front door, jimmying it open. They had found a woman first, in one of the ground floor rooms, gagged her, and bound her to a chair behind a desk. Then one of the fellows, a short, dark-haired man, brought two children into the room—kids who looked frighteningly like Justin and Claire. The men kept the woman and children bound for a long time, as if they were waiting for someone else to arrive. In the dream I walked into the room and was bound and gagged myself. I watched as the woman was shot first—blasted through the face with a shotgun. Then the children were shot. I had been made to witness it all. I woke, sweating through the T-shirt I had worn to bed, when the shotgun was pointed at me in the dream.

The next morning I didn't tell Allan or the children about the dream, but on my way downstairs to eat breakfast I stopped to look at the new snow globe. The blue front door of the Victorian house was closed, the windows on the top floor were dark, and where I and my son had once seen figures on the front steps, now there was no one. But the snowing had not stopped inside the globe. In the kitchen, I was about to confess my bewilderment to Allan, but he complained first about being unable to sleep again the night before. While Claire and Justin were eating their cereal, he whispered to me his own version of the nightmare I had had. He had dreamed he was in an old house and had been reading a story to the children when he heard something downstairs—a crash, as if a window pane had been shattered. He had stepped outside the room to check on the sound but had found nothing, and had gone back to reading with the children when he heard footsteps creaking on the old stairs of the house. Again, he went to check on the sound and found nothing. "We were asleep when they came into the rooms," he said. "They brought us all to one room and shot us. We had to watch them shoot the children."

"It was just a dream," I said, not daring to tell him of my own nightmare or any of my other suspicions.

Claire interrupted us by asking, "Allan, can Ben and Sally play in my room?"

"Who are Ben and Sally?" Allan asked.

"My friends!" Claire answered.

"We'll have to ask their mommie first," Allan said.

I would have explained to my partner that Ben and Sally were Claire's imaginary friends and he would have to ask their imaginary mother, but the phone rang and I went to answer it. It was one of my bosses from the office, explaining that the senior managers had held a special Saturday morning teleconference to respond to the damaging analyst's report, and I was expected to be in the office later that day to help formulate the company's response. I had taken the cordless phone and walked to a corner of the kitchen, away from Allan and the kids, and when I realized that I was being asked to leave my family for the day I turned and looked at Allan, as if to let him know I was going to have a change of plans. That was when I felt the cold air surrounding me and I saw a ghostly shape of gray haze standing beside Allan. "I can't be there," I suddenly told my boss. "I can't do it. I'm having a family emergency."

I hung up the phone and faced the perplexed stare of my significant other. The gray shape beside him had disappeared and I said, "Get the children ready. We're all getting out of the house for a while."

"What's going on?" Allan asked me.

"I'm not sure," I answered. "But I don't think we should be in the house."

The kids were ready before Allan and I were, and on my way out to the car, I stopped in the dining room and placed the new snow globe in a paper sack. When I got in the car, I handed it to Allan with the instructions, "Don't open it. Don't look at it." I'm not sure why I said that, except that perhaps I feared he would see something he had only imagined happening. As I backed the car out of the driveway, I noticed Claire, in the backseat, whispering to someone.

"What is it?" I asked my daughter. "Who are you talking to?"

"Nobody, Tom," she said, her eyes wide and full of fear.

I knew she was lying. I stopped the car and said more sternly, "Tell them to get out of the car."

"Why Daddy?" Claire whined.

"Tell them to get out."

There was a confusing scene—Allan asking what was going on, Claire bursting into tears, Justin crouching against the other car door. I hopped out of the car and opened the door next to Claire. "Tell them to stay with their mommie," I said.

"No, Tom-eeee," Claire said. "They don't want to."

"Tell them."

Claire mumbled something through her tears, and once I was satisfied that she had left her imaginary friends behind I started the car and we were headed away from the house. The kids had never seen me act this harshly before, and I had a palpable fear that these moments would be the ones they would remember about their childhood and their overbearing, strict parent. Allan was confused and irritated with me and tried to play good cop to my bad cop, but the trip to the village was longer and more frustrating than I had anticipated. There was an accident on the highway, one of the lanes was closed for construction, and the exit was clogged with weekend tourists hoping to shop at the discount outlet stores that ringed the area. I parked our car in the parking lot of the coffee shop where I had eaten only a few days before. I told Allan that it was best if all of us stayed together in the antique store. The kids didn't understand this protective urge of mine—Claire had no interest in the store, and she let out a high-pitched whine as we passed by the toy store. Allan was now pressed into the role of being the stern parent. He pleaded with Claire to behave better, while Justin looked on, his face dismayed and unhappy.

In the antique store I found the old man who had sold me the snow globe. Allan had managed to keep the kids nearby and distracted, looking through a rack of vintage comic books, while he remained close enough to overhear my question. When I lifted the snow globe out of the bag, I asked the man, "Can you tell me something about this? I bought it here a few days before."

"That's the old Hartman-Monroe house," he said. "It was the first of its kind in the village. They tore it down more than thirty years ago."

"Tore it down?" I asked him. "Why?"

"Spooks," he answered, smiling. "Said it was haunted."

"Haunted?" I said. "By whom? What happened?"

The old man walked away from the counter, stepped into the aisle near Allan and the kids, and came back with a small paperback book—a tourist guide to the area. "It's all right here in this section," he said. "The Monroes—the family that built the house—were murdered one night in 1932. By drifters. It was the Depression, and the legend goes that the drifters had helped build the house and came back to ransack it for money out of a safe. Mr. Monroe had died the year before. Freak accident in the snow; his sister had moved into the house to help his widow take care of the two kids. The two fellers shot the entire family. There was a nationwide search for the killers. When they were finally caught, they were tried and both of 'em got the chair."

I took the book from the old man and asked, "Are there any more details in here?"

"Sure, lots more," he said. "Clippings from the newspaper. A few photographs. Lots about the Hartmans."

"The Hartmans?" I asked.

"The family who owned the house in the 1950s," he said. "Same kind of thing happened to them. Mrs. Hartman divorced her husband and a lady friend moved into the house to help her raise the kids. Lots of gossip about them two women. Then, two drifters came and killed the whole family one night."

I looked over at Allan and saw that he had gone pale. I told the old man that I wanted to buy a copy of the book, and as he was ringing up the sale, I asked him, "Who made the snow globe?"

"The snow globe?" he answered. "Not sure about that. It's been here for years—it was part of the inventory when I bought the shop about six years ago. No one never wanted it until you came along."

Allan and I agreed that it was best to keep the kids occupied and entertained while we discussed what to do next. Somehow it was late afternoon when we had finished shopping through the stores and I had read in the guidebook what had happened to Melissa Hartman and her friend, Dianne Sanderson, and the two children. Two men, drifters, one just out of jail and the other waiting for him, had driven past the house one day and decided to rob it. During the robbery, the man just out of jail lost his temper, and killed the family in the downstairs parlor. The coroner had established that Mrs. Hartman and Miss Sanderson had watched the drifters kill the children first, then Mrs. Hartman had watched her companion shot. All of the family had died from gunshots through the head. The children were ages six and eight—a girl named Sally and an older brother named Ben.

We stopped to have dinner in the coffee shop before the long drive home—the kids were restless and hungry. While we were ordering it started to snow outside, not a light snow, but a sky full of thick, fat snowflakes that quickly coated and covered everything in sight. I knew this would mean a long and difficult drive home, and since I was the one of the four of us facing the large picture window, I sat and watched the snow come down harder and harder on the parking lot of cars and the old Victorian shops, feeling anxious and uneasy. "I don't think we should drive in this," Allan said first. "How can we see?"

"We'll give it a bit," I said. "Or there's a motel near the highway if we need to stop."

"That's too far to drive," he said. "We should try to find something here. There was a place across the street in one of the old houses."

When the waitress came and took our order, Allan asked the name of the guesthouse across the street, then he used his cellphone to see if a room was available. The clerk told him one room was left and Allan asked if it was big enough to accommodate a family of four. The man put Allan on hold while he checked on portable bed arrangements, and when Allan hung up he seemed relieved to have it all worked out so quickly, telling me that we could stay at the inn across the street until it was safe to drive back to our house.

The kids were delighted with this plan, and their spirits improved. Claire thought this meant that she would be able to sleep in the toy store, and Allan explained to her that we were going to be across the street, and that the store would be closed. Claire was disappointed, almost to the point of tears, but after dinner we stopped in the store and bought the kids books and a board game to keep them amused. This seemed to redeem us once again in the eyes of our children.

The inn was not a duplicate of the house in the snow globe, but it was eerily similar—a large front porch, bay windows, and a front door with a tiny stained glass window. Electric candles were glowing in all the windows, and the gabled roof and gingerbread trelliswork had been covered with tiny icicle lights, so that through the falling snow it looked as if we were approaching an enchanted cottage. Inside, the rooms of the inn were painted in frosty gumdrop colors, but they failed to hide the slightly musty odor of the aging wood and antique furniture, and I greeted every suspicious creak and crack as if it were a bad omen.

It took me a long time to settle in the room. I kept looking out the window at the snow, hoping it would stop, or just lessen, and we would be able to leave the inn and make the two-hour drive back to our home. I didn't feel safe in the inn. I'd had this crazy notion running around my mind that we were actually staying inside that house—inside the Victorian house in the snow globe—and that somehow we had changed homes with the ghosts and now we were going to be assaulted. I didn't tell Allan this, of course, but he knew I was jittery and uneasy. Once the kids had calmed down and were watching TV, he picked up the guidebook and began to read about the village, asking me questions or reading passages out loud. I had kept the snow globe in a bag in the closet, and once Justin had fallen asleep and Claire was just about to drop off, I went to the closet to get it to study again.

"Do you really think that Claire saw the kids?" Allan asked me, looking up from his reading.

"I think so," I said. "Because she did leave them behind. But it's strange. Look at the picture of the Monroes, the family before them. Is that the woman you saw in your dream?"

Allan flipped through the pages of the guide and found the picture of the Monroe family, looking at it silently without commenting. Finally, he breathed in a nervous gasp of air and said, "It was a dream. It wasn't real."

"But it was her," I said. "I'd swear in a court of law that I had seen her before."

"Is that what spooked you? In the kitchen this morning?"

"I sensed something that told me we had to get out of the house," I told my partner honestly. "I can't say that I believe in ghosts."

He closed the book and said, "It's all really silly and coincidental. I used to read ghost stories all the time when I was a boy. They never frightened me, because I always felt there was a reason for the ghost; like it was in the house because the spirit wasn't settled into death—murdered, or hidden inside a wall, or buried beneath the floor of the basement. Sometimes they were after revenge, or trying to warn another generation about trouble." When he stopped talking his expression froze, as if he were imagining confronting a ghost, then he sighed and said, "It will all work out." This admission seemed to calm him, and I knew he was ready to sleep.

There was nothing unusual now about the house in the snow globe. The second floor windows were dark and shut, the front door was closed, the figures I had seen on the steps and the front porch were no longer there. But the snow continued to swirl inside the globe, and its movement kept me wondering about what could happen to us next. I set the globe down on the night stand and turned out the lamp beside the bed. The light from the TV set flickered eerily through the room, until I found the remote control and turned it off when I felt sleepy. I didn't fall asleep quickly, however. The creaking and cracking sounds of the inn shifting under the weight of the falling snow kept me awake and nervous.

The ringing sound of a phone awakened me sometime later, when I had managed to drift into a light dream. It had a faint, muffled sound to it, as if it were in another room or hidden away somewhere. Allan, too, awoke when he heard it, and he stumbled out of the bed to the chair on the other side of the room, where he had left his coat with the cellphone in the pocket.

After a few seconds he turned to me and whispered, "It's the alarm company. Someone's broken into the house."

I took the phone from him and we went into the bathroom together and turned on the light, where I could wake up and talk calmly, without disturbing the children. The man from our home security company said that a windowpane on our back door had been broken and the house entered. The police had arrived quickly and nothing seemed missing except the downstairs TV. We talked quite a bit with the security representative, as he asked questions about where the TVs were located in the house, if we had a computer or stereo equipment, and what kind of valuables we might have owned. Allan had nothing of real value except a Rolex watch he never wore, and it sounded like the robbers were in search of quick cash. The man assured us that the house was again secure and locked—a board had already been placed over the broken glass pane of the door. Before I hung up, I asked the rep how heavy the snow fall was in the area. He seemed stumped for a moment, and there was the sound of empty air on the phone line; then he said, "It's not snowing here. But it's cold. Your house is really cold. You should keep the thermostat a little higher."

The next morning the snowing had stopped in the village and I was anxious to return home, but Allan said he didn't want to rush the children, didn't want them to arrive at the house frightened and worried. We ate again at the coffee shop across the street, and let the kids play a few minutes in the snow-covered field above the parking lot, before brushing them off and settling them in the car. Throughout the morning I had checked the snow globe—looking at the top floor windows, the front door, the steps—but saw no sign of any intruders or inhabitants, actual or imagined. It was if, having discovered the secret of the snow globe, the power of its suggestion had stopped.

It was a long drive home, but the kids were in a cheerful mood, Allan keeping them talking and happy as the roads cleared and the mounds of snow disappeared into icy patches and then the wet flat stretch of the highway. Before we set out from the village, Allan and I agreed that he would drop me off at the house first to check things out, and he would take the kids with him to the grocery store. At the house, the back door windowpane was boarded up with a small square of wood, just as the security rep had said. There was still a small amount of glass on the kitchen floor, and I swept that up, then made my way through the other rooms checking to see if anything else might have been stolen. Everything seemed to be in order except for the missing TV, though the house felt slightly askew, as if things had been moved and put back at a slightly different angle than before. When Allan and the kids arrived home, I was on the phone with the rep again, thanking him for his help the night before.

Late that afternoon, two detectives visited the house. They asked a few questions about the break-in—where we were at the time, what was taken. Then they asked if they could dust for fingerprints from the back door and the stand where the missing TV had been placed. Justin and Claire were upstairs in their bedrooms and Allan was on the computer in another room. Only while one of the men was dusting the glass did I find out the real purpose of their visit: the detectives were hoping that fingerprints in our house might match a crime scene a half mile away. Another house had been broken into the night before and the family had been murdered—a man, his divorced brother, and his two sons. According to the detective, they already had two suspects in custody—two men just released from prison, but no confessions yet from either suspect.

The news stunned me and I asked him to please not repeat the story to my partner or the kids—it would only spook them. "We're always a bit nervous because we're not your typical suburban family, either," I said.

I stayed with the detectives while they went about their dusting, but didn't mention that I had abandoned the house with my family the previous day. I still couldn't admit that I believed in ghosts—good or bad—and I knew it would be difficult to explain that a supernatural force had frightened us into leaving and in doing so, might have saved us from the fate that had befallen the other murdered families. After the detectives had left, I realized that I had left the snow globe inside the car, and I went outside to find the bag still beside the driver's seat. I took the globe out of the car, out of the bag and lifted it into the sunlight. The snow still swirled magically around; and there in the top window was the silhouette of a woman, now bent as if she were looking out the window at the snow falling on the roof and steps and lawn. Somehow I knew when I saw her there that things were safe with us, that no harm would find us in our house, and that this was how the snow globe was supposed to be.

I put the snow globe on the shelf in the dining room where Justin had originally placed it when I first brought it home. It stayed there safely through the years, undisturbed, the woman in the window watching over our family.

THE INCIDENT AT THE HIGHLANDS INN

Joey told Mark he would meet him after work at the gym, but he was running toward the parking lot, a target now, and instinctively he knew they would not see each other. "Don't make any plans after work," Steve had warned him, "or else you're dead." Behind him, the tall glass doors of the Highlands Inn were open, the tables on the outdoors terrace covered with white cloths and shaded by yellow umbrellas, the Sunday afternoon brunch crowd thinning out in the late afternoon sun. Carole had alerted Joey when Steve had shown up in the lobby of the inn, his work boots making the old oak floor creak under each determined step. Joey had dropped his table in the dining room in a flash of fear when he had seen Carole's warning, bumping into Walt clearing a table and sending plates and glasses and silverware crashing loudly to the floor.

Joey was a streak of white light as he shortcutted through the kitchen to reach the terrace doors, and exited toward the parking lot. Outside, the sky was high and cloudless, a solid bright blue. The days were getting longer and warmer, the edgy joy of spring morphing into the lazy mellowness of summer. Running across the bright green lawn, Joey turned and looked over his shoulder. The silverware on the terrace tables caught the sunlight, the drinking glasses glittered like crystals, the Spanish guitar music that Carlos liked to play over the stereo system drifted out of the inn like the scent of barbecue. Until now, Joey's shift had been without incident—nothing broken, no credit cards rejected, no meals returned because the food was lukewarm or undercooked or, god forbid, inedible. His tips had been good—a group of brothers taking their elderly mother out for her eighty-first birthday had been generous. Steve was only a threat to be ignored, even though the night before he had cornered Joey outside the cinema at the mall, pinned him against the wall, and hurled his threat before Mark had started yelling for the cops and Joey had been able to break away. This morning there had been a circle of bruises at his collarbone and scratches on his back from hitting the cement wall, which he had hidden beneath his white shirt. Last night, Mark had urged Joey to file a complaint with the police, but Joey didn't want more trouble. He only wanted Steve to go away. Steve would never try to kill him, Joey told Mark; he knew Joey would only come back and haunt him and make his life *more* miserable. But now Steve was there, *here*, a black silhouette emerging through the terrace doors, his footsteps heavy and resolute, heading toward the stairs to the path that led to the side of the inn and the lot where employees were encouraged to park their cars.

The questions were stuck at the back of Steve's throat: *Why? Why me? Why did you use me?* He squinted as he stepped outside on the terrace, felt the handle of the gun pressing against his hip bone through the pocket of his jeans. The jeans were too snug for this hot weather, they pinched his waist and made him feel anxious to draw the gun. The questions tensed his body, stuck in his spine and shoulders and neck and eyes. *Why? Why? Why?* Steve saw a figure running across the grassy land toward the rear parking lot. Dark hair. White shirt. Khaki pants. It was Joey. *Why is he running away? Why won't he stay? Why won't he say he's sorry and come back?*

Joey sprinted toward his car, the old reliable blue-gray Toyota hatchback he had bought from his older brother when Tad moved to Dallas. Joey didn't want another confrontation with Steve. He was going to jump into his car and drive away. He'd be gone before Steve reached him. There was nothing else to discuss or rehash. They were finished. It was over. He'd explained that several times. Too many times. It had been almost three months since he had moved out. He'd moved on. Why hadn't Steve? They were not getting back together. *Ever.* Joey would threaten to call the cops on his cellphone if Steve didn't leave him alone. He'd file a complaint this time. Get a restraining order. He'd create just as much trouble as Steve was causing if he didn't leave Joey alone. *Starting now.*

No one else had given Steve this trouble, and he'd had his share of troubles over the years. Divorce, bankruptcy, starting over. Finding a boyfriend had never been a problem. He had broken up with several before he had met Joey. At thirty-eight, Steve was solid and in shape—he ran ten miles twice a week, took a spinning class on Wednesdays, and spent one day a week in the weight room of his gym. Only a hint of gray at his temples betrayed his aging. He'd let plenty of opportunities with other guys slip away because that wasn't what Joey wanted and he wanted to keep Joey around.

Joey had wanted to be serious and committed and in love. He wanted a gay version of what his parents had, everything a partnership, everything together. He'd been struggling to come out to his mother and father when he met Steve. He'd graduated college with a degree in American history only to find himself drifting from one interview to the next, never connecting with the interviewer or the company or the job. At twenty-four, he felt useless, immaterial, and confused. Nothing like a career seemed to be opening up to him. He had taken the waitering job because he needed to find a way to begin paying his bills. Even though he liked his coworkers and loved the old creaky inn and its restaurant, he was disappointed in himself because he hadn't found a "serious career" and worried his parents would be let down too. At first, Steve had provided a distraction for Joey, a way to forget his frustrations. Sex had made him forget other things. By the end of their second week of dating, Steve had asked Joey to move in with him in his midtown apartment. He offered free rent, a way for Joey to escape remaining in the bedroom of his parents' house. Joey had ached for someone exactly like Steve, someone to change the course of his life, pull him away from relying on his family, give his life meaning and direction. Joey thought it would be easier for his parents to accept the news that he was gay if he were already in a relationship. But the opposite happened. They urged him to see their minister or talk to a counselor. They were sure he was making a mistake, and they thought Joey could be cured of his homosexuality.

Steve had responded with anger and distrust. Joey's parents were using religion as a wedge to break them apart. Steve loved Joey. He loved Joey's thin chest, the black pebbly stubble that grew only at his chin, the way his dark hair swept back from his forehead, the way he walked on cold mornings, on tiptoe, as if his feet were lifted with wings. Joey was his lover, the kind of relationship he had never had with another guy, that thing he'd always kept at a distance, not wanting to be hurt if it didn't work out. Why didn't Joey understand this?

Joey had loved Steve's bulky muscles, his swarthy chin, his black eyes and the swirling curls of gray in the hair above his ears. There was a certain coarseness that had both repelled and attracted him to Steve, but by falling in love, Joey could lay a fine tissue over the rough spots and feel protected from his own troubles. He didn't need to have his parents' approval. He didn't have to find a career. He admired Steve's strength and self-confidence, his ability to rebound from setbacks; Joey had made him recount the obstacles he'd overcome. He had considered Steve as much a mentor and a guide as he had a lover. He tried hard to believe that his love was a spiritual one and that he wasn't using it to hide from the future, but the future did scare him, and he began to doubt himself and his relationship.

Steve wanted control. He didn't want Joey going out to the bars without him, didn't want him to go drinking or dancing after work with his friends from the inn. Steve wanted to know where Joey was at all times, what he had been doing, why he had taken money out of the checking account; why he hadn't used the money to buy groceries or toiletries, things they *both* needed.

Joey snapped. He wanted a break. He felt smothered and controlled. Things had become too serious too quickly. And nothing was equal or a partnership. After ten months of their living together, Joey decided he had made a mistake about Steve and abruptly moved out. He couldn't go back to his parents' house, so he slept on Carole's couch, then on Mark's, then stayed at Walt's place while he was out of town on vacation. His parents offered him help, but at a price: *Change and you can come home. Change and we'll help you get back on your feet.*

And then the stalking began. At first it was a game, running away from Steve, hiding out of sight, driving a little recklessly when he knew he was being followed. Joey treated Steve like a crazy ex-boyfriend story. Carole and Mark laughed at it. So did Walt. Until the death threats began. "Tell Joey not to make any plans after work," Steve warned them all. "Or else he's dead."

From the terrace, Steve tried to yell to Joey to wait, but his voice caught, paralyzed by anger. He fingered the trigger of the gun in his pocket and lifted it out so that he held it at his side as he strode across the terrace. His boots sent shock waves bouncing across the planks of the decking. He'd never fired the gun before. It had sat for years in a box on the top shelf of his closet, the only thing he'd been able to salvage from the warehouse safe in his office before the bank and the liquidators took possession of everything except the broken electric stapler and a no-good coffee machine. At the terrace stairs, Steve stopped to look down at the gun and undo the safety catch, wondering if the gun even had any bullets in it, then looked up and saw Joey breaking into a run.

Joey's strides became leaps, though the Toyota seemed to be growing farther and farther away from him. He felt the heel of his sneakers hitting the pavement, the impact traveling along his foot till his toes pushed off the ground to do it again. His left hand moved into the front pocket of his slacks and touched his keys. He fingered the ridges till he was certain he had the one for his car. Ahead, the black tar of the parking lot shimmered with heat, the glare now bouncing off hoods and side mirrors and windshields. He could feel the impact of his feet in his ears and how it challenged his balance, and his hands rose up to steady himself, but instead one arm shielded his eyes from the glare, the fist of the other now clutching at his key ring. The first hint of sweat—at his back and beneath his arms—made him aware of the heat and his fear. What did Steve want from him? What good would a confrontation do? Why would he ever want to go back to him? What could Steve say or do that could make him change his mind?

Steve felt his pulse in his ears. There was the dull beginning of a headache that he had chased all day with caffeine and aspirin. He hadn't slept the night before, the confrontation outside the cinema had left him angrier, unable to reconcile being pushed away again. Long ago he'd tried to work through this fear with a therapist, abandonment issues that had started with the death of his mother when he was seven—the fear of being alone, having to struggle to find affection. *Overcome the monster*, his therapist had advised. *Start with the problem and take control of the situation.* The gun felt lighter at his side, his grip was firm, even though his palm was sweaty. He strode evenly across the green grass, freshly cut the day before but still long enough to retain his heavy footprints. His arm holding the gun began rising as he grew closer to Joey and his car.

Joey reached his car. The key did not slip in easily to unlock the door because Joey had allowed himself to panic. He steadied his hand and pushed the key in, twisted the lock open, and clasped the door handle. The metal was warm from sitting hours in the sun, and he used his weight to pull the door open and swing it to the side as he edged around it and threw his body into the seat. He could feel Steve closing in on him, the sound of his boots reaching the pavement of the parking lot as jolting as a stalking dinosaur. Joey reached out and pulled the door shut and used his thumb to press the lock. Inside the car, the air was stifling hot. Joey inserted the key into the ignition and started the car. There was a hesitation in the engine, as if the car were unsure how to act in a time of crisis.

Steve reached the Toyota and looked at Joey through the windshield. Joey saw Steve's confused expression. Steve pushed a hand against the window of Joey's car door, tapped it with his knuckles. Then he raised the gun and tapped the tip of it against the glass three times. *Click, click, click.*

"Go away!" Joey shouted. "Leave me the fuck alone!" Joey threw the car in reverse and backed out, the car trembling from the surge of gas.

Steve didn't shake as he stepped into the spot the car had vacated, lifted the gun, and aimed at Joey's head, trying to catch his eyes when Joey turned around. Ungrateful boy. Never any thanks. A hungry stray dog would have stayed, accepted the love and discipline and advice. But not Joey. Joey was unappreciative of everything Steve had offered him.

Joey turned and saw the gun. He stopped the car with a braking squeal and ducked. Steve straightened his aim and squeezed the trigger.

The window exploded. The glass cracked into a geometrical pattern like the optical ones Joey had studied in a toy kaleidoscope as a boy. The pattern seemed to sigh with breath, turned opaque and shattered apart, the sunlight pouring through a thousand fragments of glass. Joey's expression was a combination of astonishment and pain. Instinctively, his arm went upwards to shield his eyes from the flying shards of glass. The car engine chugged to a stop. Joey felt a burning sensation at his stomach. He pressed his left hand against his shirt and felt the warm sticky gush of blood. He held up a bloody palm toward Steve, tried to say "Why?" but could not make the sound.

Steve took two steps back to avoid the exploding shards, the gun and his arm thrown upward from the discharge. "Why?" Steve yelled. "I warned you. *Why?*"

Joey scooted across the seat as though fire were approaching him, aware that he was covered with sweat from the heat of the car. Only when he reached for the door handle on the other side did he realize that the blast of the gun had made him momentarily deaf. His hand was bloody. It had smeared on the seat covering and the door handle. He opened the car door and rolled his body outside.

Steve looked down at the gun, touched a finger to the barrel to feel the heat of the discharge, and kept it there, trying to feel the pain. He watched Joey squirm across the front seat of the car, jiggle the door handle, trying to flee. He raised his arm to aim again, but Joey was crouched too low. He stepped closer to the Toyota, his boots trampling pieces of glass and gravel on the cement.

Joey landed on his hands and knees. His first thought was that his clothes were ruined. How much would it cost him to buy a new outfit for work? How much would *this* set him back? There was always a problem with money. Not enough to pay Steve rent. Not enough for gas. Not enough for a drink at a bar. He was always relying on the help of his friends. He'd borrowed money from Carole and Walt. Mark had paid his admission every time they had gone to the movies together. Joey brushed his hands against his knees. There was more blood. Scrapes on his hands, his white shirt bloodied and flecked with glass.

Steve felt calm. Level headed. He saw the car. The glass. The tables on the terrace. The yellow awnings. The gardener's wood chips in the flower beds. The withered daffodils at the edge of the parking lot. The air felt thin and it pierced his lungs. He took a deep breath. He was squinting and smiling. Summer was around the corner. He felt like he was finally getting his way.

Joey used the open door to lift himself off the ground. He saw Steve over the hood of the car. The same pained expression. The glare was unrelenting. He was sweating heavily. Breathing harder. He used a hand to wipe his forehead. Steve raised the gun from his side and pointed it at Joey. This time Joey felt the "Why?" rise from his stomach to his throat, but all that came out of his mouth was a breath of confused air.

Steve saw Joey's confusion. The pain. *This is what it's been like for me. This is what you've made me feel.*

Joey turned away from Steve and took a few steps. He was trying to run. Trying to make one foot go in front of the other. He felt blood pumping in his palms, at his temples, his stomach. He stopped to look at his stomach. There was more blood. Had the bullet hit him there? Or was this from cuts of the glass?

Steve followed, worried that Joey was in pain, and angry that Joey continued to run away. Disgust settled in his throat, his chest tightened. He gripped the Colt 38 tighter. Sweat filled his palm, rivered beneath his arms, the pressure of his pulse made his field of vision throb. He raised the gun and shot Joey in the back. Once, twice, and then a third time. The shots echoed off the hot metal of the cars. Boom. Boom. *Boom.*

Joey felt his foot rise from the ground and fall; his hands clenched into fists as he used his arms to move faster. He heard the bullet before he felt the sting below his left shoulder. It was like an insect bite that grew into an itchy rash that turned into a merciless punch that knocked the wind out of his lungs. He wobbled as though he were a drunk, forced to walk a straight line at midnight in a small town. Sound fell away again, all except the scrape of his loafers against the cement surface of the parking lot. The silence was followed by the sound of more bullets, though this time he didn't feel the sting of them. When the third bullet hit, he lifted his foot high enough to make it over the curb of the parking lot and reach the edge of the lawn. He thought that if he made it back to the inn he would be free of Steve. That this would all be a mistake, an illusion, a nightmare.

The details of the afternoon and the landscape became sharper for Steve: the swirl of the pattern of stucco waterproofing that partially covered the old red bricks at the back of the building, the hanging baskets of red geraniums in the opened windows, the bright white cotton T-shirt of an overweight man at the side of the terrace as he stood up at the sounds of the gunfire in the parking lot, flattening his palm against his forehead to shield the glare and look at Joey only yards away. Steve pivoted his body so that he could watch Joey fall to the ground. He felt certain that this was what he had wanted, no doubt that this was the right and natural path for him to take. His self-confidence restored, he lifted the gun to his temple.

The sun on Joey's face felt good now. He had a clear view of the terrace. Carole had stepped through the glass doors. Her blonde hair was pulled toward the back of her neck with a silver clip, ending in a wave. Joey saw her head turn to recognize the sound of the gun, the wave of hair bobble and the silver clip catch the light. Carole adjusted her posture to register the source of the sound of the gunfire by tilting her head. Her body followed her turning head and she melted in the bright light, which was when Joey let go of her image and felt the sick sensation of falling. He was full of regret. He had not said goodbye. To Carole. Or Mark. Or his brother. Or his parents.

Jealousy was the monster. It was impossible to own someone's affection—hadn't Steve preached that himself? He couldn't control another person's life. He couldn't *make* Joey love him. Of all the things he had learned in his life, why couldn't he accept this fact? He was afraid of Joey forgetting him, moving on to someone else. Someone younger. Someone more fun and willing and less demanding and without all these issues and imperfections that aging and surviving had brought about for Steve. Joey was in his mind, in his blood and muscles and tendons and limbs, and it pained Steve to lose that part of himself.

Joey's left foot went first, disappearing as if it were suddenly sawed off. He lost his balance. His right knee began to bend, and he felt his thigh muscles burn as though he were doing squats at the gym. His hands began to rise, his fingers lengthening and spreading to cushion his fall. For a moment he was tipped forward from the waist, as if bowing. He saw the flecks of quartz in the black pavement, catching the sun as Carole's hair clip had.

Steve felt the sound of the trigger at his ear. There was a blinding light and his hand was pushed away with the force of the bullet. The gun dropped to the ground with a clackety echo that was lost in disbelief. The bullet traveled through Steve's skull and lodged in the black cement twenty-one feet away.

Joey's right knee reached the ground first. His hands were at his shoulders and the dark pavement of the parking lot rose up to catch them. His forehead followed, but it was just a tap that was enough to make him roll his face to the left and crush the weight of his body at his cheek. His left hip disappeared, just like his thigh had, and he pitched to the left and the breath of air that remained in his lungs was pushed out. The pavement was warm, like an inviting bed on a winter's night, and he felt the warmth travel through his skin as he closed his eyes to accept the exhausting sleep that had suddenly come upon him. There was a burning at his nostrils because his lungs had stopped working, and a deeper burn in his chest as it accepted the fact of what his nose had learned.

Steve was now in full possession of his physical senses. They were, indeed, preternaturally keen and alert. Something in the awful disturbance of his organic system had so exalted and refined them that they made a record of things never before perceived. He looked at the cars and saw the detailing, the grimy bumpers and the veining of tires, saw the very bits of dirt and pebbles wedged within their treads. The colors were more vibrant. Reds were redder. Blue was really blue. The humming of gnats that danced above the hoods sounded like helicopters one moment and butterflies the next. The light broke into fine particles of sand, lifeless grains that seemed easily swept away. Without the energy of life to hold them in place, the grains of sand crumbled to the ground. Steve felt the slow wave reach up and catch him and pull him down. Shoulders fell on top of his chest on top of his waist on top of his hip on top of his thighs on top of his calves on top of his ankles on top of his toes. His pain was suddenly gone, for the first time in months.

Joey accepted the darkness as fear. Fear that it was coming too soon. That not enough had been done to prevent it. That he wasn't given enough chances. That he had never loved the way he wanted to be loved back. A tiny white light arrived above him, a pinprick that twirled and sparkled and caught other tiny fragments of light. The light grew yellow, the black edges turned gray. The gray became lighter and lighter until it was all white, hovering above him like a solid pane of frosted glass.

On the ground, Steve felt the energy of confusion return. Something remained unfinished. Death had not conquered what had disturbed him in life. He still wanted Joey. Wanted to make things work. Understand why things had not worked out. The why remained unanswered. Nothing was resolved.

Joey moved headfirst toward the light, hands stretched out in front of him as if he were swimming. Ahead, there was something like grass. Thick, green blades of it. He moved slowly because he was weightless. He looked down at his shirt and saw that it was clean again. No blood. No tears. A fluttering momentum kept his body moving upward. He was facing skyward where the white plane of light was glowing brighter.

Steve felt the particles begin to rearrange themselves and take shape. He felt pulled and tugged and lifted off the ground and saw that he was standing again. The visible world wheeled slowly around with him as the pivotal point. He saw the terrace, the parking lot, the lawn, the trees, the cars, the gun, and

Joey's body on the ground.

The plane of light above Joey split into shafts and patterns, shifting and rearranging themselves. Joey saw the yellow awning. The white tablecloths. The gleam of the sun on the glasses and silverware. He seemed to remember that they had been connected in some way with his physical body on the ground, but the nature of the connection was not clear; and he did not associate the dead body with himself. He turned his body, the living spiritual one. His mind had no past and no future, no sharp-edged, coherent memories, and no idea of anything to be done next. Then his memory came together with a palpable click of recognition. He could hear the music from the terrace. He had traveled back into a definite space and time, and recovered a certain limited section of himself. He remembered the sunlight on the hoods of the cars, the heat of the car door, the stifling air inside the Toyota, then moved further back and saw Steve's ominous silhouette at the terrace door and the glint of the barrel of the gun as it tapped against the car window. He was aware of a light heaving, a rhythmical rise and fall, the faint sounds of footsteps and gunshots. He saw Steve on the black pavement of the parking lot, pushing himself up with the palms of his hands and lifting his head up. There was a look of agony and horror and determination on his face, and a bloodiness to him that washed away in the sun. Joey locked eyes with Steve and saw that he was back inside the dining room of the inn, seeing Carole rush into the doorway and mouth the words to him, *"Steve's here!"*

Steve was again in lobby of the Highlands Inn, his heavy steps sending a creaking terror through the oak floor. The gun was in his pocket and he was looking for Joey. This moment was substantial, but drawn back behind a sheet of air that shimmered over him like thin glass. The energy opened out, floated past and away from him, and instead of drawing him forward it drew him back to the moment he had discovered Joey's note in his apartment telling him he had moved out while Steve was at work—no discussion, no word of explanation except, *Steve, This isn't working out for me.—Joey.* The sunlight beat on him with the hard impact of reality; the white tablecloths, the yellow umbrellas, the glittering tableware. He was driven forward by some irresistible compulsion toward the path that led to the parking lot. Even as the staff and customers of the restaurant began to assess what had happened—the flash of fear seen on a young waiter's face, a stranger's heavy walking through the lobby and dining room and onto the terrace, a chase across the lawn, the gunshots in the parking lot. The question of why—the energy of it—remained. Why did the stranger shoot the young waiter? Why did he shoot himself? What went wrong? Why did this happen?

Joey remembered dimly that there had once been a thing called time, but he had forgotten altogether what it was like. He was aware of things happening and about to happen again; he fixed them by the place they occupied and measured their duration by the space he went through. He saw Steve raise the gun and aim. Joey thought if he could go back to the place where it hadn't happened, he would be able to get away. He turned the key in the ignition and felt the engine hesitate. The window shattered, and lives which had once been filled with love, lived once again in fear.

THE COUNTRY HOUSE

Arnie always graciously warned his guests about what to expect at the country house: slamming doors, crashing plates, flickering lamps, the dogs out of control, even a spike in their own temperaments. "Mitch and I have been fighting more and more since we bought this house," he would add after he had extended an invitation to his friends to spend a weekend with them in their haunted country house. "I think our ghosts get a kick out of seeing us irritated with each other."

After five blissful years of living together in a tiny cramped studio in Greenwich Village, Arnie and Mitch found the large, rustic rooms of their weekend retreat both liberating and aggravating. Arnie, who fell in love immediately with the giant kitchen and new appliances, wanted to cheaply furnish the other rooms, but Mitch was headstrong about scouring the local flea markets and estate auctions for deals and had soon developed a taste for overpriced broken furniture.

"The drawers won't open," Arnie complained about an oak hutch Mitch had found at a garage sale and brought back to the country house. "And the legs wobble."

"It's art deco," Mitch pointed out. "Look at the carving on it."

"And the shelves are missing. You got pinched on this one."

"I can get someone to fix the leg and put in a new shelf."

"And it'll end up costing more than it's worth. We should've bought something new."

"You can't buy a new antique."

"If it was new, you could have gotten a discount," Arnie complained, "not a four-hundred-percent markup. What a waste of money, if you ask me."

"No one's asking you," Mitch answered. "Which is why I bought it."

◈

Mitch and Arnie's country house is a ninety-minute drive from Manhattan, not far from the Delaware River and the canal and the quaint village shops of New Hope and Lambertville. Originally a small two-room stone cottage built in 1823, it was expanded in 1871 with a second floor and renovated and enlarged with a new wing a century later in 1983 by a well-known interior designer and his significant other. The property is outlined by the low-rise stone walls made from clearing the land for crops, and branches of the gnarly-trunked oak and maple trees shade the house in the summer and blacken in the winter months. A stone path, blistered by roots, leads from the road right up to the kitchen door. Inside, in the kitchen, is an enormous working hearth where the meals were cooked in the original house, along with the modern-day upgrades of a double-door Sub-Zero refrigerator, granite countertops, two ovens, and a six-burner grill. Upstairs, the master bedroom has a cathedral ceiling and a hot tub in the bathroom. Neither Arnie nor Mitch were any good at husbandry—carpentry, gardening, plumbing—and luckily all that was necessary before they moved in was to have the rooms painted and central air-conditioning installed, a process Arnie was insistent on and that meant sawing through the old floorboards and plastered ceilings of the house to install the vents, which had probably dislodged and disturbed the already restless resident spirits.

"Money well spent," Arnie confided in me one weekend when I was a guest at their house. "Or the humidity would have done us all in." I have known Arnie since our college days, long before we both reached our late thirties and he had settled down into this high-maintenance relationship. Arnie loved to tease me with the details about why he felt he might soon be back on the market for a new lover: Mitch's overanalysis of every conversation, Mitch's dysfunctional home purchases, Mitch's ill-mannered table habits. And on and on. Arnie also confessed to me that he and Mitch had purchased the house with a significantly low bid—it had been on the market for more than a year after a series of married couples had bought and resold the property after they had been unable to abide living with the cranky poltergeists.

"If I can live with Arnie, I can live with any sort of irritable ghost," Mitch would joke with their guests when they were entertained in the dining room with an elaborate three-course dinner by candlelight that Arnie had spent a day preparing. "You don't have to guess which one is easier."

This sort of banter always seemed to amuse their weekend visitors— usually other dramatic couples from the city: a gray-haired film director and the young actor-boyfriend he had rescued from hustling, the hefty lesbian couple who ran a pet-grooming salon in Chelsea, the anorexic European fashion magazine editor and her chain-smoking photographer-husband from Greece. During a weekend in the country, Arnie's seething resentment never failed to bubble to the surface. "I spend my entire time cleaning and cooking, while Mitch shops for old paintings and broken furniture," Arnie would pout, rattling his dishes and pots through the warm water in the sink, since he had neglected to notice that his new state-of-the-art kitchen did not have a dishwasher (and he had not a clue of how one could be installed). "It's an ideal arrangement for *him.*"

Sometimes their argument would escalate—Mitch might criticize the pot roast as being too dry or that the lemon-apple tart was store bought; Arnie might announce how much money Mitch had been fleeced for on a seventy-year-old cracked cookie jar in the shape of a clown's face—and if a second bottle of wine had been opened the conversation could turn nasty and wounding, depending on the familiarity of the guests, the heat of the weather, or the difficulty of the recipes. Sometimes the dinner would be interrupted to clean up an accident created by one of the two hyperactive cocker spaniels that the couple had adopted in an effort to seem more like country squires—a swift swipe of a chicken bone from a guest's plate that could send it crashing off the table or a puddle of piss shot onto the wooden floor intended to garner their masters' attention (and hopefully deflect all the rising bad tempers). One weekend when I was there with my new boyfriend Scott there was a threat by one lover with a carving knife that ended in the other lover performing a headlock on him. The sudden and sheepish apology by both men to all in attendance occurred over after-dinner drinks poured from an expensive (and fractured) crystal decanter Mitch had found at an estate auction.

But much of the conversation during the couple's elegant inedible feasts would be spent on the ghosts of their country house, particularly if a guest had heard one of the phantoms slamming a door upstairs or tapping noisily at the window. Arnie was rather fond of the door-slammer, in fact, except on those occasions when he wanted to take an afternoon nap. "Lucy—Lucinda was her real name—was the wife of the original builder of the house," he would explain, usually after Mitch had cut him to the quick with a wicked remark about a filmy fingerprint on a wineglass or a too-heavy hand with the garlic in a recipe. "Overworked and underappreciated. No wonder she just dropped dead one day. A little thank-you now and then always does her good."

Arnie liked to proudly explain that he thought himself particularly receptive to vibrations from the realm of the supernatural and Mitch loved to point out to their guests the hot spots of paranormal activity within the house, or, rather, the locations of strange, chilly drafts and severe drops in temperature. "Emma's bedroom, upstairs, at the far end of the house," he would usually begin his list. "There's a cold spot at the foot of the bed where she must have died. The dogs won't even go near it—they yelp as if someone has just stepped on their paws."

Emma was Lucy's daughter-in-law and believed to be the true source of any vicious disturbance in the house. "One morning I was standing at the top of the stairs and felt something push me," Mitch might tell the lesbian groomers or the European editor. "It was deliberate, like I was expected to lose my balance and fall and hurt myself. I could feel the anger in the air. It was as if something had conjured up all of Arnie's bitterness and I had stepped right inside it."

"Pity she didn't succeed," Arnie added.

◈

No one had ever actually *seen* any of the ghosts at the country house, at least not during Arnie and Mitch's tenure, only heard them or felt them in the dark of the evening hours, which usually meant their weekend guests would greet one or both of their hosts the following morning with an odd source of their insomnia—an anecdote of sensing someone at the foot of the bed, the creaking sound inside the armoire, an eerie light going on and off in the hallway. As for myself, I never seemed to be any kind of spiritual magnet and have generally reached a deep and unencumbered slumber on my visits to their country house, particularly since I am out of the city and away from the noisy traffic beneath the window of my third-floor apartment on Ninth Avenue. One guest, Cheryl, an overweight and middle-aged out-of-work actress, said she sensed something strange in the guest bathroom one night, where there had never been a spirit presence detected before. "I felt as if someone were looking at me when I got out of the shower," she explained in a dramatic fluster of over-the-shoulder gestures. "I felt so vulnerable and exposed, like something was going to happen."

Mitch told Cheryl she had been watching too many teen slasher movies, but over an elaborately concocted cup of vanilla roast coffee served in a disfigured and chipped set of ceramic cow mugs that Mitch had found in a thrift shop in Buckingham, Arnie commiserated with Cheryl that perhaps it was because the ghost recognized her from the low-budget insurance-fraud commercial she had filmed over a decade before. Later, in private, Arnie told me that perhaps Cheryl had only *wished* someone were looking at her. "She's desperate for attention," Arnie said. "She hasn't been on a date for over a year and can't seem to get a callback audition."

Though Arnie and Mitch had never seen any of their ghosts, they had never regarded them with frivolity or contempt, especially since the quarrelsome couple prided themselves on being progressive, inclusive, and multicultural (even when they were at odds). Mitch, a psychiatrist, liked to think of their ghosts as part of their extended family, more welcome in his home than his demanding parents, needy siblings, and pampered nephews and nieces. Arnie, a corporate travel planner, was the more compassionate one, always trying to find a reason for the noise or the cold air, hoping that if he helped change the course of the haunting he might also alleviate any eternal pain; lighting a stick of incense to change the mood, for instance, or leaving open a book of poems or family photographs to soothe the restless soul.

"Emma likes all my divas," Arnie might explain to the theater director and his ex-hustler boyfriend about his selection of background music during dinner. "Show tunes. Opera. Madonna."

"But she goes wild when two men sing together," Mitch would add. "Duets. Chorus boys. Something always goes flying to the floor."

"We've been wondering if she was some kind of feminist or suffragette, but that is clearly anachronistic," Arnie said. "More likely she was abused. Put upon. Like some in this house are *still* treated."

But there is one haunting that the couple deliberately warn their weekend company to steer clear of at all costs—the linked spirits of two soldiers who fought in and survived the Civil War only to meet their grisly end in the stone cottage. The bodies of the two young men appear only at daybreak by the giant hearth in the kitchen, or so goes the legend, and a curse falls on those who witness them. "Never find yourself alone in the kitchen when the sun comes up," the real estate agent who sold Arnie and Mitch the property told the new homeowners. The sight of these two ghosts was a bad luck omen and the last straw that had driven all the married couples away. "A very unhappy ending," the agent whispered to Mitch. "And a bloody mess you wouldn't want to clean up," she told Arnie.

✦

Peter Altemus was the son of the original builder of the stone cottage, Robert Altemus, who had built a new and larger house when his son became a teenager. By the time he was twenty Peter was broad-shouldered and clean-shaven, dark and sullenly handsome, and had the strength of one of the horses he used to plow the upper pasture in the spring. When Peter married Emma Frey, a woman from Philadelphia, the young couple moved into the stone cottage. In the years before and during the Civil War, Robert Altemus was part of the underground railroad movement, shepherding slaves northward by night to their hopeful freedom elsewhere. Peter had sat out the first two years of the Civil War—there were the crops to attend to and a colicky but pretty new baby girl, Sarah Ann, to take care of. The young couple were used to seeing figures coming and going from the barn they shared with Peter's parents—Robert's hired hands, the escaping slaves, a wandering Union soldier—but it had never aggravated the women as long as the men were there to keep order. In late fall of 1862, Peter joined the Philadelphia regiment and left his young wife and sickly daughter in the care of his aging parents in the larger house, leaving the stone cottage empty and abandoned. The following spring, Robert Altemus was shot and killed while attempting to prevent a Union officer from taking one of his horses from his barn and Emma had written her husband with the news, begging him to return to the farm. That October, Peter Altemus was captured and later, in 1864, was transferred to the Confederate prison camp in Andersonville. In the last days of the war, Peter and Will Ogden, the Confederate officer who protected him at the camp and became his close buddy, left the prison and made their way on foot back to Peter's home in Bucks County, Pennsylvania.

At dusk one day Emma had seen the two men from the upper window of the larger house, approaching about a mile away on the main post road. She did not recognize her husband, his gentleman's posture changed by a broken foot and a bullet wound through his shoulder, and thought instead that he was just another of a number of aggressive strangers the women had had to chase off the land. She saw them headed in the direction of the barn and the stone cottage and decided to let them spend the night, knowing that in the morning she might be faced with a difficult confrontation if they still remained on the property.

Before daylight the next morning, Emma arrived at the barn with her father-in-law's rifle, found no one there, and fed their last horse, a lame mare named Molly. The war and hard work had streaked Emma's brown hair with gray wisps that she was forever pushing away from her forehead with the back of her hand. It was daybreak when she approached the front door of the stone cottage. She found the two men in the front room, asleep by the hearth atop a pile of straw and a rubber coat, their arms and bodies entwined like those of lovers. She had only noticed the Confederate insignia on the discarded jacket when the first of the two men stirred, saw her standing by the door and reached for a knife he kept tucked in his belt. Emma Altemus shot Will Ogden in the heart before he was fully standing. She did not recognize her husband—he was slimmer and gaunt, his hair thinning and his face covered by a scraggly beard. She shot him as he was opening his eyes from sleep, awakened by the blast that had killed his mate.

Emma did not know what she had done until minutes later when, searching through jackets and pockets, she discovered a letter she had written her husband more than a year before. She looked at his name on the envelope, studied her own handwriting as if it were in a foreign language, then fell to her knees and began to cry.

The plan came to her about an hour later, as the dark red blood traveled along the floor to the place where she had collapsed. She dragged the bodies to the barn, burying the two men in a hole she spent several hours digging. She burned their uniforms and clothing in the hearth, which created a great and unnatural stench for most of the day. A slow, northeasterly wind prevented the odor from reaching the new house and her mother-in-law's notice, and Emma burned her own bloody clothing to hide any trace of the crime. No soldiers had ever been in the stone cottage, she decided. She would tell nothing to her mother-in-law. Her husband had died in the war, in prison, a Confederate retaliation for the Union victory, not from the trigger of a gun held by his own nervous wife.

All this had been recounted in a letter Emma Altemus had left for her daughter when she died in 1914. Emma had moved back into the stone cottage almost immediately after the murders; the felony had never been discovered, and when she remarried years later, her new husband added the second floor to the stone cottage. The larger Altemus house had been sold decades before Emma's death when Emma's mother-in-law Lucinda had died. By the time of her mother's death, Sarah Ann had married a printer in Easton and had had four children, and she had been too disturbed by her mother's news to have the barn floor excavated and the bodies located and properly buried. When no immediate buyer could be found for her mother's stone cottage, it lay abandoned until after the Second World War, when Sarah Ann's grandson began renting the property to an artist and his companion. From there the hauntings began, or, rather, began to be recorded. In his diary, the artist, Michael Franz, wrote of slamming doors and tapping sounds throughout the cottage. One morning, at daybreak, he smelled a strange odor in the kitchen and witnessed the bloody corpses of the two men on the floor beside the hearth. He fell ill later that same day, dying of pneumonia a month later.

During the next thirty years the legend of dual ghosts was widely publicized, primarily due to the posthumous renown of the artist and a big-ticket auction that included his Pennsylvania paintings and diaries. In the following years, however, the appearances of the ghosts of Peter Altemus and Will Ogden were sporadic and infrequent, though they were always preceded by a strange burning stench and witnessed at daybreak, always in the same spot beside the large hearth in the kitchen. Their embracing last moments became entwined with mysterious or suspicious meanings, particularly since Michael Franz had referred to them in his diaries as "the tragic lovers of years past." And calamity, misery, tragedy, or just an endless run of bad luck seemed to haunt any living soul who saw them. Reese Tanner, the interior designer, who had the misfortune to see them in 1983 in the middle of his expansion of the stone cottage into a two-story country retreat, fared particularly badly. He saw them at sunrise, pooling in their own blood. He went upstairs to where his partner, Don, was sleeping, roused him, and said he had just seen the two ghosts.

Afterward, Reese and Don had only experienced some minor handicaps with the expansion of the house—a contractor who deserted them, a foundation that cracked and had to be repoured, windows built to the wrong size and then installed upside down. Reese was a handsome and persuasive man, thirty-eight and well built, and he often chose workmen who also liked to party after hours, particularly if Don had remained in the city or was tied up with supervising another design job. One morning, about four months after his observance of the soldiers by the hearth, Reese noticed a reddish patch of skin by his collarbone, about as big as a one-carat diamond. Other lesions appeared quickly thereafter, on his thighs, his arms, his chin, his nose. In the final stages of the disease, he lost his eyesight and never saw the completion of the renovations of the country house, which Don reluctantly finished on his own. Don never spent another night in the house after Reese's death, however, selling the property to the first married couple who would take it off his hands.

And as for the fate of the more recent slew of married owners, the details I heard were secretive and limited, but among the words Arnie and Mitch whispered to me one night at the dinner table were "miscarriage," "adultery," and "cancer."

◆

When my boyfriend Scott first heard the tales of the ghosts of Arnie and Mitch's country house he disbelieved my theory that the two soldiers in the Civil War might have been murdered and buried by a jealous Emma Altemus. "I don't doubt that the two soldiers may have had some kind of sexual intimacy with each other—or certainly some kind of intimate bond with each other from having survived the war and been in a prison camp together—but I doubt that the wife would have displayed such a furious jealousy," he told me. "That's such a modern reaction. She killed them because she thought they were intruders."

This started our own little quarrel. Scott, an intensely focused businessman concerned mostly about "net worth" and "the bottom line," thought my jealousy theory was inappropriate. In his estimation the concept of homosexuality was a modern-day psychological invention, perhaps because he had only recently discovered his own inclinations toward the same sex. Married for sixteen years, Scott had only been out as a gay man for four months when we began dating one another, so everything about gay life—and gay history—was new and a surprise to him. He was amazed to learn that Hadrian, Alexander, da Vinci, and Lincoln all had gay pasts (not to mention quite a few of the ancient popes). "During the Civil War men used to dress up for the prison balls," I told him, when our argument about Peter Altemus and Will Ogden began. "They strung blankets around their waists for dresses."

"Then why aren't the ghosts seen in drag?" he asked. Scott was a no-nonsense sort of man. There was a logical explanation for everything. He saw nothing spooky about a squeaky door, for instance; it only needed to be oiled. (And he had all the husbandry skills our hosts lacked, a talent that resulted in our frequent weekend invitations to the country and Scott being peppered for handyman advice.)

"Technically, it would have only been one in drag, not both of them," I answered him. "And it would have only been occasionally, not a daily thing, especially since I doubt that there were a lot of prison dances or that Emma Altemus would not have noted that one of the men was dressed as a woman. So they appear the way they lived and died—soldiers embracing as lovers."

"They were probably embracing because it was cold," Scott said. "You've been reading too many gay books," he said. "Not everyone in the world is gay."

Though Scott was often amused by my anecdotes of gay history, he believed that I saw life from a narrow gay perspective. I worked as an editor for a gay news service that syndicated stories to gay newspapers, gay bar rags, gay blogs, and gay Web sites, and I enjoyed looking for historical precedents of current news items that I was reporting on. Scott never took my job seriously because in his estimation I didn't make a serious income from my gay work, certainly nowhere near his nongay six figures. I believed that Scott diminished his homosexuality, hiding its existence as if he were ashamed of it. Scott was only out to a small circle of gay friends. Neither his ex-wife, his two children, nor his coworkers at the bank knew about our relationship, nor did Scott expect to change this arrangement anytime soon with new disclosures—a continual source of irritation between the two of us, because I always felt that he undervalued our relationship in comparison to those he had had with his girlfriends and his wife.

"Peter could have written Emma a letter about what it was like at the balls," I said, not ready to drop our little discussion or let Scott think he was off the hook. "*Dear Emma, the privates of our brigade had a ball last night,*" I began, reciting an imaginary letter. "*Some of the boys got themselves up in ladies' clothes and were right pretty. A few of them even looked good enough to know better and I guess some of them did get things on with each other. I know I slept with my favorite pretty one. He kept me warm all through the night.*"

Scott arched an eyebrow at me as if I were the queerest man he had ever met. "Maybe you should direct your imagination toward solving global warming," he said. "The planet really needs someone like you to step up to the plate and make things better for *everyone.*"

◆

Scott and I were close to breaking up the weekend of Arnie and Mitch's Independence Day party. The arguing had started the day before our drive to the country when Scott had introduced me as "a friend" to one of his coworkers we had run into at a restaurant near Times Square. We had spent the night together in the city at my apartment discussing the pros and cons of coming out. (Scott felt that he would be discriminated against at work; I felt that I was being discriminated against at home.) On the drive to the country the next morning, we had reached an icy stalemate and had managed to avoid each other during the barbecue alongside Arnie and Mitch's new pool, talking with the other weekend guests—mostly a couple who had driven up from Washington, a closeted lobbyist and his very out and flamboyant boyfriend.

That evening Scott and I spent the night upstairs in "Emma's bedroom," avoiding any intimacy. (Sex was the primary thing that kept us together—

usually we couldn't keep our hands off each other, but that night we slept at opposite ends of the large king-sized bed, deliberately shunning each other.)

The next morning the chill remained between us; the sky grew gray with thick, dark rain clouds; and fearing that we would all be trapped with one another in the country house because of the miserable weather, Arnie proposed an outing to the nearby movie theater, purposely to prevent his guests from escaping to the city early and leaving him alone with Mitch.

Scott wasn't interested in seeing the movie—a romantic comedy—and decided to stay behind, saying that he needed the time to prepare for an office meeting on Monday morning. In his own way, Scott was as high maintenance as our hosts. He always traveled with a cellphone, a Blackberry, a laptop, an iPod, and a thin briefcase full of thick files. I didn't protest or plead for him to join us on the outing to the movie, thinking he was hitting the last nail in the coffin of our relationship. Before we left the house, Scott had spread out his papers on the small café table that was beside the giant hearth, flipped open his laptop and was contentedly at work, oblivious to the rest of us scrambling for parkas, caps, and umbrellas.

It was raining when we left the house and, during the course of our movie, the sky blackened and the rain came down harder. Back at the house, Scott abandoned his work at the table for short intervals to stand in front of the windows and look out at the sloping countryside and the water puddling on the stone path that led to the kitchen door. Alone, he was attuned now to all of the old house's quirky noises and motions—the tapping of the rain, the wind blowing sheets of water against the window, the creaking floorboards in the kitchen as he shifted his weight, the muffled, wet swinging chimes by the door. Scott was not a superstitious man and his practical mind was as far from wondering about the ghosts as it could be. He was thinking of the power of the rain, the solidity of the structure of the old house, how much it would cost him to put a down payment on a similar place, how he would redecorate it if he were its owner—how he would reorganize the kitchen counters and change the configurations of the guest rooms. Somewhere in there he imagined himself the resident owner and in that imagination he saw me as his partner in the kitchen cooking, reaching for a mixing bowl to make pancakes (his morning favorite) or experimenting with the color of margaritas (my favorite).

He returned to the table and his reading material and became absorbed in his work. Outside the sky darkened more, the rain continued, and Scott worked away. Upstairs a door in the house closed with a violent shudder, obviously pulled shut by the wind of the storm coming inside the house, and Scott was forced to look away from his laptop for a few seconds. Next, the overhead light in the kitchen sputtered and went black, and the laptop on the table slipped into the auxiliary power of its battery. Outside flashes of lightning flickered and a burst of thunder was so sudden and fierce Scott felt the table vibrate. He waited in the darkness for the power to be restored, for the lights to flicker and resume burning brightly, but when there was a dark quiet for several seconds, he sighed, then began to take note of where he was in his work, saving the documents open on his laptop. The kitchen was as black as night, the rain hammering the shingles of the roof and sliding down the gutters and windows and stones. For a moment he wondered where the circuit breaker was located in the house and then, realizing he didn't know, he folded his arms and sat back in his chair and waited a few minutes till the rain suddenly stopped and the black clouds blew away and the sun began to break through the darkness.

Light broke across a page of his notes first—bright and yellowish as if the morning had just arrived. The light widened over the table, then moved up his arms and chest and across his shoulders. For a moment he was conscious of the warmth of the sun and he squinted to adjust his eyesight to the fast-rising light in the kitchen. The sunlight was accompanied by a strange burning smell—like that of wet wood and scorched hair—and Scott lifted his eyes away from the table to make sure that nothing was cooking on the stove top. Immediately, he felt a change in the kitchen and within himself and he knew he would see the ghosts before they had even appeared.

The trail of blood appeared first—initially as a crimson light against the wooden floor, then thickening and darkening into a river of red. His eyes searched out the edges of the red liquid, then followed it back across the room to where he sat by the hearth, and the deep red covered his legs and shoes. His heart was beating faster but he was not frightened or panicking. He was awestruck, in fact, as if he were watching a common phenomenon of nature such as the aurora borealis or comets streaking across the nighttime sky.

He thought about closing his eyes and avoiding what was next, but he refused to give in to fear. Beside the hearth, just beyond his shoes, a blood-soaked pile of straw covered with a tarplike cloth appeared, and then the shape of the bodies.

One man was lying on his back, his eyes and mouth opened wide with astonishment, the center of his shirt and chest blown apart with a bloody hole. The other man was on his side, his eyes closed in a wince, a blackened wound at his neck where the bullet must have hit.

As the sunlight moved farther into the room, the pool of blood began to recede, as if time were reversing itself. The red edges shrank toward the hearth and the bodies and the smell changed, or, rather, disappeared. This was what worried Scott—he had not heard of this aspect of the legend.

But he didn't run away. Instead, he sat and watched the blood draw back, disappear toward the hearth and the men. When he looked again at the bodies, he saw that their positions had changed. They were lying on the tarp face-to-face, embracing each other as if to draw their bodies closer together for warmth. The wounds and the blood were gone and there was an unmistakable intimacy between the two men—one man's lips were nuzzled against the other's neck, reminding Scott of how he had liked to sleep with me, before our testy dispute. As he watched the two men sleeping, he realized that they were alive and breathing and there was nothing to be afraid of.

And then they were gone—vanishing as quickly as sunlight could fill the kitchen.

◆

Scott was napping in the upstairs bedroom when we returned from the movies. The violent rainstorm had tumbled branches and leaves off the maple trees closest to the house, but had left the air cool and sharp and fresh. The power had been restored and I cleaned up the papers Scott had left on the small table beside the hearth, replacing them in the manila folders, and brought them upstairs to the bedroom, along with the laptop he had left behind. He stirred lightly when I entered the room, then rolled over and shook off his sleepiness when I was beside the dresser and placing the folders and the laptop near his briefcase.

"I'll do it slowly," he said. "The kids first."

"What do you mean?" I asked him.

"I'll introduce you to Wesley and Jennifer." Wesley and Jennifer were Scott's children, aged thirteen and fifteen, who lived with his ex-wife. "There's no sense in meeting Melissa. I'm sure she knows, but there's bad blood there already." Melissa, Scott's ex-wife, had pressed him hard for extra money and child support during their divorce settlement.

"Why the change?" I asked him, sitting on the edge of the bed.

He looked up at me, met my eyes, and said, "Don't be afraid. I saw the two men."

"What men?"

"The soldiers. The ghosts of the two soldiers."

The blood drained from my face and my mouth opened as I looked for some kind of response or appropriate form of sympathy.

"When the rain stopped," he said. "They were there, lying together by the fireplace. There's nothing to be scared about. I don't believe they'll cause us any harm. You were right. They were in love. I saw what they felt for each other. It's how I feel about you. They were simply two guys who felt like us."

◆

Scott was right, no harm or misfortune or calamity came to him. Or us. The two soldiers were never seen again, nor have their remains ever been searched for in the barn or relocated to a more acceptable final resting place. But Scott and I often credit the ghosts of Peter Altemus and Will Ogden with turning around our relationship and creating a solid union between us, or so we like to tell our guests when we entertain them at our own country house. In the six years we've been together, Scott has come out to his coworkers at the bank, I've stopped pressuring him for proof of his feelings for me, and we bought a house down the road from where Arnie and Mitch continue to spend their weekends. Our country house is not haunted, except on those occasions when we invite Arnie and Mitch to join us for dinner. They arrive bearing quarrels and wounded feelings, though they always seem to be in better spirits when they leave.

THE AFTER PARTY

Luke stifled a yawn. Because of his new job he'd worked extra hours to get the day off and the lack of sleep was catching up with him. He had tried to nap on the plane trip down to Miami, but his seat had been next to a young mother and her month-old baby and he had spent the flight being jostled and prodded just as he was about to nod off.

"This place was the real OC," Mike said.

Mike was broad shouldered and muscular, with shortly cropped hair and pierced nipples. Since Luke had last seen him, about six months ago in Philadelphia, Mike had gotten another tatt, this one on his right pectoral, an elaborate two-colored dragon that snaked out beneath the tank top Mike wore and curled around to his back. Luke squinted from the sunlight and used a hand to cover the yawn. He wanted to crash because he was exhausted, but he was too excited to be out of town and ready to have a good time. It was his first trip to Miami. They were sitting at a café table on the outdoor terrace of the hotel with four other guys who had shown up for the White Party weekend, each as skimpily attired as Mike and Luke were, all wearing sandals, tank tops, and shorts. Luke, the youngest of the group, had met Dan and Cliff two years ago at a party in Palm Springs. Both guys were short and beefy. Cliff had a goatee that made him look like the angrier of the two, though Luke's experience with the couple had proved otherwise. Dan was an alpha male wanting to flash and fuck his way through a crowd. Cliff was a pussycat, ready to roll over and be admired. Luke might have met Frankie before, there was a familiar, old-school clone look about him: hairy-chested with a thick, wide black moustache. Luke had just been introduced to Raul when he took a seat at the table, a slick, dark-haired guy with big, round brown nipples he thought he might like to know better.

"OC?" Raul asked. "How so?" Raul was from Los Angeles, Hollywood Hills to be exact, and genetics and the California sun along with a high-priority gym membership had bronzed and buffed him well.

"Overdose Central," Mike said. "This was a real flea bag before they fixed it up. The first time I came down for the Party you could get a room dirt cheap. A couple of guys staying here OD'd that weekend—one who was staying on the fifth floor, another they found out at back. The next year I heard about a couple of guys who were sharing the same room where the guy OD'd and saw the dude. Nude, on the bed."

"A ghost?" Luke asked.

Mike nodded and folded his arms across his chest. The dragon flexed and shimmered.

"Dude said he had sex with it before he realized it was a ghost of a dead guy."

"No way, man," Dan said. "He was probably coked up."

"So it goes," Mike said. "I'm just the vessel containing the story."

"I've heard about your vessel," Dan said. "It's got its own domain name according to my sources."

"Hey, when you're a legend you're a legend."

"I don't believe in ghosts," Dan said, "but I've had plenty of spooky tricks."

"Spare us," Cliff said and the tension at the table rose a few degrees. He had been silent since Luke had joined the group because he was seated in the chair with the best view of the sidewalk traffic. Dan and Cliff had been lovers up until a few weeks ago. They were doing the trip together because neither wanted the other to have a better time. In Palm Springs, Luke had had sex with Dan first, before he had sex with them as a couple. "You'll make all of us want to sleep alone."

"Speak for yourself," Mike said, and chuckles rippled around the table. They were all in town for the same things: Dancing. Sex. Drugs. The beach. A weekend party in the sun and under the stars.

Dan went ahead and started talking about one of his spooky tricks, a tale that involved a bathtub and a catheter. Luke was mildly disgusted and turned his attention to the street, catching the cruise of a blue-eyed guy who was walking with another tattooed boyish-looking fellow. The neighborhood was filled with good-looking guys, all of them the kind you'd see on a bar float in a gay pride parade. Luke's senses had been on overload since he had stepped off the plane. Too many available men in the same place. He turned back to the group just as Dan was summing up his trick. "...He'd locked the door so I had to crawl out onto the roof!"

Luke yawned again.

"Must not have been too bad," Cliff said. "You got off, didn't you?"

Luke smiled at the double entendre and Cliff's edge of sarcasm.

"What about the other guy?" Raul asked.

"What other guy?" Dan said.

"Exactly," Cliff added. "It was all about you. It had nothing to do with ghosts. Except the ghost of your youth."

The table fell silent as everyone looked away from the trouble at the table to the trouble cruising by them, a group of men wearing sequined thongs and feathered headdresses. Mike smiled and made a comment about the party starting earlier every year that was generally ignored or acknowledged only with silent nods.

"Ghosts aren't real," Dan said tensely. It was directed at Cliff. "They're hallucinations."

"I knew one of the guys who OD'd here," Frankie said. Frankie was not much of a talker. In another life he might have been a cowboy, the strong silent kind always at the edge of the horizon.

"The ghost?" Raul asked.

"Not sure about that. He was a young guy. Kid, really. A runaway who hustled himself here and there. He'd run out of drugs to sell, so he was selling himself that night. Word had it he was tricking to get high. That might be true. But he wasn't a rough kid. He was a real sweetheart who was just looking for a steady boyfriend. Some guy to help him out."

"A boyfriend doesn't 'help someone out,'" Dan said. "I don't get these guys who are so needy that they've got to have a daddy to get them off the street and dress them up before they say they're in love."

"Not all of us are as richly endowed as you are," Cliff said.

"You can't expect to find your doppelganger as a boyfriend," Mike added. "Even Narcissus was disappointed with himself."

"Didn't he OD too?" Luke asked, trying to bring some levity back to the table.

They were distracted by another group of guys walking by, this time thin, scruffy-looking teenagers who ogled them and playfully began barking, "Woof! Woof! Woof!" toward the group at the café table. Laughs and smiles followed and Luke took the opportunity to stand and politely excuse himself. He air-kissed Cliff and patted Dan and Mike on the back. "Gotta crash," he said to Frankie and Raul, feeling a bit like a wimp leaving the party before it even got started.

"Joining us for dinner?" Cliff asked.

"Not sure," Luke said. "I'll look for you."

Inside the lobby, he stopped at the gift shop to buy a health bar and bottled water. His plan was to nap for a few hours, then get dressed and walk over to the event. He didn't want a big meal sloshing around his stomach all night. At the elevator, Luke found Raul waiting. He must have left the group shortly after Luke.

"Funky place," Raul said. The hotel was decorated in shades of blue: blue carpet, blue walls, blue fixtures. The lights inside the elevator were dim and blue.

Inside the elevator they discovered they were staying on the same floor. The *fifth* floor. "Not spooked, are you?" Luke asked.

Raul shook his head. He asked if Luke's room had a terrace.

"Out of my price range," Luke said.

Raul was slightly taller than Luke, with a slender neck corded with muscle. But his big chest overshadowed the rest of his physique and those large nipples peeking out of the side of his tank top made Luke smile and want to lean over and lick them.

"Stop by and check mine out," Raul said. "I had this room last year. I could watch all sorts of things going on all night."

"Will do," Luke said.

"I've got plenty to help you sleep," Raul said. "Or stay up."

"Party supplies!" Luke said and smiled wider. He had a good smile and knew how to use it.

"Come on in and check it out."

Luke seldom did any kind of pharmaceuticals because it messed up his system more than it elevated it and the unpleasant aftereffects often lasted longer than the short high. But he knew that Raul's invitation had more to do with fooling around with each other than it did looking at the view or sampling drugs, and the prospect of having a quickie energized him. So he followed behind Raul to his door.

Inside, Raul's room was twice the size of Luke's. Luke left his water and health bar on a desk and walked to the terrace and looked out at the view. "You've got this all to yourself?" Luke asked.

"Me and whoever wants to party," Raul said. Raul was behind him. He placed a hand on Luke's shoulder and Luke turned and draped his hand around Raul's waist. They moved into a kiss, testing and tasting each other before their hands began exploring each other further.

They moved from the terrace to the bed. Luke was used to guys being aggressive with him and Raul didn't disappoint. Luke devoted some attention to Raul's nipples, which Raul encouraged. Luke had thought it would all be over fast, a quick jerk-off session, and then he would be back in his room napping, but Raul was taking things slower, massaging Luke's crotch and reaching for lube and condoms. Soon Raul was deep inside Luke and Luke was somewhere between exhaustion and ecstasy.

Luke felt his orgasm rise naturally. Raul smiled and shuddered at his finish. They were both covered with sweat. The sheets on the bed were damp from their bodies. They snuggled for a while before Raul said, "Sleep here, if you want." Luke felt a warm glow inside his chest lengthen and cover him like a blanket. He was out moments later, sleeping deeply.

When he woke the room was dark. The sun was gone. The terrace door was open and the music from the street and the beach made its way lightly into the room. Raul was sitting on the terrace, his legs propped up on a chair. On the small table was a sweating, half-empty glass of amber-colored drink. When Raul saw Luke at the sliding glass door he stood and draped himself around Luke's body. Luke could taste the alcohol—rum—as they kissed.

Again the kissing was slow and long, their hands exploring each other's body as if they had forgotten what they had found before. "Let's shower," Raul said, and he took Luke's hand and led him into the bathroom. They kissed and groped some more, before turning on the water and continuing under the spray.

Afterward, Luke was clean and content, a light film of exhaustion lingering in his lungs. He went down the hall to his room and dressed. Raul knocked at his door a few minutes later. He was wearing white slacks and a thin linen shirt that showed his chest off underneath. They kissed and groped again in the doorway, before Luke led him inside. Luke was willing to skip the dance, willing to sleep and snuggle and wake to have sex again and again before collapsing into sleep. He was deeply attracted to Raul, which meant he was no longer looking for something else. They stood in front of the mirror by the bed admiring themselves admiring each other.

Raul thought they should party. "Take this," Raul said, and slipped a pill onto Luke's tongue. Luke trusted Raul because he had reached that part of himself that was "somewhere short of love." He swallowed and smiled and Raul took a pill too. They kissed some more, then Raul took Luke's hand and led him out into the night.

They made their way through the Vizcaya event holding hands. They saw Dan dancing with a buff guy with silver earrings and a shaved head. Frankie greeted them with deep tongue-kisses and Luke looked away when Raul passed him some drugs. Luke pushed away the idea that Raul might be a dealer, then pushed away the idea that what he might feel this weekend for Raul might continue longer, then pushed away both thoughts because he was dancing with Raul and admiring the way he moved his hips and legs.

They stopped for drinks and found Mike with a guy who looked similar to himself. There were kisses, nipple tweaks, and more drugs exchanged. Raul gave Luke another pill and said, "This will make everything look beautiful."

"*More* beautiful," Luke said, and he realized he was already high.

They walked with Cliff and a guy who had a large tatt of a Celtic cross on his back to the after party a few blocks away. They passed around a joint that Raul had tucked into his pants pocket. Raul danced with the cross-tattooed guy and Luke followed Cliff to a hallway where Cliff gave him a blow job. "Just like old times," Cliff said, and they danced through several songs, till they spotted the cross-tattooed fellow dancing with a thin blond guy with great abs and Luke remembered Raul.

Cliff was stopped by two bearded guys he knew and Luke continued on through the crowd without him to search for Raul. He stopped at a bar to get a drink and started a conversation with a guy wearing a white baseball cap backward. Luke was wasted but having a good time. The music was good. The lights were fun. Yes, everything was good and fine. He was giggling a lot. There were so many guys it was hard to focus on only one. The guy he was talking to had a great smile and stubble on his chin that Luke wanted to kiss and taste. Before that happened, Raul had found him and was holding him from behind and kissing Luke's neck.

Raul had more drugs and Luke took another pill. Raul took one himself and gave another one to the white-capped guy. The three of them danced until the lights began to brighten and the dance floor began to empty out. The white-capped guy left, but Raul wanted to dance until the music stopped.

An hour or so later they walked outside. It was morning and bright. Luke asked Raul how he was feeling, if he had done as much as Luke had. "Of course," Raul answered. They walked hand in hand back to the hotel.

They snuggled in the blue elevator and lost track of time, surprised when the door opened and they were on the fifth floor. They stopped at the door to Luke's room because it was the one nearest to the elevator. They kissed in the hallway and lost track of time again, till Luke unlocked the door and Raul followed him inside. In bed, they snuggled and groped each other, till both of them realized that they were too wired to fall asleep and Luke found the condoms he had brought in his suitcase.

Again it was deep and slow and pleasurable and when they finished they continued to cuddle. Luke fell asleep for a moment, then rose a little later to urinate. He wanted to shower. Raul said he would sleep a bit. Luke stood at the edge of the bed and looked down on Raul and smiled. Luke thought he might be beyond that "somewhere" place. He thought he could be serious about Raul.

Luke turned to go to the bathroom and saw his reflection in the mirror. His profile pleased him but he noticed that the bed behind him was empty. He turned and looked at Raul and Raul was not there. The bed was empty.

A jolt went through him, then a recollection of the story he had heard hours before at the café table. It couldn't be true, could it? He called out to Raul, thinking he might have slipped away from the bed and gone to the bathroom while Luke was busy admiring himself.

There was no answer. The bathroom was empty. Luke wrapped a towel around his waist and opened his door and looked out into the hallway. It was empty. He walked down the hallway to Raul's door and knocked, but there was no answer, so he knocked again, louder and harder.

He went back to his room and called the desk clerk and asked to be put through to Raul's room. Again, there was no answer. He called the clerk back and said he thought Raul might be in his room unconscious. He was put on hold, another clerk came on the line, then a few minutes later a hotel security guard was in Luke's room asking questions.

"I just *know*," Luke said. He kept insisting that Raul was in his room, though he kept hoping that Raul would show up at any minute, having gone downstairs for breakfast or for a dip in the pool. He knew he was asking for trouble if the security guard opened Raul's door. There were more parties that day and Raul had not planned to go back to Los Angeles till later in the week. He had tried to talk Luke into staying a few extra days to party more.

An hour later another security guard showed up with an executive of the hotel. All three men went down the hall and unlocked Raul's door. Raul was in the room in his bed. He was dead.

The coroner and the police showed up. Luke answered more questions and several he had already answered before. Raul's body was taken away. The time of death was estimated at around ten that morning, about the time Raul and Luke had left the after party and walked back to the hotel.

"Are you sure he was in your room with you?" a policeman asked.

Raul had been discovered lying on his bed fully clothed, still wearing the linen shirt and white pants and shoes he had worn to the party.

"Yes," Luke answered. "I'm sure."

Luke's certainty crumbled as the drugs wore off and his exhaustion returned. He told the officer the last thing he remembered was dancing with a guy wearing a white baseball cap backward. After that, everything else was cloudy. The white-capped guy was never found because Luke didn't know his name. Cliff and Dan were staying at another hotel. Frankie wasn't in his room, nor was Mike.

Luke remained in his room waiting for the next thing to happen. Soon the questions and the visitors and the phone calls stopped. Alone, he looked into the mirror hoping to find Raul on the bed. Something in his memory told him this was the way it had happened. Something in his heart told him he wouldn't forget what he couldn't remember.

THE HAUNTED HEART

The ghost was waiting on Commercial Street. He was bored with the couple and their two children who had rented the upstairs rooms for the month. They were not easy to frighten—slamming doors, flickering lights, billowing curtains meant nothing to them, the whole lot self-absorbed and scattering sand everywhere they walked. He preferred more drama, more purpose to his mischief. It was late, after midnight, when he gave up on them and left the house where he had been shuttered up for years, the last of his tricks—a shattering vase—unable to rouse the sleeping parents.

Outside, the street was crowded in front of the pizza shop. Young men were waiting to connect with one another. He had watched them for years from the upstairs bedroom, sometimes even entertaining a few of them if they rented one of the bedrooms of his house. He had come to long for their freedom, their ease, their adventures here one summer, another summer somewhere else.

He had been a sailor while alive: first, as a boy, the cook of a fishing schooner for a crew of twelve, then later, in his twenties, the captain of his own vessel. He was comfortable with the company of men, though he had given up the seas at the age of thirty-four when the great gale of 1841 had shipwrecked the *Peerless Troubadour*. Grief had done him in. He had survived where others had not. Seven of his crew had drowned. In the village, wives and children and parents and families had been left behind. He had returned and married, raising five children of his own, four daughters and one son, and turned a small nautical shop into a thriving grocery and hardware business. The urge to explore continued to nag him, but he never sailed again, the sound of the waves and the rain compelling him to remain inside on stormy days. As the years blew by he learned to use his pain to remind others of their fear of it, what can happen when you least expect it, how heartless the world can treat you no matter how honestly or truthfully you abide. He had died at the age of sixty-six: a clap of thunder, a heart attack, a rain of memories of the sea.

He had remained inside the house, a ghost, stricken with grief, while outside the seasons passed, the train tracks disappeared, the artists arrived by motorcars, the fleet of ships thinned out, replaced by noisy motorboats and gunning engines offering hourly expeditions. The ghost slept, woke, sighed, and puffed out the curtains of his house until it fell into neglect. Rain seeped through the roof. More time passed and outside the windows the crowds became more openly obvious. Men holding hands. Women with their arms slung around the shoulders of other women. A couple of men had renovated his house, replaced the rotted beams and nailed down new shingles, and turned it into an inn. The ghost had liked the smell of fresh paint, but not the steady stream of new tenants. Too many different faces angered him and he gave the inn a reputation. The house was sold and resold. But lately, year after year of the same childish pranks and mindless families had left him bored, and he had been looking for a reason to leave it behind.

Now, outside, on the darkened street, he felt his power diminished, his spirit lessened. He was not a traveling ghost, though alive he had traveled more than most men of his generation—far out into the Atlantic, from Cape Breton to Cape Horn. He watched a remarkably handsome man approach where he was standing in the darkened doorway of a house, the ivy on a trellis disappearing in the blackness beside him. The young man had a lopey gait, a long, thin torso, and curly black hair. He watched the man catch glances until he stopped to talk to another man, shorter, darker-haired and stocky, like the Portuguese sailors who used to work the *Peerless Troubadour*.

"Hey," the tall guy said.

"Hey," the shorter one answered.

The ghost rolled his eyes, dismayed by these meaningless introductions. He would have glanced elsewhere had he not sensed something that passed between the two men, something that made him, the ghost, brighten and sway and speed in their direction. The shorter one had shown this something first, but it was the taller one who felt it, deeper and more poignantly. The ghost sensed something other than just lust for each other—more of a need or a hunger or a thirst to understand something elusive. Most of all the ghost sensed cruelty if this game of emotions were played out wrong. Drama. Hysterics. Heart-shattering pain. He swung through the air, blowing a puff of air in front of their eyes.

"You want a slice of pizza?" the tall one asked.

"Sure," the other one responded.

The two men sat on the steps of the very same house the ghost had left. They ate their slices, drank their sodas, and talked about their favorite TV shows. The shorter one, named Wade, was disappointed in the conversation, since he'd hoped to meet a smarter guy than this one named Josh. The ghost was not at all disappointed, however; he kept the wind blowing between them, the expectations rising. Josh asked Wade what he did for a living. "Waiter," Wade answered. "You?"

"Musician," Josh answered, but felt it sounded arrogant and incomplete. "But I teach in Boston. Little girls wanting to play the piano. Little boys wanting to do anything else."

A musician? the ghost thought. *What a lucky a find—a man with a soul and a dream.* He could certainly spook and frighten and inspire a man as sensitive as a musician. He roared up another funnel of air and tossed it at the musician, but it was the other one who felt it first.

"It's too windy here," Wade said and looked up at the starry sky, as if expecting a storm, and for a moment the ghost felt as if he had been detected, then realized it was Wade's ploy to stir Josh to his feet. "We should get inside before it rains," Wade said.

The musician did not even question this. *Rain?* The ghost shivered and followed the two men along the street. Within a block it had been decided they would go to Josh's apartment instead of the guesthouse where Wade was staying. The ghost sensed passion brewing, though the men did not touch as they walked, nor stop to kiss and grope as others did in darkened nooks. The musician unlocked the door of a house on Carver Street, and the waiter followed him up two flights of stairs to a tiny apartment on the top floor. The ghost was delighted. The house was old, almost as old as his own; the stairs and doors creaked and wobbled. The musician explained that he had been renting the apartment for a month. Inside, the two men sat in different chairs; Josh rolled a joint. The ghost billowed in the smoke, disgusted by the scent, then relaxed and drifted between the two men as they shared the smoke. When the conversation ran out, when the passion should have stirred between them, the musician moved to a piano that was in the room and began to play softly. It was an awful tune, unmelodic and fragmented. It left the waiter confused. "Did you write that?" Wade asked.

"Yes," the musician answered proudly. The ghost moved closer, intrigued to discover the musician was also a composer, even though he found the music discordant and tuneless, too. "It's based on a fragment of Schubert," Josh said and slowed the notes and his fingers and the music changed into a beautiful melody. The ghost was astonished. Wade moved in closer, amazed.

The ghost waited through another song, another fragment becoming another lush melody. In his day courtship had taken much longer than this, though he was aware he was now waiting for one man to begin what the other man feared to start. Nothing like this happened this slowly in this village today. This was Provincetown in 1978 and the ghost was impatient for the fun to begin.

◆

The ghost remained with the musician because he thought Josh snobbish and condescending and should be taught some manners. Alive, the ghost had been known as Raymond Hennegar, the grandson of a poor Irishman who had sailed to Cape Breton from Limerick. His father had traveled farther south and become a drunk after his wife died from smallpox; the ghost had been given up by his father when he was only eight. At sea he had been forced to do more than cook for the crew; the needs of men were not unfamiliar to him.

Josh, the musician, was from old money. The ghost had recognized this while waiting that first night on the street. Josh had grown up in a Boston townhouse with a nanny and godparents, had never known even the hard labor of mowing a lawn. The ghost felt he deserved to be toughened up with a few scares. Raymond Hennegar had taken nothing for granted; he had had to earn every penny he made through long days and bleeding hands, bad backs and weakened knees.

That first night, when the musician and the waiter finally kissed and undressed and fell onto the bed, the ghost stood by the window rattling the blinds. The waiter was the aggressor, pushing and prodding and twisting the musician into one embrace and then another. The waiter was a descendant of Eastern European immigrants—Hungarian grandparents and a Czechoslovakian mother. The ghost knew that was why the waiter was stocky and taut; he had been a bag boy and a janitor's assistant before taking orders and delivering meals to tables, which was why he worked harder to be liked by a guy he found attractive. The two men fell asleep sticky and stained, first the waiter's arms around the musician, then later, the musician embracing Wade, as if reaching out for a stuffed animal to keep himself warmed against the night breeze. The ghost blew in between the cracks of their bodies, rustled their hair and dried their sweat. The next morning there was an awkwardness that Josh would not attempt to alleviate—his upbringing kept him cold and contemptuous. There was no offer of breakfast or coffee or even a shower before leaving; Josh wanted the waiter gone and to be alone with his music. It was Wade who left his phone number and expressed the desire to get together again, which is why the ghost decided to stay when the waiter left the apartment discouraged. Raymond Hennegar was angry and shattered a plate, thinking that the musician might have to be frightened into showing civility.

That was not what happened, however. The musician did not change and the waiter did not give up. Wade was back later in the day with flowers and a note that included the word *love*. The ghost now roared through the room with contempt and rustled through a pile of manuscripts on the piano, indignant to find the waiter groveling to be liked by a man who did not appreciate the easiness of life. The musician was alarmed and pissed by the note and the reappearance of the waiter— he sat Wade down near the window and said that nothing else would be possible between them—Josh had a boyfriend back in Boston and he had no desire to make his life more complicated than it was.

Complicated? the ghost thought. What was so complicated about balancing a checkbook that was never without funds? The ghost sensed that the boyfriend was only a prop to use when he was needed. He stirred up a draft, sent a glass rolling off the table and smashing to the floor. The waiter cleaned it up, thinking it was his fault, and the musician let him believe he was the clumsier and foolish one. The ghost slammed the bedroom door and knocked over a bookcase. The waiter bent down to reshelve the books and when Josh reached to stop him, he found himself without willpower. He kissed the back of Wade's neck, then moved around to his lips. They had sex again, this time on the floor. The musician pushed and groped and twisted Wade. That night, before the waiter left—Josh had decided another evening sleeping together was an intimacy he could not afford—Wade had suggested that they could be friends. They didn't live far from each other in Boston and Wade was only a waiter because it was his means of paying his way through college. And then the waiter confessed that he didn't know many gay men.

"I'm afraid I'm not a very good gay man, myself," Josh said; he was dismayed at being labeled in this particular way because he did not consider himself gay, other than desiring sex with men. "You would find me boring. I don't go to clubs or bars and have never been to a bathhouse."

"So I won't hold that against you," Wade answered.

Josh was as uneasy with the idea of friendship as he was with intimacy. "I would probably be a lousy friend," Josh said. "I think too much of myself."

The ghost was surprised by this admission, and amused that Wade handled it with humor. "So it would give you something else to talk to your therapist about," Wade said. "Someone other than your mother and boyfriend."

"It's that clear?" Josh asked in his most patronizing tone.

"We're all fucked up in our own way," Wade said.

The ghost was shocked to find the waiter so full of insight, brighter and more ambitious than when he had been spotted on the street—someone more than just a luggish hunk with an old man's face. When, at the end of the week, Wade returned to Boston, the ghost followed along, tucking himself up in the pocket of a knapsack. Raymond Hennegar was tired of being a phantom, hoping instead he might become a guiding spirit.

◆

Josh and Wade did not have sex with each other again for almost eight years; instead, they became best friends. They went to concerts and baseball games together, met for brunch on Sundays, helped one another pick out presents for family birthdays and holiday gatherings. Josh complained of his boyfriend's apathy and egotism. He felt no one took his compositions seriously and he didn't want to be a teacher the rest of his life. Wade talked about politics and economics and the injustices inherent in the American dream. He also told Josh of every trick he found and what had happened between the sheets (or in the steam room of his gym, if that were the case). The ghost settled into the pipes of Wade's apartment off campus, scratching the metal risers like a rat when the weather was warm, banging and clanking the radiator with gusts of steam during the winter months. The ghost helped Wade select the proper utensils and equipment to use in the kitchen, helped him decide to give up the crates and futons and buy a grown-up couch and a decent bed. He helped Wade into a better haircut, helped him buy tailored, well-made clothes, made him realize he needed a dentist to cap his chipped front teeth so it would soften his smile. The ghost thought Wade showed poor taste in his selection of men, however, or rather, perfect taste for finding a guy with a terrific body and a lousy attitude, and he felt Wade worked too hard in bed to please a guy who would not remember his name five seconds after reaching an orgasm. Raymond Hennegar knew that this sort of sex was too mechanical for Wade's passion, though he blithely tagged along as Wade experimented with bondage, dildos, and watersports, and hopelessly groped for Mr. Right in darkened back rooms and clubs.

Raymond Hennegar always liked it best when Josh reappeared in Wade's schedule. He knew they were destined for each other, could see that they were to become something more than just good friends, though he could not foresee the future in detail, other than what should happen was not what usually occurred. The ghost liked to use this knowledge to heighten the sexual tension between the two men, however; he brightened the lights when Wade was still pumped and flushed from working out, tossed windmills of air through Josh's curly hair to make him look more accessible and boyish, flickered candles and ruffled shirts to make the atmosphere more romantic when the subject of lousy dates and bad boyfriends crept into the conversation. The ghost had a deeper dislike for Karl, Josh's boyfriend, than he felt toward any of Wade's tricks; Raymond Hennegar could see right through Karl's indifference toward Josh's rising dependency on his boyfriend. The truth was that Josh was never sexually at ease with anyone, the boyfriend or otherwise. He was never sure if what he felt was pain or joy or even what he *should* feel during sex. The ghost realized this confusion translated itself into the atonal mess at the keyboard. Wade was right when he told Josh he was too uptight to believe in a simple melodic line; that Josh was a frightened and repressed romantic who couldn't admit that what he really wanted to believe in more than anything else was the pure, unadulterated power of a simple, melodic line. The ghost laughed at this, though Josh did not appreciate the bluntness. "I know what I'm doing," Josh said. "Deconstruction is very hip right now."

"But it's boring," Wade said. "And it sounds awful."

Provoked, Josh composed a discordant string quartet that was technically brilliant and difficult to perform. Wade was more supportive when this work was panned by a reviewer in the *Globe*; he tried to convince Josh to continue composing and suggested applying for a fellowship in New Mexico or Vermont. Instead, Josh joined the faculty of the conservatory where he had trained, using his misfortune to shape the technique of his students and hoping his own music would one day merit reassessment.

Josh used a tough approach in his friendship with Wade, too. Since graduating with a degree in history, Wade had bounced from one temp job to another. Josh told Wade that he had no ambition, no goals, no ideas other than the next bar he might try. Wade countered that it was Josh who was really purposeless—he had been born with a silver spoon in his mouth and could not even summon up a bad fragment anymore. The ghost swarmed up to the ceiling during this bitter exchange, writhing in the anger of the air; abandoned by his father, poverty was a tarnish that Raymond Hennegar had never polished away. These boys—yes, *boys*—knew nothing about the true horrors of struggling to find the next meal or a piece of clothing to make it through winter. He burned and seethed and decided to let them continue to torture each other. Instead, they did not see each other for a period of several months.

Josh tried to break it off with Karl, though Karl, every time he thought he was close to being dumped, played a little harder to keep stringing Josh along. Josh tried to see a few guys on the side, but found it more pleasurable to be anonymous at a bathhouse than out on a date and hoping to fuck, then gave up on the practice when first crabs, then amoebas left him sidelined and Karl protested enough was enough or else.

Wade took a job working in the library of an insurance firm, a thankless position that gave him benefits and paid vacations. The ghost followed Wade to a new apartment, a bit more upscale if certainly not deluxe, and took up residence in the back of a large closet, the door of which he could simply unhinge by slithering along the latch. Wade went through a string of men until one of them decided to stay. His name was Liam and he made Wade happy at first, then miserable a few days later. The ghost did not like this arrangement at all. Liam was sloppy (sloppier than Wade), left milk cartons on the counter and used Wade's clean underwear instead of washing his own. He never had a problem finding Wade's wallet, however, or asking Wade for money. This behavior horrified Raymond Hennegar and he no longer cared to be a guiding spirit, instead turning himself into a demon—pictures fell from their hooks, books tumbled to the floor, favorite shorts and sweatshirts were ripped to shreds, all with the hope of driving Liam away. Wade began going out on his own and staying out late, which was why the ghost decided to tag along one evening. In spite of everything, Raymond Hennegar thought he could guide Wade toward finding a better boyfriend.

Was it fate or chance that took Wade to the same bar where Josh was drinking that night? Or, the ghost wondered, had it been planned all along? The two friends sat together in a darkened corner, apologizing, and then catching up. The ghost stayed close between them, drawing their hushed voices together. Wade was not happy with the way things were going in his life but it was Josh who seemed more unfulfilled. The ghost listened to Josh's complaints of a lost commission and his diminishing desire to compose. "I don't know why I keep doing it," Josh said. "When nothing seems to work out."

Raymond Hennegar was horrified that the musician could so easily abandon his talent. The ghost knew it was time to leave Wade to work out the kinks in his life; it was time to stay with Josh. The ghost would now become a muse.

◈

And so began a period of romantic creativity for Josh. On their daily routes through the city, the ghost tinkled through balcony chimes, swayed through buckets of flowers, sprayed moist gusts of air up from the riverside, anything to catch Josh's ear and heighten his senses. The ghost knocked books off of library shelves for Josh to find and hummed old melodies of his days at sea in his ear. Josh heard the notes, one by one in his mind, thought at first they were folk songs or children's tunes, mesmerized by their repetition, then discovered by research and reading that he was thinking of chanties and ballads sung long ago by men working on ships. As a teacher his lessons began to soften as well; he taught his students that interpretation was as important as technique. Away from the classroom he broadened his repertoire, studying manuscripts by Schumann and Brahms and Chopin, listening to recordings in his office and cassettes while he walked through town. He grew sideburns and let his hair grow out long enough that it covered his ears and tapped against the collar of his shirts, and he stopped wearing T-shirts and dark jeans, favoring instead loose-fitting clothing and pleated pants. Karl liked this quixotic transformation in Josh, but as Josh worked harder at his compositions his appetite waned; he grew thinner and soon there were small dark rings beneath his eyes from late nights hunched over pages of notes. Sex was still on his mind but it was now coupled with a yearning for fulfillment, something he understood he was not capable of finding with Karl. At first Josh sought partners in darkened pockets of parks and the campus grounds where he taught classes, believing the heightened sensations of being outside, at night, the chill and dampness of the air and the wet sensation of a mouth at his crotch was what he sought, but he soon realized he needed more intimacy, and he began to go to a neighborhood bar desiring a short conversation first, hopefully followed by a longer, more arousing score.

Wade was alarmed by Josh's dramatic changes, not by the long hair and the vintage costumes, but by the continued restlessness and the persistent, feverish way Josh said he felt most of the time. Josh had developed a way of clearing his throat before he talked that had turned into a light cough that wouldn't go away.

"You should get that checked out," Wade said, after they had seen a movie together one night. Josh had coughed throughout the film.

"It's nothing," Josh answered. "It'll go away when it turns warm again."

Wade, of course, was worried about every ache and blemish he uncovered on his own body; young gay men everywhere were falling sick. Was a cold something more than a cold and a bout with diarrhea caused by something other than reheating old Chinese takeout? Wade started calling Josh every morning with a roundup of the news: Did you see the story on the front page about the blood bank? Did you read the obituary of the actor in New York? Do you know what they think is causing it now?

The ghost let out a tormented moan after every conversation Wade had with Josh, but the momentary distraction the ghost created—a falling book or a creaking door—was never enough to frighten the subject away. Wade's fear of death summoned up Raymond Hennegar's own dread, reminding him of the night the *Peerless Troubadour* sank and he clung to a wood plank for sixteen hours waiting to drown until he spotted the coastline. Martin Gillis was lost that evening; so was young Manuel Pavao, only nineteen years old. Raymond Hennegar had seen Luis "Zarco" Camara wash overboard when a great swell tipped the ship and he lost his grasp of the rigging. Carlos Benevides' body washed ashore two months later. Raymond Hennegar had avoided the horrors of the great wars after his death by shutting himself up in his own house and ignoring the news of other young men lost in battles and ships. Now, he wailed and whined as the current news became more grim: A virus in the blood? A growing epidemic? What the hell was going on in this world?

Wade's reaction was to look more seriously for a long-term commitment from a guy. (Liam had long ago moved out, dropping Wade for a man who was willing to shell out more money for his unpleasant company.) Wade continued to parade potential new boyfriends in front of Josh, calling him up the day after a dinner party or a concert for a bout of questions: Do you think this one had a sense of humor? Do you think he was too self-absorbed? Do you think he's too tall?—too short?—too old?—too boring?

Josh's response was to channel his anxiety into his work; Raymond Hennegar's hummings had finally paid off, inspiring Josh to write a song cycle for male chorus, adapted from chanties and ballads of men working at sea. The ghost guided the musician's hand when he was in doubt, dried the ink on the staffs and clefs, floated up to the ceiling as Josh revised and rewrote at the piano. The ghost was unprepared for the grief the music unleashed in himself, however. Josh dedicated the work to the "lost boys" and used the first performance as a benefit for gay men with AIDS. The concert hall was packed for the debut and the ghost hovered near the vents where the sound was best. Raymond Hennegar enjoyed the chanties, some sung in unison or a capella, others harmonized in four parts. But when a solo baritone began singing a slow, plaintive version of "All My Sailors" to the accompaniment of a harmonica, he was startled and overwhelmed, sending a gust of air down to the aisle that toppled the music stand and stopped the performance.

The performers recovered and started the song again and the ghost of Raymond Hennegar left the hall but did not stay out of earshot. Zarco Camara had sung "All My Sailors" aboard the *Peerless Troubadour* the night before the fatal storm. Zarco had a clear, deep voice but seldom sang, instead using his harmonica to keep the other men going. In the lobby of the concert hall the ghost rose into a funnel of anger and sent a wall sconce smashing to the floor. Zarco had been his mate, his best buddy, since the days when they were both boys working on the *Blue Parrot*. Zarco was the soul of the schooner—part mediator, part nurse, part teacher—who kept the crew in line and the captain enlightened.

After that night, the ghost sulked and pouted inside Josh's armoire for days: how could the musician have known of his love for Zarco and the grief of the *Peerless Troubadour*? He had only given the musician clues, not facts. He rattled through the old clothing, tossing shirts and jackets and coats off their hangers and onto the floor. Why was he so spooked? He was the one who was supposed to be haunting. Was this why he was confined to this unending limbo? Was he haunted because of grief or was grief the reason he was haunting others?

Zarco Camara had saved him from the crew of the *Blue Parrot*. Young boys were often abused by the older men while at sea, but Zarco, four years older than Raymond and taller than some of the crewmen, had kept the seamen away from the young cook by bunking with him, in essence claiming the boy as his own. Raymond Hennegar had promised Zarco that one day he would repay the favor, and he did, over and over again, hiring him first for the crew of the *Integrity* and then later for the *Peerless Troubadour*. Raymond Hennegar had taken care of Zarco's widow and daughter after the gale had swept away five boats and fifty-seven men. But he had never loved anyone else in his life as much as he had loved Zarco. Not his own wife, not his five children, not his mother or his younger brother. Was this his curse? The reason for his wanderings? Was this God's retribution against him? Was this the sin he was repaying? Was this why he was consigned to limbo, to haunt the living?

The ghost grew weaker and weaker; grief now disheartened and dissolved him. He could no longer rattle the hangers or dislodge the bottom drawers of the armoire. Only when Josh opened the doors and began packing did he find the strength and courage to move on, slipping inside a suitcase on a wisp of air to follow the musician to New Mexico. Josh had been awarded a two-month fellowship in Taos and the ghost thought the change in climate might do them both good.

◆

The dry climate suited Josh. His two-month residency was on a small estate between the desert and the mountains. Josh had decided to use his knowledge of the sea chanties as the basis for a larger work, a symphony with the working title of *The Voyage*. During the morning Josh worked on the manuscript at the desk in his small bungalow, then took a break for lunch and a short walk, then worked and napped in the afternoon.

The ghost grew lazy in the bright sun, enjoying the solitude of the artists' retreat, and only moving from his spot in the folds of the curtain when Josh needed reminding of a melody or a specific note. During Josh's second week, a new turnover of fellows arrived—there were fourteen artists in all at the colony, a mix of writers, painters, playwrights, and photographers who stayed for a varying length of terms—and at the communal dinner that Josh went to every night he met a graphic artist named Gavin who had arrived from San Francisco. Gavin was tall and blond and as nonchalant about his talent as he was about his beauty, a welcome change from many of the other high-strung or complex-karma fellows who thrashed out their neuroses or insights over their meals.

The ghost always joined Josh for these gatherings and was delighted to uncover the subtle ironies of the other residents—the watercolorist who painted languid, hazy landscapes and yet worried about minute, germ-carrying insects, for instance, or the novelist who was hard at work on a memoir of her string of short, fleeting love affairs yet couldn't understand that she might have bored her lovers to tears. The ghost took an immediate liking to Gavin, however. Gavin produced poster-size prints of bold, simple images emblazoned by contradictory words or slogans, such as a coffee pot with the word *COLD* or a beach umbrella with the word *WARNING.* He had earned two college degrees, one in art history and the other in psychology, and he could hold a conversation on any subject when he wanted to, and it was this asset, along with his boyish attractiveness, that made him an accessible target for the companion-seeking fellows.

In his first few days at the estate, Gavin moved through a flirtation with a screenwriter and a resounding rebuke of the female novelist, before settling into an ongoing friendship with Josh. Gavin wasn't as disciplined toward work as Josh or the other fellows were, and he began showing up at Josh's bungalow in the afternoon and talking about a recent book or article he had read. Josh had not broken the habit of his afternoon naps, but he would chat with Gavin for a while and then excuse himself and lie down to sleep. The first few days Gavin would read while Josh slept, but the ghost found this behavior too discouraging and frustrating; he liked listening to Gavin talk and enjoyed heightening the sexual tension between the two men, and so by the end of the week Josh and Gavin were sharing the bed together and Josh's afternoon naps were replaced by other activities.

Till now, Josh had never allowed himself a lover who was as willing a student as he was a teacher. Gavin admitted he had a low threshold for boredom (attributable, he explained, to his being a Gemini). Gavin loved to talk during sex, not with the "Uuhs," "Oohs" or "Aarghs" of porno films, but by revealing details of his prior sexual partners (tattoos, piercings, favorite body parts, and what they could do best with the equipment God had provided them). Gavin liked to flatter Josh about his own attributes as they kissed, and Gavin's willingness to be spontaneous and rough kept Josh from being sentimental about the affair, though it did not keep him from silently fantasizing about something more long-lasting with the artist. Josh always hesitated about revealing this desire when he was with Gavin, worried, instead, it would reveal his vulnerability. Josh must not have hid this yearning too well, however; one afternoon, during Josh's final week at the retreat, Gavin said while they were in bed, "You're definitely a water sign. I'm going to miss that."

Instead of hinting that it did not have to be the end of things, Josh, instead, said he was not a water sign.

"No?" Gavin asked. "But there are waves all around you. There's definitely water nearby."

Josh explained that perhaps it had to do with his music—the sea chanties, the ballads and song cycles, the new symphony he was writing—he tried to use the fluidity of water in all of his compositions. The ghost, who had been watching them have sex from a chair in the room, blew himself into the folds of the curtains and then onto the bed beside Josh, prompting the musician to continue. Josh, then, admitted that he was a Libra, hoping it would somehow reveal his wish for long-term compatibility, particularly to Gavin.

"Ah yes, the closeted romantic," Gavin responded a bit too critically.

Josh took offense at the comment and said, rather coldly, "You don't believe all that stuff, do you?"

"I don't disbelieve it," Gavin answered. "I keep an open mind about everything—tarot cards, tea leaves, psychics, ghosts."

"Ghosts?" Josh asked.

Raymond Hennegar, shocked and worried that he was at last about to be revealed and exorcised, rose to the ceiling to remain elusive within the white stucco.

"Sure," Gavin answered. "Ghosts, daemons, guiding spirits. You've had one with you this whole time."

The ghost began to circle the room, still hovering near the ceiling, concerned, now, that Josh was disappointed and distressed.

"What are you talking about?" Josh asked.

"A guiding spirit," he answered. "Something moves you that doesn't move everyone. A gift. A talent. A muse. Call it what you want. But it's with you."

This was not the direction Josh had hoped the conversation would take. He wanted to talk about the two of them as an ongoing couple, not about himself and his talent. "And you?" Josh asked, still a bit icy, aware he was inching himself further and further away from Gavin out of a habit of self-preservation. "Do you have a muse?" When he asked this, he realized—perhaps for the first time in his life—that he was more in love with someone than that someone was with him, and he was frightened about going any further—or asking for anything else from Gavin. The ghost realized this too, and felt, for the first time himself, that he was holding Josh back—holding him from falling deeply, intensely, and intimately in love with someone—something that had never happened in all his time with the musician. And Raymond Hennegar understood that he had reached another crossroad, too—that if he stayed with Josh he would continue to hamper the musician's emotional growth in the interest of brightening his talent. Someone like Gavin could also use a muse—his artistic spirit needed both inspiration *and* discipline. It was not an easy choice for him to make—he'd grown to love Josh like a lover himself. But three days later when Josh's residency was over, Raymond Hennegar stayed behind in New Mexico. And then he followed Gavin to San Francisco.

❖

Josh knew when he arrived back in Boston that something in him was lost, or had disappeared, or that he had changed in way he could not quite name. At first, he felt it was due to leaving Gavin behind, that something had not been resolved between the two of them, and then he thought it was because he had reached a crisis point in the writing of *The Voyage*— the climax where the churning, rhythmic pattern of waves overwhelms the melodic line of the ballads, meant to symbolize the wreck of the vessel in an unexpected storm. Josh stayed away from the manuscript for days because he did not want to end it, fell into a moody depression, then noticed his cough had become worse, deeper, perhaps, because the weather was more burdensome in Boston than New Mexico, and he became sick with a feverish cold that did not go away.

It was Wade who suggested the blood test. He was glad that Josh was back in Boston, but worried by his own health concerns—he had detected a sore on his ankle that did not seem to go away, and Wade, unable to face the possibility of learning his HIV status on his own, took Josh along with him to the clinic for the bloodwork, and then back for the results. Wade tested negative, but Josh tested positive. The news brought Wade more resolutely into Josh's life. Karl dumped Josh, breaking off their nine-year relationship without even a consolation or benediction, and Wade's daily calls turned into a necessity, at least a necessity for himself, if not for Josh. Wade found a support group for Josh to attend, but Josh balked about moaning and groaning in public with a group of gay men. Instead, Josh found a new doctor through his academic network, enrolled in a protocol study and began volunteering at a hospital—delivering books and magazines twice a week to patients in a cancer ward.

Josh's new doctor treated the persistent cough and it seemed to go away, or at least was subdued, and Josh, not about to be weighed down because of a virus in his blood that might or might not be the cause of AIDS, went back to work on finishing *The Voyage* and threw himself into the dating pool. Wade was surprised by the ease with which Josh now moved from one guy to the next; Wade complained voraciously about his own dates—the guy who paid for his meal in quarters, the guy who fell asleep during a blow job, the guy whose vocabulary consisted of three syllables—"Oh," "Yeah," and "Uh." Once, at a reception for one of Josh's students, Wade stood beside Josh and some of his music colleagues and entertained the group with a list of the lousy dates he had the week before. A professor, a thin, short-haired woman who worked in the office beside Josh's, simply responded to Wade's litany with a question that seemed to be on everyone's mind, including Wade's. "So when are you two going to get together?"

Josh clenched his jaw and blood rushed to Wade's face. "Why mess up something that works fine the way it is?" Wade answered, finally, after a space of what seemed like hours to him.

Unfortunately, things were still changing. In another week, Wade went to three memorial services—one for a guy who had been one of Josh's students. After the service, the two friends walked to a bar and sat and had drinks. Wade was light-headed after his first few sips of beer and this made him bold enough to ask Josh, "Well, what do you think?

Should we give it a try?"

Josh pretended not to understand what Wade was suggesting, then, after Wade had repeated himself, answered. "I don't want you taking care of me."

"Why not?" Wade asked. "And what makes you think you're going first?"

"I don't want to talk about this," Josh said, stood up and left Wade in the bar alone.

A few days later, over brunch in a Back Bay restaurant, Josh broke down and cried, and confessed his love for Wade. Wade held himself together, did not reach for a drink to celebrate, but asked Josh if he was certain about taking steps to redefine their relationship. Josh outlined his weaknesses (all of which Wade knew) and Wade confessed his own (some of which surprised Josh, though they did not make him change his mind). Then they made plans to get together the next day to see a movie in Cambridge and spend the night at Wade's apartment. Two months later they moved into an apartment together in Beacon Hill, a bit too expensive for Wade's liking, but large enough for Josh to assert some independence.

◆

The ghost of Raymond Hennegar had just found a comfortable niche in the damp spot of Gavin's bathroom when death sent him weeping through the corridors of the building. He cried through the water pipes, short-circuited fuse boxes, and sent garbage tumbling down the stairwells. Gavin went swiftly, drowning overnight in fluids which had collected in his lungs from an infection. Once again, grief caught Raymond Hennegar unaware. Why was this happening? These young men did not deserve this fate. Nothing in their lives—from the most sexual to the most purposely cautious—warranted these random killings. Yes, *killings. This was murder.* The ghost refused to attach himself to only one man now, not after the loss of Gavin and his memory of losing Zarco. Raymond Hennegar howled at the unfairness of it all and his lack of good fortune, riding on the back of one guy to that of the next, from one bar to a support group to a single bed in a hospice to a four-poster canopy in a townhouse near the wharf. It took weeks before he could decide how to work through his depression. He felt best at community vigils and demonstrations, raucous gatherings protesting rising costs of medications and ill-treatment of patients where angry, AIDS-impacted men swore and chanted and marched and yelled. Once he rode on the back of an activist into a city councilman's office; another time he flickered candle flames at a benefit concert. One morning he would wake and feel fine until more news—more obits and more wakes and more memorials—sent him out sobbing and shrieking through the streets of San Francisco. Some nights he would wail like a banshee because of his unhappiness; he once shared a hospital room with just such a revenant—a pale Irish woman with long blonde hair and a hooked nose who viciously wept as her family's heritage came to end with the death of its final son—a young gay man tied to IV tubes and a respirator machine and with a living will that instructed his best friend not to make any attempt to revive him. Raymond Hennegar's contact with the rest of the spirit world was only what fate allowed, and there were nights when he floated along the rising mists of the bay watching departing souls on their way to Heaven.

This was an idyllic time, though, for Wade and Josh. Wade got a new job and then a promotion; Josh remained healthy and his T-cell count stable and he was able to finish *The Voyage* and the work premiered in Houston. The two of them took trips together to Ireland and Spain and spent Thanksgiving with Wade's family in Connecticut and Christmas with Josh's sister in Maine. The next summer they rented an apartment in Provincetown, not far from the spot where they had met more than a decade before. Wade talked about investing in real estate, buying a summer place on the Cape—he'd been promoted once again and was now part of the senior management team of his firm. "Do you want something close to here?" he asked Josh. "Or out of the way?"

"You should decide," Josh said. "Since you'll be the one using it the most."

"What do you mean?" Wade asked. "I don't want to come here without you."

"I won't always be around," Josh said. "Don't do anything because of me."

"I'm not going anywhere without you," Wade answered and dropped the idea.

Wade always looked back to that summer as the beginning of the end, aware that Josh's cough had returned and was changing for the worse, and that the night sweats and the loss of weight were a symptom of Josh's declining immune system. Josh moved through a slow and painful descent, and when neuropathy crippled his legs, he refused to use a wheelchair, relying instead on a cane and Wade's shoulder. His sunken brown eyes still had a warm sexiness to them, even as he became weaker and weaker; Wade, however, was the one who began showing his age, his hair graying and his brow furrowed with worry.

Meantime, Raymond Hennegar knew that it was time to leave San Francisco; his heart could bear no more grief. He followed a man to Sacramento and from there hitched a ride to Tahoe. He was fascinated by the casinos, and the loud sounding clink-clink-clinks as he moved from slot machines to the blackjack tables to the more exclusive back rooms where the stakes were higher. He was somewhat in awe of the gamblers, people risking their life savings and hard-earned wages for the dim hope of winning more. For days he intervened against fate, sending tumblers and chips and cards in directions that could not have been predicted— he helped one woman—a diabetic on insulin—win big-time at the slots and forced a businessman to cash in more than he had planned with a losing hand of cards. He loved watching the anxiety of losers hoping to turn around their luck, loved the exhilaration of winners ready to celebrate, for in these feelings of happiness, excitement, and defeat he found reminders of what it was like to feel alive. After every great loss he wanted to walk away, but he returned to play again, aware, however, that when each new game began he grew harder, colder, less willing to give gifts or help to the gamblers, because he wanted to watch their failure. He soon wore himself out on this vicious cycle because he knew at the core of himself he was not a malicious man, and overwhelmed by shame and nausea, he knew it was time to move on again.

Then one day he followed a woman from the casino to the airport where she caught a flight to Oklahoma City. He rode with her back to her house in the suburbs and stayed there longer than he had anticipated, moving from the woman's house and in with her sister Maggie, a much prettier and younger and practical version of the gambler. Maggie reminded Raymond Hennegar of Elizabeth Sharper, the woman he had married a few years after the sinking of the *Peerless Troubadour*. Maggie's family provided him the distraction he needed—three kids, two dogs, a cat, and an aquarium full of guppies. They drove around town in a minivan, ate raucous meals together, tumbled out into the yard onto swing sets and into vegetable gardens. Raymond Hennegar became happily mischievous again, puffing up the cat's fur and watching the dog howl with fear; he loved spooking the youngest child, Emily, because she reminded him of his own daughter, Tessie, when she was five years old.

Wade had one single goal during these months—to keep Josh alive; for himself, he found ways of "getting on" and "getting by," ways of avoiding the drama and hysterics that welled up inside himself. He learned to sit quietly, to save his breath, and to manage with little breathing. He learned, while slowly breathing in, to quiet his heartbeat until he found an inner calm. Josh resented the decline of his looks; some mornings he begged Wade to help him end things. Wade ignored the requests, or at least tried to find a reason for Josh to want to continue to live—reminding him of a concert they were going to or a film he wanted to see or a friend's birthday he should not miss.

"It doesn't mean anything," Josh would say, disheartened.

"It means something to me," Wade would answer. "So don't dismiss it so easily."

Soon, Josh was so sick and thin his pants would fall off of him. He went in and out of dementia and Wade breathed slowly in and out to keep himself from going mad. In his final weeks, Wade helped Josh write as much music as he could, inking in the notes and rhythms where Josh had pointed to on the page. Even on his deathbed, Josh was humming the songs of the sea, the melodies Raymond Hennegar had implanted in his subconsciousness.

And Raymond Hennegar knew when Josh died. One morning, an icy chill stole over him and he realized something profound—not how out of place and isolated he had made himself in Oklahoma City—but how lonely Wade was now feeling, hundreds of miles away. *Wade, Wade, Wade*: Why was he feeling this and about this particular man? He shivered and followed Maggie into the minivan and then waited in the parking lot of the grocery store for another ride. He made it to the interstate and another town six miles away and then had to wait in another parking lot for another ride in what proved to be the wrong direction. Finally, he reached a diner where he waited for a trucker who was heading northeast. He slept through the ride, waking up near Providence to send a shriek through the brake pads so the trucker would pull off the highway. At a rest stop, the ghost waited for another ride, sensing the deepening humidity of the air, the closeness of the sea. He thought again about Zarco and the nights they spent together in their small berth of the *Blue Parrot*. And then the years afterward consumed him—the death of his wife, the loss of his daughter from diphtheria, his middle son's wedding on the wharf, holding his first grandchild in his arms. He tried to understand the right and wrong choices of his life but could not distinguish between the two. He was thankful and grateful that he had had the love of a wife and a family, but he also wished he had never lost Zarco. Since then he had felt an emptiness in his soul; loneliness had settled into his heart, haunting him both day and night.

◈

It was late when the bus pulled into Provincetown. The ghost followed a man off the bus and into the station and then out onto the street. He found his way easily to Commercial Street and stood outside the house where he had once lived for forty-one years. It was still an inn, the sign outside read *No Vacancy*, which Raymond Hennegar thought meant his devilish reputation had finally waned. He could not enter the house unless on the shoulders of a visitor or resident—such were the ways of being a ghost—and so he waited on the corner, in the dark of the alley where he had stood years before waiting to embark on a new journey.

It was late, after midnight, and the street was crowded in front of the pizza shop next door. Young men were still lingering to connect with other young men. A light mist filled the air as if it were weeping. The ghost wanted to warn the men of the potential sorrows and misfortunes ahead, when he realized that it was not sorrow or misfortune that had governed and guided his time as a spirit, but adventure and the quest for companionship, just as it had when he was alive.

In the dark of the doorway where he waited, he watched a remarkably handsome man approach. He had a lopey gait, a long, thin torso, and curly black hair, just like Josh had had fourteen years before. He watched the man catch glances until he passed by another man, shorter, darker-haired and stocky. It took him a few minutes to realize that this was Wade, waiting in front of the pizza place, a bit dazed and confused to find himself here again. Raymond Hennegar knew at once why Wade was alone and back in Provincetown; he had come to scatter Josh's ashes, as Josh had wished, along Herring Cove beach.

Wade stood staring at the printed menu that hung over the counter of the pizza shop. He was aware of only one thing—that he could not go back to the way things were. His dream was finished. The music was gone. Over. He was full of misery and sorrow and guilt for surviving when so many other men had perished. He deeply missed Josh. He felt there was nothing else in the world that could give him pleasure or solace, and he thought, then, about his own death. To be at rest. Outside the store, he looked skyward, at the dark starry night above him. A widow's walk caught his attention and he wondered if he were to climb up to the wooden terrace and then leap toward the ground below it, things would finally be over for him; if the impact would be strong enough to kill him. Or if he could only take some kind of poison, fall asleep and never wake again. He felt his life was full of mistakes and wrong choices and despair. He wondered if it was ever possible to feel human again—to eat, sleep, cradle a man in his arms.

He had no reason to go any further. For what purpose? There was nothing but a deep, painful longing to shake off this whole confused time of watching Josh die. Yes, he was at the end. He looked down at his feet, ready to climb and leap and die. Then, from a remote part of his soul, from some place in his past, he heard a sound. It was a fragment of a melody—an atonal, discordant tune, as if someone was sucking air through a pipe. As he looked up he felt the sound change, brighten, gain harmony. It became a line of "All My Sailors," a melody Josh had used years ago in a concert.

Wade was horrified with himself—so this was what it felt to be so lost, so confused, so devoid of reason that all he wanted to do was to die. The music blew through the street now—someone, somewhere in a room, was playing a harmonica. Wade felt the music overcome him and he smiled. Raymond Hennegar heard the song, too. He rose up in the air, determined to find the source of the song, then waited, not wanting to spoil the moment, not wanting the music to end. He knew, then, why he had returned to Provincetown the moment he spotted Wade. Wade possessed the soulfulness of Zarco Camara—the same ease, humor, protectiveness, and desire Zarco had displayed. Why had he not detected this before? Why hadn't he realized that this was his fate? Raymond Hennegar was never meant to be a haunting or roaming spirit. He was always a companion and a partner. He had remained behind to find a way to absolve himself of his grief for Zarco and their unexpected abandonment and tragedy.

Out of the darkness another man approached the pizza shop. He was older, tougher-looking, as if he had been weathered at sea. To Raymond Hennegar, he looked exactly as he remembered Zarco the night before he was lost. The man carried a harmonica in his hand, which he slipped into the front pocket of his jeans when he turned to study the menu over the counter. He turned and asked Wade if he wanted a slice. Wade shook his head no. The man did not let this deter him. "Then come sit with me while I eat mine."

They sat on the steps of a house while the man ate his slice and asked Wade questions. Wade's answers were perfunctory at first. "Boston." "Thirty-seven." "Getting over a bad time." But he gradually began to talk more, his sentences and thoughts longer and warmer.

Raymond Hennegar was lost in his own disbelief, even when the man introduced himself as "Bobby Dublin" who was "fortysomething, from Baltimore" and pointed to the house where the ghost had once lived and haunted and said it was where he was staying for the weekend. The ghost flickered the outside lights of a storefront and blew a thick mist around the two men. This new couple could embody everything he had missed of Zarco. Raymond Hennegar was no longer homeless or lonely; he climbed on Bobby Dublin's shoulders and curled himself around his neck and chest like a warm scarf. Wade followed the older man up the stairs and through the front door of the house, surprised to find his grief replaced by a mixture of happiness and relief. He felt as if something was starting over again. He felt he had been saved, as if a guardian angel had been watching over him. He felt lucky and blessed. This was 1993 and he was alive, his heart haunted and full of music.

THE THEATER BUG

It was a buggy summer, even on the Island. At the summer house we began to spend more time indoors than outside, our poolside lunches, barbecues, and cocktail hours hampered by the increasing number of flies, mosquitoes, and other biting, flying insects that seemed drawn to our place. There were sixteen of us sharing the house that season, though never more than twelve of us out at one time on a weekend, what with the shares and half-shares and quarter-shares and guests crashing on the convertible sofa. None of us could seem to deter the pesky insects, not with scented candles or torches or lotions or sprays. It got to be a running joke between whoever among us was out at the house—how these tiny little creatures were dictating our summer adventures; even the biggest, toughest, meanest-looking of us screaming drama queens were watching the surf and sunshine and the parade of beautiful men through our glass doors and picture windows.

Even the houseguests remarked how strange it was that we spent so much time inside, and David, our clever and overly handsome ever-resourceful leader, set up fans to create a cool breeze through the rooms and keep the bugs that had found their way inside the house from alighting on us. Our evening dinner parties soon turned into elaborate candlelight spectacles of gourmet dishes instead of the more light, waterside fare. One night around the dinner table late in the season (and at the height of all this bugginess) we had three guests over for dinner—a buff young couple of musical comedy junkies from another house and an older British actor who was a houseguest of Tino, our resident musclehead and exhibitionist (in spite of his visible bug bites). The tall, barrel-chested, dark-voiced actor was something of a minor celebrity amongst our youngish, urban crowd—he had trained at the Royal Academy in London and played many Shakespearean roles on the West End. He'd done several films and a failed sitcom and then, in his fifties, come out of the closet and begun playing an assortment of more gentlemanly, supporting roles—divorcés, übervillains, widowers, pedophiles—that sort of thing. He had just finished appearing in a one-man play at an off-Broadway theater where Tino was the house manager—hence the invitation to the summer house, and David, whose weekend it was to oversee the evening menu, had concocted a four-course spectacle of salads and chilled soups and seared salmon to impress our special guest.

Ian—that wasn't the actor's name but I shall call him that because I think it suits the purpose nicely—was appalled that we were dining inside on such a beautiful, starry night, but after five minutes outside with his sweating cocktail glass and swatting at the bugs, he soon adapted to our more interior, breezy lifestyle. Once the rest of us were comfortable that he was comfortable, we began relating our own comical skirmishes and wounds from our weekend pests. Neil, my well-groomed but highly anal-retentive boyfriend, ate all his meals at the summer house with a flyswatter nearby, not about to let the bugs get the better of him (or his portions of the food), and mentioned to Ian that he had abandoned all scented grooming products that could attract any sort of insect—cologne, aftershave, deodorant—much to the delight of Rick, Tino's aggressively honest, tightly built bulldog of a boyfriend, who refused to trim, clip, or groom any bit of his excessive body hair to fit in with the "fascist norms of gay style consciousness." Pale-skinned Wally, David's roommate and the only other single, unpaired man in the summer house, said cleanly shaved scent-free skin proved no deterrent to the bugs, either, their bites remaining as annoying and problematic as razor burn and acne. "The scourge of the fundamentalists won't do us in," David laughed, as he gathered us around the dinner table. "Nor will divine retribution in the guise of a gnat."

"There was a summer like this when I was a boy in England," Ian began telling us somewhere over the chilled soup. "Buggy. Flies and gnats everywhere you walked. A few years after the end of the War." Tino had explained in advance of Ian's arrival that the actor loved to entertain his backstage audiences with rambling tales of his sexual adventures, particularly with other celebrities, both minor and major, and we were prepared to listen to any and all he wanted to share with us and I assumed that this would be one of those kind of tales. "There was one particular place in the village where I lived that you were sure to get bitten—the meadow opposite the church graveyard. This was where the theater troupe set up their tents for two weeks in the summer and it had a large and flat enough space to stretch out their tenting before the hill sloped upward—the only place, really, where a stage could be set up in the entire village.

"They'd been coming here for years; the troupe was run by a London actor—a stout, middle-aged fellow who was prone to hammy monologues—and there were maybe six of them altogether in the company—mostly young chaps in their late teens or early twenties who had been too young for the War or had left it behind and were hoping for some kind of training or work or both. They all slept in the back of the tent on cots and bathed and took their meals at the public house and they traveled with a small upright piano—there weren't many of them in our village—and because the parson or the parishioners forbid them to do certain plays—such as *Macbeth* or *Midsummer Night's Dream* or anything by Molière—they drew their biggest crowds—about a grand total of fifty per performance—by doing pantomimes and musical skits.

"We were well behind the times with the rest of England. I wasn't even allowed to see those performances; me Pa and Mum were convinced that anything on the stage was the work of the devil, but we were the first house outside the village (or the first house on the edge of the village, depending on how you looked at it) and it was easy enough for me to sneak out and see the shows with me mates. There was always a way for us to weasel our way into the tent without paying and stand at the back and watch—and sometimes I think the old fellow—Osborne was his name—would have been disappointed if we didn't. The first time me Pa found out that I went to the shows he slapped me and threatened to take a belt to me, but I know it was all tied up with his own pride—we couldn't really afford to pay to see the shows, even as cheap as they were.

"They weren't a great troupe but the younger boys dressed up to play women and even at his worst, old Osborne could rattle you with a good monologue from *Hamlet* or *Anthony and Cleopatra*. He was always flirting with the village women—both from the stage and after the show in the public house—but it always seemed he had a special boy around—someone in the company he doted on and gave the best parts to—and during the day he would sit on a crate outside his tent while the other boys mended costumes or patched the tent and ask passersby what they thought of his latest protégé.

"There were plenty of gossip and scandals going on whenever they were in town—Osborne was always trying to keep his lads from chasing some young townie lassie—or laddie, mind you—even his special one was always up to having a go with someone else—they were a real randy crew, all them boys. There was one particular fellow that Osborne had a fancy to the year I was fourteen or fifteen—fifteen, I think—not so long ago I should hope—and he was a beauty—dark floppy hair, long lashes, pale blue eyes—Kent Kiernan, was his name—and he took up with one of me mates—Trevor, the butcher's son, who was older than the rest of us—sixteen, seventeen, I guess, because he was working in his pa's store and itching to set out on his own to London."

Ian paused his story long enough for David to clear the soup bowls from the table and bring the dinner plates from the kitchen, gossiping for a moment about the "beautiful wisp of a divine youth" Tino had noticed on the ferry ride who kept staring at Ian as if they had met before, until "the dawn of enlightenment occurred and he realized I was that actor from that hideous children's show I did a decade ago."

From the kitchen there was some banging and clanging of utensils and drawers and David returned; platters of steaming vegetables and potatoes were passed around, silverware reached for, and Ian took a taste of the salmon and said, "My goodness, you should become professional at this."

"Pride and manners are my downfall," David answered, relaying a short anecdote of his aborted enrollment at a noted culinary institute because he realized it was "as vicious as working in the theater."

"And what did I do?" David laughed at himself. "I went out a got a job as a stage manager."

We all laughed at both his fortune and his misfortune. All of us in the house were connected in some way to the theater, presently or in our pasts. Rick was an electrician, who worked for a lighting designer, which is how he met Tino one night at a theatre two years before. Wally had the highest profile job, as a casting agent for theater, film, television, and commercials, which was how he had met Neil and invited him to take a share in the summer house. Neil was an advertising executive, whose many accounts included three off-Broadway productions. As for myself, I was a freelance copywriter, which was how I had met Neil, trying to earn some money while I was working on writing my first play.

"It was a small village, did I tell you that?" Ian said, resuming his story after an acceptable pause in the dinner chatter. Across the table I noticed Tino's eyes were bright and engaged in the tale, while Rick's seemed distant, distracted inward—they'd been fighting about something all weekend that the rest of us had not been privy to, most likely over a telephone message that had not been relayed properly, since both fellows liked to keep their weekend schedules "open and independent of each other."

"North of Lancaster—almost up to the lakes," Ian said. "Lots of folks still didn't have cars then—rode into the village to see the shows on their bicycles, a few even on horses, I recall. There were plenty of country houses up on the fells by then—owned by bankers, businessmen, gentry, those sorts—some of them came into town for the shows, too.

"One morning one of the cooks who worked up at Benton Hall—one of the larger country houses—they had a year-round staff of about eight, I think, and it was one of those warmish, damp and foggy summer mornings, and, well, she had to pass the church and the tenting on the other side and the slope of the meadow on her way into the village. As she passed the southern gate, she noticed a dark lump of something up on the hill near where the slate fence divided the property and another meadow began.

"At first she thought it might be one of the sheep that had died or been slaughtered by another animal or something during the night— because what had caught her eye was a dark patch on the meadow that could have been blood. Well, when she walked closer to check it out, she realized it was old Osborne, lying there dead and still wearing the long dark coat he usually performed in, and the dark patch on the ground around him was indeed his own blood. When she turned to look away from the site, she noticed another dark clump near the stone wall that ran along the side of the road. She took in a big gulp of misty air and ran straight on to the parsonage on the far side of the graveyard and told the parson what she had seen.

"Edward Sadler was the parson then—and oh, he was a quare old cat himself, but I'll get to him later—and he rounded up a few parishioners and the postman and soon enough they were all up on the hill behind Osborne's tent, looking at the body. Osborne had been hacked in the chest by a large blade—some kind of hatchet or cleaver—and it was a grisly sight, mind you—you could actually see the breastbone exposed.

"In her misery, the cook who had discovered the body had forgot to tell the parson about the second body she had thought she'd seen—over by the stone wall on the other side of the tenting. And by then all the lads in the troupe were waking up—most of them visibly upset over the state of poor old Osborne—and one of them started saying that Kent Kiernan was missing—he wasn't in his cot or upstairs at the public house, where he also sometimes slept or went for baths.

"Then, one of the fellows spotted Kent's body over by the stone wall—dead the same way—sliced through the chest and all. When I heard that later that morning it just tore out my heart—even at fifteen. Kent was something breathtaking to watch—singing, 'All follow this and come to dust.' I remember I could not keep my eyes off of him—still not sure if it was because he was such a beautiful girl in that gown he was all dressed up in or because I knew underneath he was also a beautiful boy."

Ian's tale continued while David returned to the kitchen in search of second portions for Wally, whose appetite never seemed diminished (or visible on his lanky frame). Stuart, the taller diva from the house next door, stopped the story to ask Ian a set of perfunctory questions about the profitability of the troupe and the amount of villages they played at in a season, and Ian did his best to indulge him with some kind of professional answer. Stuart was also the more business-minded of the two young neighbors and was part of the advisory board of a nonprofit theater company that specialized in reviving old, forgotten and no-good musical comedies. Stuart's boyfriend, an actor (and the youngest and cutest of us, in my opinion), did not look pleased with Stuart's deflection of Ian's story, nor did the others at the table, but soon enough David was back at the table, more portions of food were being passed around, and Ian was back on track before his small, but captivated, audience.

"Well, my dears," Ian continued, "soon the coroner and the magistrate were there and the rest of the villagers and plenty of people milling around and a reporter showed up from Lancaster—seemed someone phoned someone in another village and the news had started spreading elsewhere. They laid Osborne and Kent Kiernan out on the stage while they tried to sort out the crime and who the next of kin might be and what the other lads might have known. It turned up that Trevor was missing—the butcher's son—and so were some knives from his pa's shop—and one of the boys in the troupe cracked under pressure and started talking about seeing Trevor and Kent Kiernan going at it one night in the back of the churchyard, hot and heavy.

"Trevor was never seen again in the village and they buried Osborne and Kent Kiernan outside the church wall, on the north side of the graveyard where they buried all of the village questionables—stillborn babies, unwed mothers, *illegitimate actors*, that sort of thing. The theater lads left town—the tenting and costumes were left behind—they were torn down and finally burned when no one showed up after a few months to claim any of Osborne's belongings.

"As I recall there was something of a trial—some sort of mock jury assembled to review the charges—and Trevor was charged but not convicted because he was nowhere to be found and could not face up to the accounts, though me Mum told me a few years later that she thought he was in London and had changed his name and was trying to make a go at being an actor himself. But the real reason he got off was that his parents still lived in the village and were good friends to almost everyone and were thought of as decent, hardworking people.

"They did establish some kind of sequence to the events of the murders, however; Osborne was killed first, it seemed, possibly due to a disagreement with someone, and young Kent was killed later, probably while defending himself from the same attacker."

A jolt that shocked us all shook the dinner table and once again stopped Ian's tale. My boyfriend Neil was standing beside his seat with a smug, victorious expression on his face and his flyswatter in his hand. There was a good six years between the two of us and I always felt this translated into Neil's younger, unapologetic restlessness and dramatic flair for being noticed. I turned to our guest and gave him a weary sort of smile and said, "Well, that's one less to worry about."

Ian nodded to me and since we were seated so close to each other, he reached out and placed his hand against my shoulder. It stayed there for a moment while he said, "But like I said it was a buggy summer—don't worry, I didn't totter off there—just had to provide the back story and all, you know."

Ian's hand continued to remain at my shoulder, suggestively shifting to massaging the back of my neck while he continued to talk, though it was unclear to me whether it was a manner of flirtation or out of sympathy for my plight of having to endure such a boyfriend as Neil. "And after they moved Osborne's body to the stage of the theater, flies began settling where his blood had been on the meadow, so many that the slope where he had lain looked like it was covered with his shadow. And this went on for days while more people phoned and spoke to the parson for details and asked more questions of the troupe and more reporters showed up in the village.

"The meadow where Osborne was murdered got to be a great gathering spot for a while, and one day I was there and one of the reporters thought he would take a picture of the shape of the flies against the grass—it was of great interest to the media of the day—you know how the British press are—flies settling in the shape of a body and all—it was certain to attract them and it was quite a big to-do.

"Well, I was helping this fellow set up a photo, tagging along with him and assisting him up to the ledge of the stone wall where he could look down at the meadow and snap his photograph. He used a flash that day—not exactly sure why, might have been a mistake or, no, it was another one of those misty days, so he might have needed the light—but the flash startled the flies and they rose up in a great mass as if it were the ghost of old Osborne himself awakening from the dead. They swarmed about for a minute and somehow I was caught in their path and bitten several times before they settled again on the side of the meadow."

Ian removed his hand from my neck and used both hands to demonstrate his battle with the bugs and we all laughed at the performance. Neil stretched out his swatter to him as if to offer a stronger weapon, which made a few of us laugh even harder.

"I didn't think about it right away," Ian continued. "I was swatting and laughing and then sort of itching from the stings or bites or whatever they were. But I started to feel strange—dizzy and such—and as the day went on my arms and legs and neck where I had felt the flies land started to swell up. Soon I was home and in bed and the doctor from the next town was dispatched to come look at me. I was quite feverish and spouting gibberish. I was later told that in my delirium I recited a passage from *The Taming of the Shrew* that Osborne had done one night—he was always testing the rules a little bit more, to see every year what the village audiences would allow him to do.

"I was sick for several days and me Mum was so worried she had Edward Sadler visit me regularly. He would hold my hand and say prayers or recite passages from the Bible, and, as I began to feel better, I noticed he was as hammy as old Osborne had been in some of his line readings.

"I remember one day—one of the dizzy days—telling him how much I wanted to be an actor, like Kent Kiernan had been, and he laughed and said the stage was a fine and noble profession to chose if I were to be serious and committed to it. Me Mum twisted her hands and then they prayed and consulted their Bibles. The parson was a great help in convincing me parents that theaterfolk were not devil-worshippers.

"One day when I was better, the parson brought round a book

that had belonged to Osborne—it was a collection of speeches from Shakespeare—and he told me I should try memorizing one of the passages and try it out one night at the church for the parishioners. He touched me a little longer that day than he ever had before—a sort of lingering graze first at my thigh—and then later against my forearm."

Ian continued talking while I helped David clear the finished plates from the table to make room for a lemon ice pie he had made the day before (which was greeted with a chorus of ooohs and aaahs when I carried it out to the table). In the kitchen, David swatted at a gnat and then slapped the side of his neck, drawing his prey into the tips of his fingers and then washing his hands at the sink. Back in the dining room, the candles were flickering and the tale was continuing as we took our seats again.

"I know that summer was a changing point for me," Ian said. "Something in me began to stir as I started to get stronger. I memorized Petruchio's speech from *The Taming of the Shrew* that was in that book and I went around town reciting it and gesturing like a fool. It got me talking to a lot of people I didn't normally talk to—older folk, stopping to listen, who would then ask me questions about how I was until I had expired all my news and then they could confess their own—ailments and such, at first, like arthritis or sore joints, but the longer I spent with them, the easier the complaints would turn to gossip.

"It seemed as if everyone in that village was having sex—quare or otherwise—with someone they were not supposed to be having it with, and I soon learned myself that a good little monologue could get me into any girl's britches or a fella's trousers that I wanted to get more special with. What a thing, mind you—and it still works today, most of the time, a good tale can still charm the pants off of some folks. I let the parson believe he had deflowered me that year, even though by then I had already been with Bobby O'Hare and Sean Matthias and Lizzie McTarnahan, an older woman who worked at the public house, whose specialty was deflowering young fellas. Everyone was always telling me how good I was with the Shakespeare, so one day I upped and left town, just like Trevor had done, and went off to London to study and become a professional actor.

"Of course there were no more theater troupes coming through my village after that particularly buggy and tragic summer—I did a few stagey things for the villagers—some on my own, some with some other local fellows—but in a year or so there was a picture show held twice a week at the local hall and that sort of killed all the desire to see live theater.

"After I left, me Mum wrote me once in London that the flies had never disappeared from that hillside of the meadow. I was back there about fifteen years ago and I saw it for myself. They were still at the same spot where old Osborne's body had lain, as if he had only been murdered the day before."

At the completion of the tale, Stuart did not waste any time asking Ian another question about his career, then inquired about the size of a particular West End theater Ian had once performed in, and soon Ian's story was completely forgotten. The conversation lingered for a few minutes on the recent influx of American musicals being revived on the London stages, and then the evening seemed to be over, or, rather, the group had dissolved into more intimate conversations and I wandered into the kitchen, helping David wash and dry the last of the dishes.

◆

It wasn't long after that dinner party that Rick and Tino officially broke up, though all of us had seen it coming all summer long. I always thought it was because Rick was fooling around on the side with David that summer—they'd hook up downstairs late at night in front of the refrigerator or in one of the bathrooms for a quick thing, but that wasn't the case at all because David told me later that Rick was fooling around with a lot of guys that summer (not just him). I also heard—from my housemate Wally—when I ran into him in a lobby of a theater in the city sometime that fall after we had closed up the summer place for the season, that Tino had followed Ian to Hollywood, where he was hoping to work as Ian's personal assistant on the film that Ian was to begin shooting soon. Ian and Tino had been having a thing going since the off-Broadway run of his show and once the play had closed it cleared the way for Tino to begin clearing away Rick (which had been one source of their testiness that summer).

Not long after that I heard that Ian had died of a heart attack in LA, and I remembered how he had pressed his hands against my shoulder and massaged my neck while telling his tale of the buggy summer and the tragic fate of the old hammy actor and his younger beau. I still feel that he was trying to impart something to me in the way he touched me—to flirt me out of my own bad relationship or at least warn me that it was in trouble—and as I recall the absence of his touch—the rise of his hands to flail away the stinging pests of his youth—I can also find an apparition of my own—a forewarning of what was to come. Neil and I broke up at about the same time Rick and Tino did. The oddest thing about ending things with Neil was how liberating it felt to me—we had been a miserable couple for too many years and it must have been more obvious to friends and strangers than I had pretended to myself that it was and maybe that was what Ian was trying to tell me, that it was time not to be so miserable anymore. Neil left me to take up with Rick and when Neil told me that I had to laugh—I didn't think it would last much longer than its announcement. Rick would have no sort of patience for the kind of needy attention Neil desired, and Neil, I knew, because of our own disagreements, would certainly not settle long for Rick's roaming, indiscreet eyes.

Still I took our split up as an opportunity to change a lot of things about my own life—I terminated my association with Neil's advertising agency, took a temporary editorial position at a newspaper, and found a new apartment downtown, as far away as I could from Neil and his crowd, though I had developed a fondness and friendship with David that I had no intention of ending. Ironically, it was David who suggested that I should give acting a try—that maybe I could write a better play if I had a stronger impression of what an actor needs to work with in material and motivation. One day after we had lunch together, David and I stopped in a bookstore and he found a book of Shakespearean monologues that he convinced me to buy. I learned Petruchio's monologue from *The Taming of the Shrew* and used it at an audition a few weeks later.

I didn't get that role, but I did get a compliment from a casting agent, and that swelled up my hope that I could improve and find a better role that I was suited to play. In fact, David seemed interested in me being an actor and I decided I was good enough to want to play *that* part. This was how we hooked up together for a little while—and how I found my way into the spotlights of the theater—and why I've decided, after my own rather long and pesty route, it has not been too bad of a place to be found.

WAIT!

Clay still had a buzz going when they reached his car. He'd driven home under worse conditions, but something told him to wait, not to rush out of the parking lot so fast. He'd only taken a quarter 'lude before he left home, but the two beers he had drank at the club had left him foggy and unfocused. Or maybe it was his luck at meeting Mack that made him feel more than just slightly intoxicated—giddy, even, like he just won a trip to the destination of his choice and now he had to quickly decide where to go or lose the prize. Clay inserted his key into the ignition, but instead of starting the car, he leaned across the seat and drew Mack into a kiss.

Mack opened his lips and steadied himself by grasping the back of Clay's neck. The clutch was firm and certain and made Clay feel luckier. They had met on the dance floor, talked a few minutes at the bar, and agreed to go back to Clay's apartment for the rest of the night. Clay knew nothing about Mack other than how he looked and that he had arrived with a group of attractive college boys. Their conversation inside the club had been about the DJ and his poor choice of songs that night. Clay had been surprised that it had been so easy to ask Mack back to his place and that Mack had been so willing to leave the club before the lights flashed for last call.

Behind Clay's car, on the far side of the parking lot, there was a thump and the sound of breaking glass. At first Clay thought someone might have opened the back door of the club and the dance track had blasted out into the night, but then he heard another thump and another sound of shattering glass and another car alarm going off. Clay lifted his face slightly away from Mack's, the heavy, humid night air helping to retain the warmth of the other man's mouth against lips. The parking lot had been a target of trouble in the past few weeks. The owners of the lot—a group of out-of-town investors—had protested to reporters and news crews that the lot was being used for the overflow crowds from the club and the police were apparently keeping track of license plate numbers. Inside the club, a notice had been posted that cars using the lot after hours would be towed away at the car owner's expense, though rumor had it that the towing company was refusing to work late in this section of town. But there was no other choice when the club's parking lot was full—parking next to the curb meant a certain traffic ticket and the next available lot meant having to walk through an unlit and unsafe corridor of warehouses and abandoned buildings. And on nights like this, when there was the certainty of rain, it made it easier to risk the uncertain consequences.

Mack had heard the noise too. "Shit," he said and turned his upper body to look through the back window. There was another thump and the car alarm stopped, but another alarm had sounded with a repeating teep-teep-whooo-op. Through the rear window Clay could see shadowy figures moving toward his car, a group of boys, it looked like, dressed in baggy clothes and caps, carrying what appeared to be nightsticks or baseball bats. There looked to be five of them weaving around the cars in the lot, glints of gold chains at their necks and wrists catching the reflections of available light. Clay heard one of them yell, "Hey, here's a faggot from Florida, let's see if he makes it back," and there was another thump against the hood of a car.

"Lock your door," Clay said to Mack. "Push it down with your thumb." He didn't want to use the electronic button on his armrest—the clunking sound could draw attention to the car and might make the gang change direction.

Clay locked his own door and saw that the gang was sweeping sideways through the lot, headed for the row of abandoned buildings where they could scatter and hide in the alleys. They would certainly pass his car. He had left his cellphone at home in the charger—he had thought about bringing it, but didn't want to carry it inside the club and didn't want to leave it behind in the car to be stolen. He felt his anxiety dampening his armpits.

"You have a phone with you?" he asked Mack.

Mack shook his head no.

"Get down as far as you can," Clay said. "Maybe they won't see us."

Clay folded and tucked his body so that he was beneath the steering wheel and the dashboard, out of sight of anyone walking past the car. He was sweating now through his forehead and temples, the humidity rising inside the car. Mack curled himself underneath the glove compartment, but he was too tall to fit comfortably and his eyes darted nervously at Clay. Clay could not see the gang now but could hear them getting closer to his car. "Keep still," Clay said. A shadow passed between his car and the next and he could hear a voice saying, "How 'bout that one over there?"

Clay realized that he'd left the keys in the ignition. He looked up and saw the keys dangling in front of him. He knew they were catching the outside light. He thought about reaching up to yank them out. He glanced over at Mack and saw Mack's eyes flickering with fear as the keys swung back and forth. "Close your eyes," Clay said and Mack gave him a strange look, but did as Clay suggested, squinting them shut. Clay reached up and pulled the keys out of the ignition. He felt a tightness in his chest, like he had run too fast. Somewhere, in another part of the parking lot, an alarm stopped honking. Clay counted the seconds of silence, listened to the thumps and rockings and shouts and shattering glass as the gang moved around his car. He didn't dare to wipe the sweat that was now running from his cheeks and along his jaw, worried that even the slightest movement would give them away.

There was another pass of a shadow and then another pass. Someone beat the hood of another car and then the gang was suddenly gone from the lot, leaving another car alarm sounding in their wake. Mack opened his eyes, waited for another thump, then shifted his leg to a more comfortable position. Clay waited beneath the steering wheel, his ears cocked as if he were a dog tuning for prowlers. The car alarm stopped and they waited in their hiding places, drinking in the silence. When Clay was certain the gang had gone, he lifted himself up and looked out the windows, lifting the ends of his shirt and drying off his face.

"It's okay," he said to Mack and Mack unfolded himself and looked around the car as he took his seat again. They were both embarrassed by their behavior and Clay gave a nervous laugh and looked through the car windows again at the lot. Mack wiped off the sweat from his own face with the sleeve of his polo shirt.

Clay hesitated about starting the car—some instinct again told him to wait a second before turning the ignition—and then there was a light thump against the back of his car. Before he could turn around he saw the guy walking toward Mack's door. He had come out of nowhere in the dark night. They had not even seen his approach.

"Shit," Mack said. He drew in his breath. The guy outside the car leaned down and looked through the window. Clay could see the guy clearly now—he had spiky black hair, a whisper of a goatee, furious black eyes that seemed to roll toward the back of his head. He looked like he wanted to say something but didn't know how to form the words with his lips. In Clay's panic, he thought the guy might have been someone who had been attacked by the gang, but that was because the boy was wearing jeans and a sleeveless vest, like he was someone who might have been inside the club. They waited for the guy to do something—to knock his fist through the glass or draw a gun from the waistline of his jeans. Nothing happened except fear rising up into a confrontation.

"What do you want?" Clay shouted. His voice startled Mack. Mack turned to Clay, his expression a mixture of distress and self-consciousness. The guy on the other side of the window brought his face up close to the glass, as if he were a giant who had heard a tiny voice inside a box and was trying to figure out what it was saying.

"Do you know him?" Mack asked Clay. "Is he someone you know?"

Clay shook his head no. They both looked at the guy. Now he looked like he was trying to read the tiny print of a phone book, moving his lips while he made out the words.

"Is he with them?" Mack asked.

"I don't think so," Clay answered.

They looked at the guy moving his mouth as if they understood what he was saying. "What's wrong with him?" Clay asked. "What do you think is wrong with him?"

"He's spinning," Mack said. "He must have taken something. Do you think he's okay? Should we get help?"

"Leave him alone," Clay said. "Maybe he'll just go away."

The boy kept reading, or imagining he was reading, his lips moving swiftly into a jumble of motions. He reached something—a phrase, a name?—that made him laugh and he pulled back into a smile and then into a soundless laugh, the kind an actor might do at an audition.

Then the guy drew his face again closer to the window, bumping his head on the glass. The bump startled him and he drew back and looked like the pain might make him start crying. He shook his head back and forth violently, as if something were lodged between his ears and then he stopped, and then he began shaking his head again.

"What if he OD's?" Mack asked. "Maybe we should try and get help."

"No," Clay said. He had become suspicious of the guy's act, unsure if he was really high or not. "What if it is a setup? What if he was part of them? What if they saw us hiding and they're waiting to see what we'll do?"

"That's crazy," Mack said. "He'd have cracked the window by now if he wanted to do something to us. He's tripping on something. What if he needs help?"

"You don't know anything about him," Clay said. "You don't know who he is."

"There's a lot of runaways in this part of town," Mack said. "They shoot up in the buildings over there."

"Then we should just let him go," Clay said. "Leave him alone. Stay out of this."

"We can't just leave him," Mack said. "He's in some kind of trouble. Something's wrong with him. We ought to help."

"We can drive up to the club," Clay said. "You can tell someone he needs help. Maybe they can call the police."

Mack agreed to the plan with a short, "Okay." Clay started the ignition of the car, put it into reverse, and turned to look behind him, when Mack suddenly started yelling, "Wait! He's standing behind the car now."

The guy had moved to the rear of Clay's car, his hands were pressed against the trunk, as if he were trying to hold the car into place, to not let them leave. "What the hell is he trying to do?" Clay asked.

"He doesn't want us to leave," Mack said. "Don't go back any farther or he'll get hurt. You'll run over him."

"Come on," Clay said. He was exasperated now, as if the danger had disappeared and the guy was now an annoyance. The effects of the 'lude and the beers had worn off. He was starting to feel edgy. The guy started tapping on the trunk of the car, small quiet drumming with his fingertips that got louder and louder until he was smacking the metal with the palms of his hands. Clay turned off the motor, turned around so he could see what the guy was doing. He cracked his window a bit, yelled out, "Knock it off."

The guy stopped and lifted his head toward the front of the car.

"Go on," Clay yelled. "Get out of here."

"Don't encourage him," Mack said. "You'll just make it worse if he understands what he's doing."

The guy crawled on top of the trunk and sat down, his back toward Clay and Mack. He started hopping up and down on the trunk with his butt, making the car jump. He kept up with this movement, as if it were a newly discovered toy and not a way to further infuriate Clay. Clay yelled out the window again, his tone harsher than before, "Knock it off. Get off the car. Go on—*get outta here!*"

The guy began hopping harder, stopped and then stood on top of the trunk. He was wearing black boots. He stamped a foot as if he were trying to keep time to some kind of music. The guy wasn't very big—but he made the car bounce up and down like a big, threatening kind of guy would.

Clay wiped off another layer of sweat from his forehead, started the ignition again, hit the brake pedal, and put the car into reverse. The car lurched but went nowhere.

"Wait!" Mack yelled. "You'll make him fall."

"That's the point," Clay said. He was breathing hard now. "He's damaging my car. Enough of this shit."

"He doesn't know what he's doing," Mack said. "He's stoned or high or flying on something."

"That's why he should do it somewhere beside the back of my car."

They both looked at the long pair of legs at the back of Clay's car. Clay tried to think of something that he might have to arm himself with if he went outside the car—a knife under the seat? A screwdriver in the glove compartment? Could he hold the keys in his fist so that they would work as spikes? He felt his anger fueling his courage. Just when he was about to unlock the door the boy fell from the car onto the pavement.

"Oh god," Mack said. "Can you see him? Is he okay?"

"I don't see him," Clay said. "Where did he fall?"

"Behind the car," Mack answered. "Don't back up. Turn the car off. Don't back up!"

Clay turned the ignition off. The vibrations of the car stopped. The parking lot was silent. "Do you see him?" Clay asked.

"No," Mack said.

"If we just wait, he'll go away," Clay said.

"He won't go away," Mack said. "He just fell off your car. He probably broke his back or cracked his head open. He's not going anywhere."

"Can you see anyone?" Clay asked. "Anyone else from the club walking over here?"

"Are you crazy?" Mack replied. "You're not supposed to park in this lot. No one parks in this lot anymore."

"Then why is it full of cars?"

"Because some idiots don't know better," Mack said. "There's always trouble in this lot."

Clay took the insult in stride. He hadn't been to this club in almost a year. He felt he was too old for the crowd, not hip enough, and too eager to meet someone who looked exactly like Mack—young, careless, and available for whatever could happen without any strings attached.

"I think we should check on him," Mack said.

"Go ahead," Clay answered. "You can have him." Bitterness surfaced in his tone. He looked out the window and took a deep breath. The air inside the car was warm, stuffy, like trying to breathe water. He felt his blood banging in his ears.

"You can't just back up and drive over him if he's under the car," Mack said.

"Go ahead and help him," Clay said. "I'll wait."

"What if he needs a doctor?" he asked.

"We'll call an ambulance for him at the club," Clay said. "Go ahead. I'll wait while you check on him."

Mack waited to open the door. Clay saw fear move through Mack's expression again. Mack unlocked the door with the electronic button on his armrest. The chu-ching bounced through the darkness. He cracked the door slowly open, then found his courage and opened the door all the way. He stepped out of the car and took a few steps toward the rear of it.

Clay could see Mack's neck slowly stretching and inching to find the boy. Clay kept his hand at the ignition, ready to start the car and head out if the trouble escalated again. Mack saw nothing, took a few steps, and kept looking. He walked to the back of the car and then back to his open door.

"He's not here," Mack said. "He's gone."

"Shit," Clay answered. "He's probably underneath it."

Mack squatted to his knees and looked underneath the car. "Nope," Mack said. "He's not there either." Mack walked again to the back of the car, looked around the parking lot, and returned to the opened door. "Nowhere," he said. "He's nowhere to be found."

"Then he's gone," Clay said. "Good. Get back in. We can go now."

"I dunno," Mack said.

"What?" Clay asked.

"I dunno," Mack said again. "I don't have good vibes about any of this. I'm gonna go back and look for my friends."

"Well, get in," Clay said. "I'll drive you back to the club."

"No," Mack said. "This is just too freaky. Like in some kind of slasher movie. I'm just gonna walk back to the club."

"But it's safer if I drive you," Clay said.

"No," he answered. "I'm gonna walk. I just don't feel like doing anything right now."

"Listen," Clay said. "Wait a minute. I don't care if you don't want to do anything anymore. Okay? But at least let me get you back to the club safely. Let me drive you over there."

"No thanks," Mack answered. His tone was certain and determined. "I'm gonna walk back."

Mack shut the door and started toward the club. Clay turned his head and watched him move through the lot. Mack weaved in and around a bank of cars and then waited at the curb to cross the street. Clay turned the ignition key and the motor jumped alive. He slowly reversed the car out of the parking space, the thought flashing across his mind again that maybe he was being set up, maybe this was a trap to believe that the gang had moved through the lot or that the guy had been buzzed and injured by the fall from his car. But as he made it out of the parking space, he looked back at the gray, oil-stained cement where he had been parked and the hoods and bodies of the parked cars. There was nothing moving. No body. No guy. Nothing. Nothing at all. If it was a setup, what were they trying to get out of him?

Clay waited in his car with the motor running at the exit of the parking lot until he saw Mack cross the highway. He tried to keep his disappointment in check; after all, he'd been luckier than he thought he would be tonight just by meeting Mack. The first plops of heavy rain hit his windshield, then fell against the roof of the car in a drumbeat of thonk-thonka-thonk. Clay pulled his car out into the street, turned into the club's parking lot, his eyes following Mack's lopey gait to the entrance of the club, hoping Mack might turn around, glance back and give Clay a second chance. Clay flipped on the windshield wipers, the few drops of rain smearing the dirt that had settled against the glass. The rush of air-conditioning from the vents made Clay feel better, hopeful again. He drove slowly up to the club's entrance and stopped at the curb and waited, giving Mack time to reconsider, thinking he might just walk back out the door having changed his mind and realized he had made a mistake.

There were a group of young guys in tank tops and T-shirts smoking close to the door, one fellow passing the red ember of a joint to a friend who stood next to him. The rain—still sparse but falling in heavy drops— pinned them single file against the wall of the building like a police line-up. There was another young man a short distance from the group—tall, lanky, wearing faded jeans, his dark T-shirt stained with sweat at his armpits and at the center of his chest. He had a scraggly, worried look about him, his eyes were cast nervously up at the rain and then out toward the traffic in the street as if he were waiting for a ride, an oily sheen to his complexion as if he had been dancing too hard and had to stop. His hair was an ungroomed mop of curls, blondish and long, darkened also by sweat. Clay estimated the guy was in his early twenties and it unnerved him when their eyes met and locked. Clay had been bending his head down in the car to be able to look up and study the guy through the side window when the young man suspiciously glanced in Clay's direction and caught his glance.

The rain came down faster now. The air-conditioning had dried Clay's sweat. Clay deflected his eyes, flipped the wiper again, and then looked back at the entrance of the club, counting slowly in his mind to ten, still waiting for Mack to emerge. When he looked back at the young man once more, their eyes locked again. The guy gave a suspicious glance toward the street, then returned his stare to Clay. He approached the side window of Clay's car and tapped on the glass. When he bent down to look through the window, Clay cracked it slightly open with the electronic button.

"You're not headed uptown, are you?" the guy said. "I've been waiting for a cab. It'll never show up now because of the rain."

Clay never picked up hitchhikers, never stopped to give stranded motorists a hand. It was too risky in this part of town. There were always reports of murdered Good Samaritans or drive-by shootings. But the guy was cute and worried. And young. Clay tried to decide if the boy was a hustler or a runaway or a junkie, but he knew there was nothing that could distinguish one or the other to him. It was all intuition. Clay's car was inexpensive, close to ten years old, a functional choice, not an expensive or sporty or flashy one. No one would want to hijack the car. And all he had on him was his driver's license, a bank card, and a little bit of cash. He didn't have much to loose if he gave the guy a lift and he turned out to be a mugger.

"Get in before you get soaked," Clay said.

Clay unlocked the passenger door with an electronic ch-chunck. The guy cracked the door open and slipped inside, droplets of rain caught in the sweaty tangle of his hair. Clay thought he looked like someone he might have met a decade ago—no, perhaps even longer back—the jeans and T-shirt and the long curly hair gave the boy a decidedly retro look.

Clay introduced himself and the guy nodded, saying his name was Jason. "My friend got lucky tonight and took off," he said. "I just got tired in there and was ready to go, so I called a cab about a half hour ago. The guy I spoke to didn't sound like he was in a hurry to send someone over here."

It sounded plausible enough to Clay. He gave one last look to the entrance of the club and gave up on Mack returning. He shifted the car into gear and drove back toward the highway.

Jason told Clay the address where he was headed. "I hope it's not out of your way," Jason said.

"No," Clay answered. "I can go that way."

The guy ran his hands through his hair, flattening the curls against his scalp, the drops scattering against Clay's arm. There was a look about the young man's face that Clay couldn't quite decipher—sadness, disgust, fear, anxiety? It made Clay believe the guy was not a troublemaker, just someone trying to get home. Jason twisted his head toward the backseat and saw that the car was empty. "Nice car," he said.

"Not really," Clay answered. "But it's reliable."

Clay turned out onto the highway faster than his usual speed, his own nervousness making the tires give off an anxious squeal. Through his peripheral vision he studied the young man's profile. The nose and chin were prominent and strong, and there was a light stubble of unshaven beard growing at the chin. "You're in school, right?" Clay asked. Clay had decided his passenger was younger than he looked.

The guy nodded. "State," he answered. "I got a ride this morning with friends. I really came to see my sister. She just got a divorce and wanted some help moving."

Clay felt a surge of lust move across his body, the second he'd felt that night. He was at a loss how to proceed; the guy was indeed younger than he had imagined. There was a gap of silence between the two men, while the rain pounded against the windshield. "Are you hungry?" Clay asked. "You want to stop to get something to eat?"

He had decided he could at least try to turn his misfortune with Mack into something better with Jason. "I better not," Jason said. "I was supposed to have been back an hour ago."

They rode in silence as the rain thickened, worsened, pounded on the roof and the windshield—tatatatatatatata. Clay leaned forward in his seat to get a better view of the road and he forgot about Jason for a few minutes. The shop signs they passed were illegible in the rain. The stoplights were colored blurs through the windshield. Clay wasn't even sure how far they had traveled from the club. When he tried to relax a bit, he glanced to his right, and saw Jason was lying with his neck tilted back, his eyes closed. Clay thought maybe he didn't want to talk. Maybe he just wanted to get home. Maybe Clay should just call it a night himself, get home safely too.

Every now and then an approaching car would materialize, appear out of the rain as if it were right upon them. One car was driving down the median. Clay hit his horn, swerved out of the way. Jason opened his eyes and said, "That was close."

Clay glanced at his passenger, caught his eyes. They were green. Even in the dim light of the car he could see their color. His own eyes felt huge, heavy, tired, ready to close. Just as he shifted his eyes back to the road he saw something in front of the car. It was a man. Someone in the middle of the road. Clay slammed on the brakes but he was going too fast. Clay stretched out his arm toward Jason, as if to prepare him for a sudden stop. Outside, in the road, the man stretched out his arms toward Clay's car, the palms flat open and the fingers wide. In the seconds that Clay's car closed in on the man the details flashed into view—the spiky hair, the goatee, the sleeveless vest, the dark stretch of legs, and the black boots. The impact sent the man under the wheels of Clay's car. Clay felt the shock absorbers fail to cushion the horror. Clay twisted the wheel, even though it was too late. The car banked, flipped over onto its side, and skidded to a stop when it hit a pole.

It took a few seconds for the accident to make its way into Clay's brain. His hands still gripped the wheel. He was aware of the windshield being cracked, the rain continuing its tatatatatata against the glass. The car door was now facing the sky. There was a sharp bolt of pain up his neck. The car was flipped so that Clay was at the higher end, his body straining to break free of the seat belt and tumble toward the passenger seat. Clay turned his head toward Jason, the pain excruciating. "Are you okay?" he asked, his voice nervous, scared.

When there was no answer, Clay shifted his shoulder and looked down at the young man. Jason's eyes were open, and blood had settled in his mouth. Clay took a sharp, sudden breath. He tried not to panic. He reached for the car door, used both hands to push it up and open. The rain fell against his shirt, his eyes, his forehead. He unhooked his seat belt and climbed out of the car, landing on the curb on his palms and knees. A river of sewage was flowing beside him.

He stood up and felt the pain in his neck travel along his shoulder and upper back. He blinked away the rain from his eyes, blinked again, and wiped his brow, the bolt of pain now back at his neck. He walked along the side of the car, afraid to reach the end. In the street, he saw the curled body of the young man he had hit. Clay jogged over, and leaned down, squatting to rest on his knees. In front of him the body shivered, as if the memory of pain were still inside the brain. Clay wiped the rain from his eyes, clasped a hand across his mouth, as if preventing a shout. It was the guy from the parking lot. How had he gotten this far so quickly? Why had he walked right out in front of the car?

Clay knew he had to find help. The street was empty. No traffic was approaching where the car had stopped against the street pole. In the distance he saw the red blur of a stoplight shift into green and a pair of tiny white headlights. Clay walked out farther into the street, into the approaching lane. The rain came down harder. Clay felt the drops hit the top of his head, his forearms, wrists, chin. His clothing stuck to his body. Why was this happening to him? How was he going to survive it? He waved his hands up and down as if he were doing jumping jacks, trying to catch the approaching driver's attention. The driver did not seem to notice Clay, so Clay took a few steps more into the middle of the lane, flagged his arms again and tried to yell, but he could not find his voice or hear the sound of it, the rain now thumping and tatatatating like the volume had been increased.

As the car approached the headlights grew brighter. Clay took a few steps backward, his hands stretched out in front of his body, waving for the car to stop. The car's lights blinded him and his chest filled with air. "Wait!" he yelled, as the rain continued to pound. "Wait!" he yelled as the headlights reached his eyes and he threw up his hands to keep from being blinded.

◆

It took Clay four days to find Jason's sister. At first he could not remember the address Jason had given him, then, after it had come to him while he was trying to nap, it had taken him another day to find a listing for the house and make the phone call. He had reached a woman named Lisa Braden who had a younger brother named Jason. On the phone she had given him a suspicious dismissal, but he had pressed harder, said he had been involved in a car accident and needed to talk to her about her brother.

Lisa lived in a small house near the entrance of a park. When she answered the door, she led Clay through a tiny room full of bookcases and chairs and knickknacks and into a smaller kitchen of crammed cupboards and shelves and to a small door that led outside to a patio deck that overlooked the park. She offered Clay a drink and he accepted, saying water would be fine. She was fortysomething and divorced, her dark hair had been lightened blonde but in a natural way. Clay recognized the similarity in the face—she had Jason's long jaw and strong chin, though she appeared old enough to be Jason's mother, not his sister.

"How long have you lived here?" Clay asked her. He was trying to make conversation first, before jumping directly toward the information he wanted.

"Almost eighteen years," she said through the kitchen window. "Right after my divorce. I never thought I would stay here so long, but I have. But it's become a bit lonely since both my children are in college now."

"State?" Clay asked, when she handed him a glass of iced water.

"My daughter's at State. My son's at Tech."

They sat at chairs beside a café table. "I'm sorry to bother you," Clay said. "I know my phone call must have seemed strange. I was wondering if you had a picture of your brother." He didn't have the stomach to drink the water and his hand was already wet from the moisture on the outside of the glass, but he didn't want to seem impolite by refusing it. Clay held the glass against the armrest of the plastic chair, the park lawn below him a bright green in the sunlight of the afternoon.

"I do," Lisa answered, though she made no motion to go and get it.

Clay began his story, starting not with his unfortunate luck in the parking lot, or his rejection by Mack, but with seeing Jason standing outside the club waiting for a cab. Lisa's eyes narrowed with suspicion and Clay backtracked, saying, "I was waiting for a friend to decide whether to go back with me or someone else," so it would not appear to Lisa that he had tried to pick Jason up. "And then it started to rain. Jason tapped on my window and I told him I would give him a ride home. Here."

"It was so long ago," Lisa said. "I don't know why you are here."

"But he told me his name," Clay said. "Four days ago."

"He had come down to help me move some furniture," she said. "We were going to pick up a sofa the next day. Something I found on the other side of town. We were going to rent a truck."

She stood up from chair and went into the apartment. Clay looked at the leaves floating back and forth from the breeze, the sunlight so bright it was like you could almost see through the green. Lisa returned with a framed photo. She handed it to Clay. "He's the one on the right."

Clay studied the young man in the photograph. The jaw and chin were just as he remembered. The hair was mop of blond and brown curls. The eyes were a bright green. He was standing with a small boy and girl that Clay assumed were Lisa's children. "Yes," he said. "That was him."

"He's been dead for eighteen years," Lisa said. "I don't believe you could have seen him."

He handed the photo back to her and said, "But I did. I know it was him. He told me he went to State."

She curled her fingers around the photo frame, pressed it instinctively facedown against her breast. She sat again in the plastic chair beside Clay.

"I couldn't find anything about an accident," Clay said. "There was nothing on it in the papers. There's no police report about an accident that night, other than mine. No one was admitted to the hospital that night because of a traffic accident. I just can't believe they disappeared." Clay had not even been able to find Mack again, to see if he might have noticed Jason in front of the entrance to the club or had run into the guy from the parking lot again. Mack was only Mack. No last names had been exchanged. The club owners had told Clay there was no such thing as surveillance tapes of the outside of the building or of the parking lot. Clay's only clue was that the responding officer at the accident scene had said that it was a difficult intersection, accidents had been happening there for years.

"There have been a few others," she said. "Otherwise I wouldn't believe you. But you're the only one who's seen them both."

She began to describe the night it rained eighteen years ago. "I wasn't worried about him, since he wasn't driving. He had been playing with the kids and a friend had picked him up around ten. He said he was going out to get a drink. The police called about three in the morning. He had left the club around one-thirty with another man. It had started raining hard. The driver had not seen the hitchhiker. Apparently the boy hitchhiking was hallucinating or stoned or scared by the rain, because afterward the coroner's report revealed that his blood levels were very high for a variety of things. The driver said he walked right into the car. And then the car skidded and toppled onto its side and hit the street pole. The impact was what killed him. Jason."

"The police didn't believe me," Clay said, "but I knew I wasn't crazy. He was as alive to me as you are now. And then he wasn't. When I stopped the car after the accident, I got the guy to call the police with his cellphone. I was lucky he stopped. He didn't believe me, either. When I went back to where my car was there was nothing. Nobody. The guy I had run over was gone. Jason was not in the car. They had both vanished. My car wasn't even on its side, like it had landed in the accident. The front wheels were up on the curb. There wasn't even a scratch or a dent on it. I don't know what happened. It was like *I* was hallucinating."

"You were lucky," she said.

He shook his head and took it all in, a slight memory of pain traveling up the muscles of his neck. "Not really," he said. "It was humiliating after that. Like I didn't believe myself. The police gave me a breath test. I was perfectly sober, like I hadn't even had a beer at all that night. I had a tow truck come and take the car away even though it was running perfectly when I tried to start it. I couldn't get back into it. I was really freaked out. I had the police take me home. I'm renting another car right now. It really feels to me like I totaled that one."

"What kind of car was it?" she asked.

When Clay told her the make and year of his car, she said, "No. That isn't the same one."

Clay took a swallow of water. He leaned forward and placed the glass on the café table. *Why me?* he thought, *why did this happen to me?* He stood up, instinctively brushed off his pants, and said, "Thank you for seeing me. I just had to find some kind of piece to this puzzle."

At the doorway they shook hands. "What happened to the others?" he asked.

"The driver survived," she said. "Though I heard he died a few years ago. Cancer."

"I was thinking about the others who saw him," Clay said. "Like I did."

"I don't know," she answered, pressing her cheek against the door frame. "They find me. They vanish quickly after that. Just like he did."

"Do they tell you anything?" he asked. "Is there something I'm missing?"

"No," she said, shaking her head back and forth. "Only that he's trying to get back here. I didn't have a key to give him that night. So I left the door unlocked. I think he must know that I was waiting up for him."

Clay nodded and thanked Lisa again and as he turned to leave he asked her one final question. "The other boy? The hitchhiker? Do you remember his name?"

"Russ," she answered. "Russell Pierce."

◈

Clay wanted the facts instead of a therapist to straighten things out for him. He began on the Internet, searching through newspaper archives, but came up empty handed. Obituaries were only archived for the past five years, so he left work early and drove to the campus library and used his alumni card to search through the records on microfilm. Over the span of three weeks eighteen years before he found news reports of the accident, the obituaries of Jason Braden and Russ Pierce, the public outing of the driver, Spencer Flynn, the citizens' petition for a stoplight at the intersection, the city council's compliance and the mayor's veto, which resulted in a backlash of more stories and editorials until the mayor reversed his decision and a stoplight was installed. Clay found no link or reason for his participation in the haunting, nothing that hinted why he might have stepped into a time warp and witnessed the accident. He refused to admit that it was a hallucination, a lapse of sanity or a fabrication of psychosis. He accumulated names, addresses, and phone numbers: the cemetery where Jason Braden was buried, the hometown and parents of Russ Pierce, the relatives of Spencer Flynn, the driver of the car who had died two years before of cancer.

He contacted Spencer's daughter in Florida, first by e-mail, and then, after there had been no reply within three days, by phone.

"There's nothing else to dredge up," Nancy Flynn, now Nancy Gerard, said. Her tone was harsh and annoyed. "Leave us alone."

"Did he ever talk about the accident?" Clay asked. "Did he give you any details?"

"Details? That car wreck ruined our family. My parents divorced. My father was depressed for the rest of his life. What details do you want? That he tried to commit suicide? That he broke my mother's heart? That he had to face one lawsuit after another?"

She hung up on Clay and he did not attempt to call her again. Spencer Flynn had not haunted him. The two boys had. He believed that they would be the source of any meaning or reason. But he couldn't help thinking that his life was changing in ways that Spencer Flynn's might have changed as well. *What had he done wrong? Why had this happened?*

◆

Russ Pierce's hometown was upstate. His father had been a minister but the home phone number Clay tried was no longer in service, so he phoned the church where Reverend Pierce had been a pastor. A receptionist told him that the Mr. Pierce had retired several years before and was now working as a youth counselor at a center not far from where Clay lived. Two hours later, Clay found Reverend Pierce in a poorly-painted office on the second floor of a halfway house for teens convicted for minor drug crimes—too young to be put in prison, too troublesome to be left in foster homes. The Reverend was a short, compactly built man, with a dark peppery crew cut and a gray stubble, looking more like an Army drill sergeant than a man of faith. Clay had interrupted a phone call and waited by the office door until Reverend Pierce was free.

"Come in," Reverend Pierce shouted to Clay. "Am I late on another report?"

"No, sir," Clay answered. "I'm here on a personal matter."

"Personal? About one of the boys?"

"No sir, about your son."

"My son?" The Reverend pushed his chair back from his desk and stood up. He was wearing a plaid shirt and jeans. He waved Clay into the office and toward a seat that was facing the desk. "My son has been dead for some time."

"That's why I'm here. I saw your son two weeks ago. First, in the parking lot of a club downtown. Then later, on the road, in the rain. It was an accident. There was another guy in the car with me."

The Reverend's neck flushed red and his eyes narrowed with hurt and anger and he glanced suspiciously around the office. On the desk was a wooden plaque that read *Trust in the Lord.* On the wall behind the desk was a poster of an eagle flying over a mountain and out toward the sea. "This isn't some kind of sad joke, is it? There's not some hidden camera recording this?"

"No sir. It happened," Clay said. He could feel his own discomfort. The sweat at his armpits. The tension in his brow. He could not see the boy in his father and he wondered if he had made a mistake. "Only it didn't happen. There was an accident and there wasn't an accident. There was a guy in the car and a guy on the road and then when the police arrived there were neither. They thought something was the matter with me. There wasn't. I'm certain of it."

"My son was there and then he wasn't?"

"That's right. He was the guy in the road. I hit him exactly the way another driver had hit him eighteen years ago. I'm trying to find the meaning of it. Why I was there. Why this happened to me."

"That accident changed a lot of lives."

"I know. If it happened to me, but *didn't* happen to me, what am I to expect?"

"That's as much of a spiritual question as a psychological one. Do you believe in ghosts or do you believe that God has sent you a message? Or neither? That you've just experienced a random blip in a freakish world?"

"I believe I saw it. That it happened. That's what I believe."

"Then how you react—or how you change—seems to be up to you. What you believe is possible. I know my son is dead and his death changed my life."

"Suppose your son died without accomplishing something that he really wanted to accomplish. Do you believe that his spirit could still be trying to do it? That somehow I got in his way?"

"My son was a troubled boy. He accused me of ignoring him. And being too strict on him. I always thought that was his paranoia until it occurred to me that he might have been right. I left my church to be here. To do this work with these boys. I ignored my son's addictions and I remind myself of that every day."

"Was he in love? Was he ever in love with someone?"

"I don't know for sure. Like I said, I didn't know him as a father should his son."

◆

For months Clay was ruled by confusion. He slept poorly. He felt exhausted and weary. He stopped going to the gym, called in sick to work, and stayed home to read and eat and sleep. He tried to accept the fact that there had been no accident. That no one had been harmed. That he had not been a part of it. He prayed. He fasted. He tried eating only organic foods and taking homeopathic remedies to restore his energy and maintain a sense of calm. Nothing changed him or connected him with a different plan. He spent time fretting. He spent time speculating. He went to a psychic to have his fortune told, only to learn that he held the key to his own future.

Time passed and he fretted less. He became more focused at work, received a raise and more responsibility. He went out with coworkers, went out of town on a business trip, took a vacation to London and New York and came back feeling different. He bought a new car, something more adult and fully loaded with extra options and features. He began to date again. No one serious, then someone serious, then another guy not so seriously. Soon he was promoted again. And then again. He became more focused on his work than on his personal life. He placed the ghosts of Jason Braden and Russ Pierce in a gray spot at the back of his mind, as part of something that had happened in his past; knowing they were what made him different, but no longer worrying about what they were supposed to mean to him.

Four years later, Clay was driving back to work from a business meeting at a restaurant. His route took him past Lisa Braden's house. As he passed the block, he noticed a moving van in the driveway. He circled the block, drove by the house again and saw a bright-red-lettered SOLD sign out on the front lawn. He stopped and parked the car.

The front door of the small house was open. Inside the front room a woman about Clay's age was working over a series of moving boxes, taping the lids shut and labeling them with a black marker. He took her to be Lisa Braden's daughter. "Sorry to intrude," he said. "The woman who lived here. Lisa Braden. Is she moving?"

"My mother died a few months ago," the woman said.

"I'm sorry for your loss," Clay answered. "I only knew her casually. Through an accident. It was an accident that we met."

He cast his eyes around the room, taking in the outlined spots on a wall where pictures had once hung. He moved toward the door to leave, and stepped out of the way of two men carrying boxes toward the door. There was something familiar about one of the men and Clay followed them out the door and watched them load the boxes in the back of the van. He felt immediately odd, as though he were a voyeur perched behind a tree. He had met the taller of the two men before. He was certain. Clay waited until the man began to walk back toward the house before he approached him.

"We met before," Clay said to the guy. "A couple of years ago."

The guy squinted, gave Clay a glance up and down. "You sure?"

"At a club. Downtown. There was a problem in the parking lot."

The guy's eyes widened, but he looked away from Clay, toward the front door of the house.

"Mack," Clay said. "You're name is Mack, isn't it?"

"That's right," Mack said. "I remember. Some freaky dude kept jumping on the car."

"Right," Clay said, tensing his mouth into a smile. His mind was shifting gears rapidly, trying to reconnect with the guy, trying to sort out the reason why he would find him here, of all places, all this time later, moving boxes at Lisa Braden's former house.

Clay sensed that the guy was embarrassed to be talking with him and they both looked at the door when the woman appeared and said, "Mack, did you look through the videotapes? Is there anything you want to keep?"

It occurred to Clay that Mack was not a moving man, but the woman's brother. Lisa Braden had been Mack's mother. Jason Braden had been his uncle. That night four years before Clay had stepped into Mack's nightmare. Not one of his own.

His mind quickly replayed the events. The rain. The boy in the parking lot. The hitchhiker in the car. He traveled backward to the beginning, how it all began: a kiss he had shared with Mack. *History*, Clay thought. *This is it. We all share a history now.*

"Wait!" he shouted to Mack, when the guy began to walk back toward the house and his sister. "Can I see you again? There's still a lot more I want to know."

The guy gave Clay a pained expression, but something in his eyes brightened. "Sure," he answered and took a step forward. "We can try it again. I could give it another try."

Sometime weeks later, Clay and Mack were seated in the car outside a shopping mall, waiting for the rain to stop before they made a dash to the front entrance. Mack leaned over and kissed Clay. It was simple and genuine and felt quite natural to both. In that moment Clay felt something in him change. He believed that love had caught him first, but in the version Mack would soon tell his sister, Mack thought that Clay was the more hesitant one. "I always regretted leaving the car that first night," he explained. "That decision haunted me for years."

DEATH IN AMSTERDAM

"Hold on tight to your purse," Brian said to Amy. "Keep a good grip on it."

They had finished dinner at a restaurant near Leidseplein and decided to walk to the Red-Light district instead of returning to the hotel. Amy insisted that she wasn't tired or the least bit suffering from jet lag. Cara, Amy's girlfriend and partner of three years, was grumpy but willing to make the trek, ready to deplore the experience and working conditions of the sex workers on display. Brian, who had been to Amsterdam before, suggested that they take the tram, but the women wanted to get a feel for the city so they set out on foot. It was a warm summer night, the sky above like a dark, velvet blanket, but there was a joyous energy on the street—tourists skirting around the trams, rowdy students circling a street performer posing as a statue, groups of gay men and women headed out to a bar or one of the weekend street fairs.

They followed the crowds along Warmoesstraat to the lane that circled Ouede Kerke and the path to where the barely dressed women sat behind the tall windows and glass doors illuminated with eerie blue or red lights. Groups of nervous young men seemed to spontaneously pause around a window, snickering and reacting to the women behind the glass, then rejoin the flow of the traffic to the next window. College boys, Brian thought, aware that they had left behind most of the gay crowds—it was Pride Weekend in Amsterdam—but the city was also packed with students and other tourists. He felt disturbingly out of his element in this neighborhood. The air was heavy and motionless in this part of town and it added to the ominous mood of the scene—everyone watching someone else—yet a distinct divide existed between the tourists and prostitute-oglers and the dark-eyed, hooded young men circling the crowd, watching the watchers—pimps and hustlers and petty thieves.

Brian had always found his Rosse Buurt visits disconcerting and unnerving—the dark nights, the narrow streets, the large, uncontrollable crowd that felt ready to disrupt or encircle a spectacle. There were warnings posted at the hotels and in the guidebooks about pickpockets and crime in this area. In his opinion, the Red-Light district and the green cafés had given Amsterdam something of a bad rap, there was so much else to experience here—the glorious architecture, the romantic canals, the sense of adventure every time you wandered into a new neighborhood. To Brian, Amsterdam was as magical as others found Venice and Barcelona. Eddie, Brian's former lover and a design buff, had always enjoyed their visits here—they had often stayed on the outskirts, near Vondel Park and the museums, and spent hours wandering through the neighborhoods snapping photographs of unusual architectural details. But Brian knew the trip to the center of Sodom could not be overlooked for first-time visitors such as Amy and Cara. It was part of the experience of Amsterdam.

Brian led his sister and her partner to a dark street where they could walk with more ease, alongside the canal that reflected the neon lights of the Bulldog bars lining the block. An ominous calm hung in the air and Brian's senses were on alert. He heard loud, confused noises from far away, rattling cups and dishes, a low dull thunder of chairs being moved across a floor. Sweat formed around his throat and under his arms. He quickened his pace so that the women would walk faster. Behind them, a man followed closely, his boots striking the sidewalk in a stalking pace. They had reached an isolated stretch where they were briskly walking side by side when Brian made the comment to Amy about keeping hold of her purse.

"Let them try," Cara said in her toughest tone, though experience had taught Brian that she would crumble and run at the least sign of trouble.

Amy didn't respond, but Brian knew his sister's posture had tensed. He could detect the strain on her face without looking at her. Their follower was now walking too closely behind them, almost upon Amy's heels, his boots landing like gasps against the stones of the street. Brian stopped and turned to get a good look at the fellow's face. The man, in a light jacket, raised up the hood and bent his eyes down to the street. He was a dark-looking fellow with a scruffy stubble, though Brian didn't want to pass an immediate judgment on him. The man veered across the street, stuck his hands into his pockets, then turned and walked in another direction. Brian watched him till he was satisfied that the guy wasn't planning on returning or didn't have associates in the vicinity, then turned to get his bearings. "Down here," he said, choosing a street that he thought would lead them back to Warmoesstraat.

Again, they were in a thick flow of a crowd and passing the open doors of souvenir shops, peep shows, and sex merchants. Cigarette smoke and reefer spilled out to the sidewalks. They had reached Warmoesstraat when Brian spotted a young man across the street he was certain was Jariel. He turned to his sister and said abruptly, "Wait here," and pointed her inside to a café. He didn't linger for her response. As he turned to cross the street, the young man noticed him and began to run away, into the crowd Brian had just left. Brian yelled, "Jariel!" and the guy turned at the sound of his name, saw Brian, then continued to run.

Brian followed, pushing his way through the other tourists as fast as he could. He ran down a block, and then another. Just before he reached the canal again he stopped, stuck his hands on his hips and bent over, defeated, trying to catch his breath. He was forty-five years old and though he went to the gym as often as he could, the sprint left him winded and flustered. All he wanted was for what had belonged to him to be returned. All he wanted was something back that had had a meaning in his life.

A few minutes later he sheepishly returned to the café where he had left his sister and Cara. "You want to tell me what that's all about?" Amy asked him when he joined them at their table. She was not happy about being deserted and Cara was not happy with the café.

"Not yet," Brian said. "Let's check out the street fair by the Amstel."

◈

He had met Jariel the day before. Brian had arrived in Amsterdam ahead of Amy and Cara. He was a journalist on assignment, covering the city during Gay Pride, writing about whether the city was still a safe haven for gay men and tourists. There had been a growing tension between the conservative Islamic immigrant community that had settled in the European city and the more liberal Dutch natives and gay tourists. A Dutch filmmaker had been killed by an Islamist extremist and a gay politician was murdered by a left-wing activist who called his victim a racist, but after an American gay editor vacationing in the city and walking hand in hand with his boyfriend one night on the way back to their hotel was spontaneously assaulted by a gang of Moroccan youths and hospitalized, the city's Tourist Board issued a warning to gay visitors to be careful in the city.

Back in the States, the mainstream media were ignoring the story, but Brian's editor wanted a firsthand account of what was happening in Amsterdam. Was it safe or was it dangerous for the gay traveler? Brian had approached this trip and his assignment with an open mind; he refused to be swayed by the hysteria that had crept into some Internet gay chat rooms with postings about the overreaction of the gay media and the under-protection of the police. Brian had done several pre-interviews before arriving in town—with reps from the Tourist Board, the Flying Pig student hostels, and the Bulldog cafés—each downplaying the brewing troubles. On an Internet message board he had found a contact for an organization of gay activists trying to set up a "Bring Back the Night" patrol group, similar to what had been organized years before in the U.S. during a spate of urban hate crime bashings, but so far he had been unable to get a response from the organization because its position seemed aggressively and suspiciously anti-Muslim, and he was uncertain as to whether it was a trap attempting to snare a victim.

Brian had all this in mind when, his first day in town, he spotted Jariel while at the train station. He had just arrived from the airport and noticed the young man when he had gone into the bank to get Euros. Jariel was thin, dark-skinned and dark-eyed, with a mischievous smile and a severely short haircut, and Brian could not imagine he was even in his twenties. Jariel was standing beside two similar-looking young men in the station passage that led to the bank entrance. Brian had immediately assumed that the young men were Muslim but it was unclear to him whether Jariel and his friends might be "casing" the crowd or themselves tourists who had just arrived—there was a duffel bag at Jariel's feet and the other two fellows were looking at a map. Brian had caught Jariel's eye when he opened the door to the bank and smiled at him, and the grin the young man had returned made Brian sincerely doubt his objectivity on the assignment. He was a sucker for a handsome face. And Jariel's was a *young* handsome face. What would he do if he were to meet someone like this fellow—a young, handsome conservative Muslim? Would he fall prey himself, Gustave Aschenbach at the hands of an angry Tadzio? A quick death in Amsterdam instead of a slow, aging decline in Venice?

The young men were gone when Brian exited the bank minutes later with his cash. Brian had forgotten about the encounter until hours later, after he had checked into the hotel and taken a nap, and then gone out late in the afternoon to sightsee. While outside the Anne Frank house, he caught sight of Jariel again. This time the young man was alone, dressed in jeans and a yellow T-shirt, sitting on a cement post near the canal and smoking a cigarette, watching the line of tourists enter and leave the building. Jariel's friends and the duffel bag were absent. Brian had taken a tour of the house, and, while in the bookstore, he had initiated a conversation with a gay couple from West Hollywood who had been in his tour group. He had asked them a few questions about their trip, their caution or lack of it while out at night in Amsterdam, and written down their response in the small notebook he carried in his back pocket. The two men—Tim and Craig—were both well built and in their mid-thirties. They had an open relationship, and had come to Amsterdam to dance on a dinghy that was to be part of the canal parade the following day and attend a private party that was being thrown by a "friend of a friend."

"But we're not looking for trouble," Tim, the younger of the two, said. "No M&Ms."

"He means meth or Muslims," Craig, his partner, added. "No drugs and no late-night street cruising."

They each responded with nervous giggles, which made Brian think they were all style and no substance. What would these men do if they were confronted with trouble? Would they run or fight or offer to bargain? Brian thanked the two men and shook their hands, and he'd written a few other notes in his pad after he had left the bookstore and stood outside the house, when he looked up and spotted Jariel smoking a cigarette across the street. Brian nodded and when Jariel politely returned the nod, Brian crossed the street, thinking there might be another story in front of him.

"A sad moment," Jariel said with a heavy accent Brian could not immediately place. He was referring to the Frank house, which he continued to watch. Brian thought that perhaps the young man's friends were still inside. In the young man's hand was the flyer that all of the guests had gotten while touring the house.

"Yes," Brian replied. He was ready to find out a few facts about Jariel and his opinions, whatever they were, and if this short interview turned dangerous, it was still daylight and there were plenty of others around who might be called as witnesses.

"Are you Dutch?" he asked the young man, knowing the response was almost certain to be otherwise.

"Spanish," the young man answered.

"On holiday?"

The young man nodded. It was still unclear to Brian whether Jariel was Muslim, or if the young man was gay, though if Brian's gaydar still worked, he felt certain the young man was, even if he wasn't open and out about it.

"A writer?" the young man asked.

Brian nodded, though he did not disclose the nature of his assignment or the paper he was working for. "You talk to me?" the young man asked. "You make me a celebrity, too?"

"Sure," Brian answered and laughed.

The young man suggested the café next door. Jariel's friends never appeared. Brian sat with the young man and learned his name and his story. He was twenty-five and traveling with friends from Los Barrios, a small town near Gibraltar where they lived. Jariel worked as a waiter and his friends worked in a village market selling food. His friends wanted to come to Amsterdam to smoke pot and find a hooker. He wanted to do "something else." Brian asked about the other cities Jariel had visited. Had he been to Paris, or Rotterdam, or London? Jariel had not been anywhere other than Seville, which made Brian suspicious whether Jariel was telling him the truth. "What about Barcelona?" Brian asked.

"No," Jariel answered, then corrected himself. "As a boy, but I do not remember it."

The subject of Jariel's faith or his possible homosexuality was never brought up, though Brian felt certain that the way they held each other's eyes, there was no doubt to at least one answer.

There was no doubt about it later, when Brian had slipped his notebook into his pocket and they were walking together toward the Pink Point kiosk. The city was beginning to swell with the arrivals of more gay and lesbian couples, enough for a stranger to wonder if something special were about to happen. Brian stopped and watched a few couples take their pictures at the Homomonument and he spoke to a lesbian couple from Northampton, Massachusetts, who asked him to take their picture. Jariel did not seem offended or act disgusted and Brian granted him a stronger level of trust than he had given the young man before.

They continued walking together along the Keizersgracht till they reached Leidseplein and Brian asked Jariel if he wanted to stop for a drink. Jariel wanted to know more about Brian's life back in America—what was Manhattan like? Did he live in a loft and had he met Britney Spears? Brian was still uncertain if he wanted to bring the young man back to his hotel room—or even if that was an option available to him. Brian knew he was not "a beautiful man." He was more ordinary than handsome, with a receding hairline and growing gut, not the kind of gay man you would notice at a bar. But he had clear, intelligent eyes and a nice smile that others found relaxing, and he used it as often as he could in response to the young man's questions. After his first drink, Brian had made up his mind he would invite Jariel back to the hotel, but it was only after the third drink, after he had signed the check for all the rounds and they were briskly crossing the street to avoid the approaching tram, that he asked Jariel up to his room.

In the lobby of the hotel, Brian stopped and asked the concierge if there had been any messages. He didn't expect to hear from Amy until she was in Amsterdam the following morning and in her room, but he wanted a witness to see him with Jariel, in case there was any problem later.

In the room, Brian asked Jariel if he wanted another drink or something to eat. He opened the minibar and found a bag of chips and a bottle of beer. Jariel looked around the room and peered through the curtains at the Leidseplein below, as though he wanted to signal to someone. Brian regretted opening the beer the moment he took a sip—it was certain to pitch him into a hangover. When Jariel went into the bathroom, Brian turned on the TV, hoping that Jariel would not return with a knife or a gun or something equally troubling.

Brian heard the toilet flush and the water turn on in the shower. He sat on the edge of the bed and unlaced his shoes, leaned back against the headboard, and drank more of the beer. The young man taking a shower surprised him. Jariel emerged a few minutes later with a towel around his waist, the white fabric in stark contrast against his darker skin. He sat on the edge of the bed beside Brian and took a sip of Brian's beer, then leaned over and kissed Brian on the lips.

Brian took in the taste of the beer and the smell of soap and shampoo and the impression of the clean skin and the wet towel against his hands. Things moved swiftly after Brian slipped his hand along Jariel's thigh and the young man did not offer any resistance.

It was only when Jariel was straddling Brian's thighs and Brian was deep inside the young man that Brian began to let go of his tension. At last, he thought, at last he was beginning to get over Eddie. This trip could turn out to be the cure he needed, blotting out the numb despair that had lingered too long. And he had misinterpreted Jariel, had not given the young man the benefit of the doubt of *not* being an angry, conservative Muslim, though Brian still had not confirmed that the youth was Islamic. Certainly not a devout one, if what they were doing was a testament of his faith. Jariel was circumcised, as Brian expected, and he made a mental note that perhaps the story he should write was about how difficult it was for a Muslim youth to accept his homosexuality in a town such as Amsterdam. He did not intend to be racist or sympathetic to any side—he wanted his story to be objective— but an article such as this could temper any sort of anti-Muslim sentiment the main article might pose. Jariel struggled and shifted atop Brian, trying to find pleasure in the pain of having Brian inside him, his skin flushed and tight at his chest and neck muscles.

"Relax," Brian said, and it seemed to do the trick. The confused expression Brian had noticed had given way to one of dawning pleasure, almost of exaltation. The young man pulled Brian off of the mattress and closer to him until there was no space at all between their bodies. Brian shuddered and fell back against the bed. Jariel smiled, as if this was what he had planned to do all along, and his orgasm soon followed, landing on Brian's stomach.

◆

The next morning Jariel was gone. Brian had been aware that the young man had left sometime during the night, but his rising headache prevented his giving it too much thought. He got out of bed, rinsed his face, and ordered coffee from room service. A few minutes later, when he went to find his wallet in the pocket of the pants he'd worn the night before, he discovered that Jariel had taken all of his cash.

The disappointment overwhelmed him. He had been hustled. His credit cards and identification were still in his wallet, so he hadn't been completely blindsided; there had been some sort of ethical behavior behind Jariel's thefts. Brian checked the room for other missing items—his passport was still inside the room's safe. His cellphone and camera and laptop were on the desk where he had left them the day before. He was just at the point where he was reconciling the pluses and minuses of the encounter when he realized his watch was missing.

The watch. The expensive gold watch. The one thing of sentimental value that he could not part with. He remembered a playful moment from the night before, when Jariel was admiring the watch. He asked to try it on and Brian had let him wear it. The young man had slid it onto his hand, and lifted his arm up in the air to catch the light.

"It looks good on you," Brian said. "A perfect fit."

"I can keep?" Jariel asked.

"No," Brian answered.

The young man's face darkened with anger, as if he were about to hit Brian. His face changed as he thought and he said, "If I come to America, I can keep?"

"No," Brian said, and slid the watch off Jariel's arm, with some resistance. He twisted the watchband so the back of the watch could be seen. "See," Brian pointed at the back of the watch and the engraving there. "It was a gift."

"You give to me?"

"No," Brian said again.

"Some day you will," the boy answered. There was still a touch of anger in his voice.

Brian let the coffee go untouched when it arrived and he went back to bed, uncertain how he should—or if he could—report the stolen cash and watch. His stomach rumbled and his head began to ache. He decided all he wanted to do was sleep. Depression was consuming him. He had no desire to do any work. He only wanted to escape his emotions. He slept until his phone rang and Amy said she had arrived at the hotel and was in her room.

◆

"Of course you should report it," Cara said, when Brian told his sister and her girlfriend the story of the encounter. After the street fair along the Amstel, they had gone to the hotel bar before going back to their rooms, and Brian had confessed his plight. "The police should be aware of it. This is a liberal city and they're trying to keep that reputation. An unrecorded crime is *another* crime. No one should have to tell you that."

"If I establish myself as a victim, it compromises my story," Brian said.

"That's old journalism nonsense," Cara said. "You have a new media responsibility to report what happened. To tell the truth."

"It's only my truth," Brian said. "It's no longer objective news."

"If your editor had wanted an objective piece he would have sent a straight woman to write the story."

"And you?" Brian turned to his sister, who had remained quiet. "What's your opinion?"

"I'm sorry you lost your watch," she said. "I know what it meant to you."

Brian felt the crush of sentiment at his chest. The watch had been more than a watch. It had been Eddie's gift to him during their exchange of vows. Eddie had been Brian's lover for twenty-two years. They had navigated college crushes on each other and other guys, initial relationships with other men, Eddie's HIV status, and their own on-and-off sexual attraction to each other. Eddie had always been the sentimental one, collecting seashells on their visits to P-Town and Fire Island, swizzle sticks from bars in Vegas and New Orleans, and shot glasses from London, Rome, and Venice. Brian had remained practical, budgeting money for rent and a down payment for a weekend house upstate. Brian and Eddie had held a commitment ceremony long before it was fashionable and politically correct. Their second year owning the old Victorian house in Livingston Manor, they invited their closest friends and coworkers to witness them "bequeathing time" to each other. It was Eddie's idea—instead of rings, each would give the other an engraved watch.

Back in his hotel room, Brian flung off his shoes, ran water in the tub, and soaked for a long time, relieved to find a measure of comfort. A song—one of Eddie's favorites—played through his mind—and he tried to use it to lift his spirits. The story about Amsterdam no longer interested him. He was too distracted to write. He replayed the vivid moments with Jariel, which led him to replay his more lasting memories of ones with Eddie. Eddie had died of a stroke three years before. After all the medication to keep him healthy and his immune system functioning, his heart just gave out. He died before an ambulance could even arrive. Irony or fate? Brian wondered. Whatever, the event had left an irreparable gap in his life, even as Brian threw himself into one new assignment after another.

He lay in the tub until the water grew cold. *Eddie,* he thought, *what would you think of my life now? How would you have handled this loneliness?*

Brian lifted himself out of the water and dried off with a clean towel, unconcerned by the chill or the dampness of his hair. In the room, he turned on the television to keep him company, but fell fast asleep on the bed, his exhaustion overpowering his disappointment.

◈

The following morning an e-mail from a Dutch gay rights organization alerted Brian to the news that two American gay men had been attacked on the Nassaukade the night before. One man was beaten and sprayed with pepper spray. The second had been shoved around, but had escaped the three youths who were taunting him.

Brian sent off several e-mails requesting further information and asking if either of the men were available for interviews or statements. He sent another e-mail to the contact at the anticrime organization of gay activists, again stating that he was in town and interested in interviewing someone from the group. He called a contact at the COC Nederland and left a message, and left another one for Nys Meesen, a gay police officer who worked as a community liaison, confirming the arrangements for an interview later that morning that Brian had arranged prior to leaving New York.

At breakfast, Cara again asked Brian if he intended to report the stolen watch.

"I haven't decided," Brian answered. "I'm partially at fault because I trusted him."

"Amy and I discussed it," she said. "We can make the report for you, if you want."

"No," Brian answered. "I'll handle it."

"I'm worried," Amy said. "I've a premonition I can't shake."

"What sort of premonition?"

"Something bad is going to happen," she said. "Maybe you shouldn't write this story."

"It's my job," Brian tried to calm her. "It's what I do. I know how to keep my eyes open for trouble."

"Prevent trouble," Cara said with a light sneer. "Not find it."

Brian was grateful when Cara turned her attack toward Amy. At issue was whether or not they would visit the Sex Museum that morning before finding a spot to view the canal parade. Cara felt that they had an obligation as members of a suppressed community to make sure women and lesbian's struggles were properly documented in the exhibitions. Amy rolled her eyes and said, "Why couldn't I find a girlfriend who wanted to just look at sunflowers?"

They parted, Brian promising his sister he would check in with her later by cellphone. He found Nys Meesen, the police liaison, at the Westerdok harbor, where the Pride parade along the canal was to begin. Brian introduced himself and explained the story he was writing and asked for comments on the recent warnings issued to gay travelers.

"The Tourist Board shot themselves in the foot with that one," Meesen said. He explained to Brian the prevention efforts the Dutch police were providing to make Amsterdam safer for gay travelers—more police, a stronger advertising campaign urging caution. He advised Brian to drop his request to speak with the victims from the night before. "You're only serving up more trouble by reporting the problems," Meesen said. "Chat up the appeal of the city. The bargains. The new clubs on Reguliersdwarsstraat."

Brian felt he was getting a snow job from Meesen, a patronizing response to the media from a spokesperson trained to hide the real news. "My sources have told me that reports of violence against gays in the city are up this year," he said. "Twice the total of last year."

"That's true," Meesen confirmed. "But more people are coming forward with stories and that can account for the rise."

"And not just hate crimes," Brian said. "Petty crime, too."

"Petty crime?"

"People show up here thinking they can get away with something they might not do at home."

"I doubt that seriously," Meesen laughed. "We're not Monaco."

"It's true," Brian said. "I had my watch stolen two days ago. Right from my hotel room." He immediately regretted telling this to Meesen, and all at once felt highly vulnerable.

"I hope you told the staff at your hotel."

"It's complicated," Brian answered and realized he was talking too much about himself to try to get a rise out of Meesen.

"You should make a report."

"So I've been told."

"It's important to be as cautious here as anywhere else that you travel in the world," Meesen said. "But I hate that it's come to this. A cultural war between religions."

Brian felt his reporterly instincts kick in again and he felt he was on stronger footing now that the subject was no longer himself. "Religion has accounted for a majority of the aggressions in modern times," Brian said.

"Religion and nationality."

"There is word that a gay vigilante anti-Muslim movement is beginning."

"You'd be well advised not to publicize that," Meesen answered. "Do you know what that could create?"

"The rising violence here is disturbing," Brian said. "But the sense of fear is more upsetting, don't you think?"

"Fear?" Meesen answered. "Fear is nothing new to gay men anywhere in the world."

◆

After lunch, Brian found a spot on the Prinsengracht where he could watch the parade and take pictures of the shirtless muscle boys dancing on the floats passing by on the canal and the drag queens in their sequined gowns and elaborate headdresses yelling through microphones at their audience to "Dance! Dance! Dance!" Brian's editor would most likely use stock photos with the article, but in case he wanted something current or specific, Brian took photos of the crowds lining the bridges and the teams of revelers dressed as leathermen, angels, demons, and nuns. He did a few spot interviews, gathering some quotes from Dutch locals and European tourists, and other than his own personal misfortune of the stolen watch, he spoke to no one who had encountered any other petty crimes except for one woman whose room service order had been taken by another guest. Two fellows from Sydney, Australia gave him an anecdote about the Muslim staff at their hotel who would not speak to them in the hallways. Brian attempted to break down the composition of the crowd into gay and nongay spectators, but it was a useless exercise and all speculation. He hoped that he might spot Jariel again somewhere along the route or even Jariel's friends, but he was again without luck, roaming through the crowds seeing men that looked like other men he had known. Nostalgia tugged and taunted him, reminding him more and more frequently of Eddie.

After the parade, Brian met up with Cara and Amy and they walked back to Leidseplein for an early dinner. He checked his cellphone for messages and e-mails, but he had not heard back from anyone at the anticrime gay group. He had no plans to attend any of the circuit parties that evening; he had long ago shed that desire, and he was thankful for it, since he was exhausted and ready to relax and stop thinking and asking so many questions. Jariel now was a memory to him, an unfortunate trick. The watch was lost and he was moving through the disappointment of it. His desire now was to fall into bed and sleep for a long time.

At the hotel, the concierge stopped Brian and handed him a package that had arrived for him in the afternoon. It was box wrapped in brown paper, a little larger than a regular shoe box, about the size that could hold a pair of men's boots.

Brian hadn't been expecting a package. There was no return address. His name was printed on the wrapping paper, Brian T. Bishop, using the middle initial which he hardly ever used except on legal documents. He carried it into the elevator and shook the package to hear the sound it made, but it didn't make the contents of the package identifiable.

In his room he worked at his laptop before turning his attention to the package. He had noticed a slight stench to the box when he had accepted it in the lobby, as if something inside had been wet and then dried. The stench intensified as he tore off the paper and opened the lid. On top of the box was a yellow T-shirt that had been stuffed into the box. It was similar to the one Jariel had worn the day he had met Brian outside the Anne Frank house. Brian lifted up the shirt and was shocked by what he found underneath it inside the box. It was a severed arm, brown-skinned, dried and stinking, cut off about midforearm. And on the wrist was Brian's watch.

◆

Hotel security arrived. A Dutch policeman stationed at Leidseplein was at the hotel within minutes. Brian called his sister and Amy and Cara were soon crowding inside the hotel room.

Brian recounted his tale about meeting Jariel and the stolen watch several times, each time to a new security official or police officer who arrived at the room. He wasn't certain if the arm belonged to Jariel, but the watch, with the engraving underneath, was his. There were several formalities; his name, address, and passport number were recorded, regiven, verified, and checked. His date of entry was requested. One officer asked to see his boarding pass. Brian answered questions about who he told about the theft of the watch, who had seen him enter the hotel with Jariel, and who knew Brian was in Amsterdam and whether he was writing an article on the tensions between the gay and Muslim communities. The security chief of the hotel went to look for the tapes from the hotel cameras that might have caught someone watching Brian and Jariel enter the hotel and who had delivered the package. Another officer with a sour expression began examining Brian's laptop.

Cara interrupted the officers' questions—the police force had grown to four and several of them were picking through the items in Brian's luggage and dusting the box and other objects in the room for fingerprints—to mention that the Islamic punishment for theft was amputation. "When they catch a thief," she said. "They cut off the limb. But was this revenge for a guy stealing Brian's watch?—Which would mean that Brian had Muslim protectors—or was it because the Muslims had detected a thief?"

Brian, annoyed that Cara was putting forward motives to the officers, was more concerned his privacy was being violated and his press privileges compromised by the officer inspecting his laptop. He asked for a lawyer to be present, then asked that Nys Meesen be contacted, then strongly suggested that the American embassy at The Hague be notified that he was being interrogated and his items confiscated.

The officers tried to subdue Brian's anxieties. The hand was fingerprinted and whisked out of the room, along with Brian's watch and laptop. The room was sealed off and the hotel moved Brian to another room on another floor and, once he was settled there, he was asked by one of the remaining officers to return with them to the police station, as a formality, he was told, to complete the paperwork and sign a statement. Brian stressed to the officer how valuable each item was to him that the police had impounded— the watch and the laptop. One was a sentimental link to his deceased partner, the other his livelihood and the reason why he was in Amsterdam. Cara insisted that she and Amy accompany Brian to the station, but Brian asked the women to stay behind, in case he needed to contact someone outside of the station.

While he sat and waited at the station for the officer to complete the report, Brian sent a text message to Nys Meesen and another to his editor in New York, informing them of the severed arm and his police visit and the need for his laptop to be returned as soon as possible. He sent another message to the anticrime gay group, requesting a meeting with a representative because of some unfortunate events that were happening to him in the city, though he did not offer any specifics. Brian was summoned to another room, where more formalities took place in front of three officers, two who were new to the case and now introduced to Brian. The new officers proceeded with more questions, and Brian, the sweat beginning to appear on his forehead, was asked to repeat his story and listen to it translated into Dutch, and then another officer repeated it back to him in English, fragmented down for "yes" or "no" answers. An hour later, he was told that the watch was being kept as evidence, and while Brian was again requesting its return, he was taken by another officer into a room and asked about the e-mails he had sent earlier in the day from his computer to the anticrime gay activist organization.

"Where did you learn of this group?" the officer asked. "What sort of contact have you had with them?"

Brian explained his rights to the officer: that the information on his computer had not been properly and legally requested from him, and that his sources were confidential, but he had only used outlets available to anyone—list servs and Internet groups. He was only probing into a wound that had opened, not creating it.

"I doubt that I'm the only journalist who has stumbled onto it," he said. "They seem rather eager to solve the problem, even if they are more reluctant to meet."

"You've requested a meeting?"

"Yes," Brian answered. "But I've had no response."

"Don't you understand?" the officer said to Brian. "If this gay vigilante group suddenly goes public, we've got a war on our hands."

"The war has already started," Brian said. "You've only been pretending it hasn't."

◈

On the tram headed back to his hotel, Brian's cellphone rang. It was a text message from a user named "QNatie," a contact at the anticrime activist group. It suggested a meeting a half hour later at a café near the Koningsplein; the contact would "be wearing green."

Green? *Green what?* Brian texted back, and confirmed the meeting. The timing was too suspicious to ignore—finally, a message from someone at the group, not long after the severed arm had arrived, minutes after he had left the police station. He looked around the tram, wondering if he was being watched or followed. He felt certain that these events were connected. He called the hotel and left a message for Amy and Cara on their voicemail explaining his whereabouts, not wanting to get either on the phone and listen to their warnings.

Off the tram and walking along Leidsegracht, there were more people than ever, the crowds walking shoulder to shoulder, like a carnival was under way. Music blared out of cafés and impromptu dance parties of gay men happened in the waiting lines, while passing tourists seized the opportunity for photo ops with the outrageously attired drag queens and their entourages. Walking had always been Brian's compulsive behavior, ready to see what was around the next corner or just over the next bridge, but he disliked having to slow down or speed up or wedge his way around too large a group of partiers. Brian arrived at the meeting spot early and he continued walking instead of taking a table at the café and waiting like a target. On Herengracht he noticed a restaurant where he and Eddie had dined years ago, and, tugged by a memory, he went to inspect the menu. While he was standing in front of the glass window of the restaurant, he noticed a reflection of someone standing close behind him, looking at him. It was Jariel. Brian turned and saw the young man running away, into the crowd. Brian followed him down the street, shouting his name, but the young man darted out of sight.

Brian continued running and looking, at store after store. Again, he was quickly out of breath and defeated. As he stopped he realized his phone was ringing. It was Nys Meesen. Meesen explained that he had been caught up on Brian's case. "There was a body discovered earlier today in the canal," Meesen said. He asked Brian to meet him at the hospital morgue in a half hour to see if he could identify the body.

Brian knew it meant missing the hook-up with QNatie. He texted the contact and said that he would not be able to meet as planned, something urgent had come up, but could they still meet a little later? *Odd events,* Brian texted, *need explaining.*

◈

The body had been discovered floating in the Oudezijds, spotted by a tourist in the canal closest to the Red-Light district. It was of a young man, thought to be in his early twenties. The left arm was severed. The missing part was the limb that Brian had received in the box. Meesen was with Brian when the body was unveiled at the hospital morgue, pulled out of a drawer of a wall of metal cases.

"It's not possible," Brian said to Meesen, when he recognized Jariel's corpse. "I just saw him an hour ago."

"Saw him?" Meesen asked. "Where?"

"On Herengracht. He ran away when he spotted me."

"And you're sure this is the same guy?"

"Yes," Brian answered. "He either has a ghost or a twin."

Brian asked if there had been a match on the fingerprints, if the young man's identity had been established.

"He was a small-time thief," Meesen said. "Jeroen Roos. Twenty-two years old. Grew up in Delft. He'd been arrested three times before."

"He told me he was Spanish."

"His family is Jewish," Meesen added. "One of the few in the area that survived the War."

"Jewish?" Brian answered. Why had Jariel—Jeroen—lied to him? "Are you sure?"

"He was arrested twice last year, once this year," Meesen explained. "Random acts against tourists. Pocketbook, the first time, right off a woman on Prisengracht. Stole a laptop from a student at a hotel near where you were staying. Same situation as yours, guy brought him home and he tried to hock it later and was caught. He stayed off the radar until he tried working De Wallen. An undercover cop got him before the Turks could beat him up."

"What about his friends? The two guys I saw him with?"

"Worked alone, as far we know. He was living from place to place, from what we understand. Falling out with his father, who wanted to him to work in the family business. His father is on his way here now, I'm told."

"I don't understand," Brian said. "He told me he was from somewhere near Gibraltar."

"No different than stretching the truth in a chat room," Meesen said. "You wanted someone exotic, so he became someone exotic. I've always found that disturbing. Why do we pretend we're not the person we are?"

"Who do you think murdered him?" Brian asked.

"The Turks in the Rosse Buurt, angry at him working in their territory, trying to sell a hot watch? Maybe the Moroccans because he was a gay man bragging about his heist from an American reporter? We're concerned now how it ties in with you."

"You don't think..."

"There's a lot more to try and sort out," Meesen said. "What are your travel plans?"

"You don't suspect me?"

"Let's just say we haven't ruled you out yet," Meesen answered. "But we're also concerned about your safety, since you say you knew this young man."

Brian's cellphone rang and he saw that it was a text from QNatie. It was another request for a meeting: same place, an hour later. Brian texted back that the meeting was on.

"My sister's girlfriend," Brian lied to Meesen. "She's concerned that I'm being treated fairly."

"Please reassure her," Meesen said. "You are not in the hands of terrorists."

◆

This time he was stood up. Brian waited an hour at the café where he was to meet his contact. At the bar, he had ordered a scotch to steady his nerves, then ordered another one to keep his light buzz going. The severed arm and Jariel's dead body had unnerved him. He was caught in a mystery—or was he already trapped in a web and struggling to get free? He scanned the crowd, trying to find someone wearing something green and trying to detect if someone was watching him. He felt like an unjustly accused criminal awaiting trial, and he defended his innocence over and over in his mind. The bar had a clubby feel to it, like it was a melting pot of locals and devoid of the tourists who scanned the menu out front and decided to go elsewhere. He had a short conversation with the bartender, a slender woman with an arm full of tattoos who said Gay Pride was always her favorite week, even if the work was exhausting—but keeping the conversation going felt strained to

Brian, his thoughts were in another place. Finally, Brian gave up on QNatie and decided to leave. He would drop this part of the story, since there was no one who could substantiate the existence of this group. He texted Amy that he was heading back to the hotel.

Outside the café the rowdiness on the street continued. Colors had brightened as the night deepened, neon signs blinked and encouraged visitors, incandescent bulbs made souvenirs look bright and inviting. On his walk back, Brian tried to plan out the day ahead. He would contact the American Embassy in The Hague and phone his editor in New York. His story was now a report of his innocence, how he had been flipped from being a victim to a suspect. The reports were correct, he thought, Amsterdam is not a safe place. The whole city is powder keg ready to blow. One day something here will ignite the fuse, but the question remained: will it be too late? And how could he write this without seeming alarmist? Racist? If Jariel was Jewish, how would he factor that in? Was the murder anti-Semitic or antigay or both? He stopped and stood by a building to make a few notes in his pad—his conversations with Meesen and the Amsterdam police, the bartender, a note to follow up with Jariel's family at some point.

When he looked up from his pad he saw Jariel again. The young man was standing there, watching him, grinning, exactly as he had at the train station two days before. This time the chase was slower. Jariel seemed to appear and disappear, evaporating into a crowd and materializing in another spot. Brian followed him through the street, around a corner, and along a canal. The young man had a definite physical substance, but also an ethereal distinction. Was Jariel a guardian angel or a harbinger of doom? Sounds sharpened and smells hung in the air before Brian—cigarettes and perfume mixed with the thick scents of European coffee and petrol. An apprehension nagged at Brian that somehow this was prearranged, that Jariel was leading him toward trouble, that QNatie had never intended to meet him, that Amy's premonition of harm was right. *Oh god*, he thought, *that's impossible, I'm becoming paranoid...*

But Jariel—or the ghost of him—was leading Brian somewhere. Somewhere that must have a meaning to this mystery. A hateful sultriness hung over the block, that airless, motionless quality he had detected before. He realized that he was near the edge of the Red-Light district. Brian took the same corner Jariel had and saw a young man wearing a green shirt. It was one of Jariel's friends from the train station. Brian smiled and approached the two guys—ready to ask their names and seek their help—they were the key to his innocence, he felt sure of it. And he felt certain that they could lead him to the contact for the activist group.

The taller of the two fellows scowled as Brian began to talk with them, explaining how he knew their friend Jariel—or Jeroen. The shorter one, the one wearing the green T-shirt, took a step back and said something in Dutch which Brian didn't understand. He spat at Brian and called him "flickr."

Brian immediately realized his mistake. "Flickr" was Dutch slang for "fag." He stumbled away from the young men and wiped the spit from where it had hit his cheek. What had he done? These were the boys who had killed Jariel. He was certain of it now. Jariel had bragged about the watch and how he had gotten it from a gay American journalist, shown it to them, and they had reacted with shame and disgust and violence. Just as they were doing now. They had severed Jariel's arm and sent it to Brian as a warning and dumped the body in the canal. It had nothing to do with the gay vigilante group.

The taller one reached out and grabbed Brian's shirt, but Brian was able to swat the guy's hand away. He turned and began running along the canal. The young men chased him and there was a scuffle as the shorter guy reached Brian, but Brian was able to knock his grasp off. He thought if he were only to make it round the next corner, there would be a crowd and he would be clear of danger.

Brian took the corner and found himself face-to-face with a dark-eyed man. He was held in place, unable to move, and an impending sense of tragedy washed over him. It was the guy who had followed them before with his eye on Amy's purse. Irony or fate? He nervously laughed. The man had a ruthless air and his lips curled back into a sneer. *Amy*, Brian thought, *how will she handle this?*

The dark-eyed man smiled and Brian felt a jab at his stomach. He covered the flare of spreading pain with his hands, and brought his palms slowly away from his stomach and saw that they were bloody. The man had knifed him. The last thing Brian noticed was the faint ring of skin at his wrist where he had worn the watch as he turned his hands to the ground to catch his fall. *Eddie*, he thought as he fell to the sidewalk, *how much time do I have left?*

THE VISION

At night, Buddy would study his reflection in the window. He'd become quite good at it. He'd push his chair as close as he could to the glass pane, the light above his bed bright enough to cast his image back to him. The reflection was not as good as a mirror, of course; there was a hazy, dreamy quality to the edges of himself that Buddy sometimes liked, even though he usually thought there was something wrong with the way he looked. He wasn't a vain young man; no, more disenchanted than arrogant. He could tell when he hadn't slept well the night before, his eyes would look small and puffy and the cowlick on the left side of his forehead would be dark and ominous, like an enlarged spiderweb ready to catch an unsuspecting prey. He liked the way the pane elongated his face and squared his chin, made him look more attractive than he was willing to admit to himself he could actually be. Sometimes he would open his mouth and pull his lips back, believing his eyeteeth long enough to be eerie-looking fangs. If his throat felt dry and itchy, he'd stretch his neck so that his sideburns became lost in the shadows of the glass, and if he tilted his head just so, he could shift his eyes so that he could scrutinize his profile for its other, less obvious, imperfections—the short, upturned nose, the weak chin, the brow that he thought stuck out a bit too far.

Buddy seldom looked outside, into the night. The scenery outside his room on the ward was nothing but another wing of the hospital. The brick wall dropped down to a row of bushes and a parking lot. Sometimes he could detect shapes coming and going through a few windows, but there was nothing he wanted to analyze further in those rooms—he cared nothing for this place or its patients. Sometimes he allowed the movement of something else to distract him from the obsessive study of himself and the horror of being trapped with his boredom in this ward, but it was always momentary; he would always return to the study of himself in the glass.

Buddy was twenty-one and under observation. Two weeks before he had failed at his third suicide attempt. At sixteen, Buddy ran away from his family in Santa Clara, living in a communal house first in Palo Alto, then later in Redwood City, before taking up residence on the streets of San Francisco. Buddy was not from an abusive family—he was not threatened or tortured or beaten. He was lazy and bored and unchallenged; he turned to drugs for quick highs and to escape his ennui. At first he used pot or alcohol as his means of evasion, until he realized he could get away with much harder stuff and he began using an assortment of pharmaceuticals. When his luck and money ran out he became addicted to crank. He learned to cook up the stuff himself when he couldn't buy it on the street. His temper flared and stung and subsided and rose up again until he was diagnosed as addicted and clinically depressed, along with an assortment of other psychiatric disorders. Buddy wanted to quit using but couldn't make the break. He fell into the city welfare system. His father did not want him back in Santa Clara. His mother was frightened of him and his older sister would not return his phone calls. His last attempt to quit cold turkey left him so despondent he swallowed every pill he could find, which was how he ended up here, in front of this window in this hospital room.

Buddy hated the ward. He hated the routine of waking for medication or waking to eat or waking to talk to a doctor or to tell a nurse when his last bowel movement had been. He hated the group therapy sessions, the ugly art hanging on the walls, the inane "personal growth" projects he was encouraged to do. Buddy found studying himself in his window's reflection more interesting than sitting in the common room with the rest of the loonies and listening to their litanies of heartbreak and misfortune. He supposed this worked against him, made him look angry or antisocial, or, god forbid, like a loony tune himself. But he could never focus on the television set in the common room; the images moved too quickly for him, and his roommate was an idiotic rocking dribbler—a hyperactive punk named Theo who was always looking for a cigarette.

It was about nine o'clock one evening when Buddy was looking at himself in the window and he noticed the reflection change. It was his second week in the hospital and Theo was elsewhere on the ward. Buddy could see the image of his head and shoulders in the pane of glass. Behind him, the door of his room was open and he noticed the white flash of a nurse's uniform in the hallway as she passed by. He momentarily changed the focus of his vision so that he could study the movement in the hallway and not himself. In a small corner of his glass pane he could see into the room on the opposite side of the hallway, the first of the two beds and the lumpy outline of a patient's legs beneath a sheet. In a moment he saw a doctor in a white lab coat enter the room.

Buddy would not have seen anything else if he had turned around and looked at the room across the hall. He was at an angle to his window that allowed him to see beyond the natural perimeters of his vision. The doctor approached the patient in the bed and Buddy realized he could now see deeper into the room. The patient—a long, lanky guy with spiky hair similar to Buddy's was saying something to the doctor. The doctor remained calm. Buddy was convinced that it was Dr. Kuttar, one of the psychiatrists on the ward, even though Dr. Kuttar never made rounds this late at night. The doctor stepped out of Buddy's frame of vision for a moment, just long enough for Buddy to glance away, and when Buddy looked back again, he noticed the doctor's white lab coat smeared with what appeared to be blood. In the reflection Buddy watched some sort of a struggle with the patient. The patient also looked bloody. The patient slowly moved out of his bed and began choking the doctor with his hands at his neck. The doctor's face turned pale. He legs buckled and he went to the floor. When the reflection of the struggle disappeared from his view, Buddy leapt up from his chair and ran into the hall, shouting, "Nurse! Nurse!"

There wasn't the least possibility of a mistake. Buddy knew what he had seen in the window. He was convinced that he had witnessed the struggle, even though he had seen everything in the reflection. He had seen Dr. Kuttar clearly in the window—his wiry black hair and salt-and-pepper goatee, his thick neck, his stocky shoulders, his bloody lab coat. Of the patient Buddy had seen only parts—the pale hairy legs jutting out of the bed, the *V* of his back when he lifted himself up in the bed, the long, stringy arms covered with scars and welts as he tried to strangle the doctor.

Buddy ran into the room opposite his own and saw that the bed was bloody. It was empty and the two bodies were now on the floor. He looked down at them and was certain one of them was Dr. Kuttar. Buddy stepped out into the hall and yelled for help until a nurse, and then a few seconds later, an orderly, arrived. They found the room empty and thought Buddy was having a bad reaction to his medication. Buddy was helped back to his own room, sedated, and slept fitfully through the rest of the evening.

⧫

In the morning, Buddy met Dr. Kuttar in his office. "So you thought I was murdered?" Dr. Kuttar said. "Would you like to talk about this?"

Buddy did not answer the doctor. He was angry and upset. His eyes felt small and puffy. He looked down at his hands and arms covered with bruises, welts, and scars from too many needles and razors.

"It's normal to experience transference," Dr. Kuttar said. "Perhaps I represent safety to you. Or health and contentment. And you are worried about losing them. Or not achieving them. Is that what you might have felt, Buddy?"

Buddy did not respond. Dr. Kuttar did worry him, but Buddy would not admit it. Dr. Kuttar was fortyish, thickly built, and carried himself like a military officer. In their sessions the doctor talked about nutrition and discipline and how bodybuilding had helped him to be calm and centered and organized. Buddy often wondered what the doctor looked like working out in the gym. Sometimes after their session Buddy carried the clean and polished scent of Dr. Kuttar back to his room on the ward. He kept it hovering in his mind, used it to fantasize and masturbate until he either reached an orgasm or boredom descended and he needed to find something else to think about.

"I did see it," Buddy said finally.

"Did that upset you?" the doctor asked. "Did it bother you to see someone hurting me?"

Buddy again did not respond.

"Or did you think that we were involved in some other way?" the doctor asked.

Buddy knew where the doctor was leading him. Dr. Kuttar was always leading him to the subject of sex. Since their first session, when Buddy had confessed his trading sex for drugs or money or a place to sleep, the doctor was always asking him how he felt about sex. Buddy tried not to feel a thing; sex was something he did for survival. He had sucked guys off in the men's room at Macy's for a few bucks and then jerked off a tourist for free in his hotel room as long as he could stay and sleep through the night. He had even let an orderly on the ward blow him in order to get a pack of cigarettes, though he didn't tell this to Dr. Kuttar. Buddy thought the doctor showed too much interest in wanting to know all the details of his sex life. Once Buddy told a story just to get the doctor hot and bothered. It was a true story about a woman who picked him up to have sex with her boyfriend to prove that he was gay. The doctor remained calm for a good five minutes until he crossed his legs and began to look agitated. Buddy knew the doctor was aroused. At the end of the story Buddy asked the doctor, "Want me to suck you off, too?"

The doctor had kept his expression calm and things between them remained professional. Except that he was always coming back to talk about sex. Or trying to talk about sex. Like now, when Dr. Kuttar asked more bluntly, "Did you think that I might be having some kind of a relationship with this patient? This male patient?"

"I saw him trying to kill you," Buddy said. "That's what I saw."

"I'm going to put you on a different medication for a few days," Dr. Kuttar said. "We'll see how that works out."

A week later the new medication was working. There were no more hallucinations or nightmares. Buddy was calm and more focused; he watched TV in the common room and began a drawing project. In his sessions with Dr. Kuttar, Buddy talked about wanting to take up some kind of sports activity and find a job and buy some nice clothes—the kind the doctor wore. Dr. Kuttar said he was recommending Buddy be dismissed from the ward and put into a halfway house. On Buddy's final day at the hospital, Dr. Kuttar said, "I'll continue to see you at the house twice a week. I'll give you a week to settle in on your own. Then we'll meet Tuesday and Thursday evenings when I see some other patients in the area."

At the halfway house, Buddy shared a room with a dark-skinned fellow named Equator who wore puka shells around his neck and his hair in dreadlocks. Buddy got a part-time job stocking shelves at a supermarket; at home he smoked on the terrace, and worked out every night with Equator in a moldy rec room in the basement. Equator had a hairless body and a perfectly flat stomach. Buddy sucked him off their second night in the rec room. Buddy also had sex with the assistant manager of the house and a fellow who worked the morning shift in the kitchen. By the end of his first week in the halfway house Buddy had a new set of workout clothes and a stash of protein shakes in his room.

When Dr. Kuttar visited him on Tuesday evening, they talked about Buddy's addictive behavior toward sex. The doctor was worried that Buddy was replacing his dependency on drugs with a dependency on sex. Buddy confessed that it hadn't felt that way with Equator or the cook or the customer he blew in the back room of the grocery store. Buddy was shrewd enough to tell Dr. Kuttar that it felt like fun because he actually enjoyed having Equator's cock in his mouth. Then, Buddy manipulated the doctor into talking about bodybuilding. Buddy asked what kind of exercises he needed to do to get a set of abdominal muscles like Equator. Buddy did not think it strange when the doctor demonstrated a routine for him on the floor of the room in the halfway house where they met, but he did get weird signals when the doctor suggested that Buddy give it a try and Dr. Kuttar kept a hand against Buddy's stomach while he went through a set of crunches. "Feel how the muscle tightens and contracts," Dr. Kuttar said, keeping his hand against Buddy's waist. Buddy wondered if the doctor wanted Buddy to suggest again that they could have sex. Buddy let the doctor keep his hand against his waist as long as he wanted, even shifting his position on the floor so that Dr. Kuttar's hand grazed against Buddy's belt buckle. Nothing else happened, though the hand remained at Buddy's waist through another set of exercises. At the end of the session, the doctor suggested that Buddy could come with him to his health club one night if he was interested. "You can try out some of the machines," Dr. Kuttar said. "Some of them even take the effort out of exercising."

On Wednesday of the following week Dr. Kuttar picked Buddy up at the halfway house and drove him to the health club. It was a clean, high-tech sort of place that Buddy thought perfectly fit the doctor's personality. The club was crowded and Buddy changed into his workout clothes in a guest area of the locker room, out of sight of Dr. Kuttar and his locker. In the large, high-ceilinged gym, Buddy's eyes roamed from one well-built guy to the next while Dr. Kuttar remained focused and guided Buddy through a workout on the machines. After their workout, Buddy undressed by his locker and followed the doctor into the steam room. They were both wearing only short white towels around their waists. When they were sitting beside each other in the steam room, Buddy was able to study the doctor's body for the first time. It was heavy with muscle around the shoulders and arms and chest; a triangle of black hairs separated and outlined the doctor's pectoral muscles and then traveled in a thin line down the middle of his stomach and disappeared beneath the white towel. On the doctor's upper right arm was the tattoo of a tiger that extended slightly over his shoulder so that it spread onto his chest and back. Buddy asked the doctor where he had it done. "I got it when I was in the service," the doctor said. "I'd had a lot to drink that night."

There was a steady stream of guys in and out of the steam room. On the other side of the room a guy sat fondling himself beneath his towel while looking straight at the doctor. The doctor pretended not to see the fellow and Buddy wondered if the doctor wanted him to leave so that he could have sex with the guy. Once, when he lived in Palo Alto, Buddy had been with a guy who took him to a club like this where everyone had sex in a steamy tiled room. Buddy felt himself growing hard watching the guy watching the doctor. Soon, another man had entered the steam room and was sitting beside Buddy. After a few seconds, the man grazed his hand against Buddy's thigh, then slowly let his hand press harder against Buddy's leg until he felt bold enough to reach beneath Buddy's towel.

Buddy let the man fondle and stroke his cock. He was aware of the doctor being aware of the man's boldness, but Dr. Kuttar made no motion to leave or to turn and watch. The guy on the opposite side of the steam room continued to jerk off while looking at the doctor and glancing at Buddy being stroked by the stranger beside him. Buddy leaned his head back against the wet tiles and closed his eyes, his chest filling with the warm, moist air. He let the stranger stroke him to an orgasm, imagining it was Dr. Kuttar who was grasping his cock. When Buddy opened his eyes, Dr. Kuttar was not in the steam room.

Buddy showered and dressed by his locker. Dr. Kuttar was waiting for him in the lobby of the health club. "I'll give you a ride back to the house," the doctor said. On the car ride across town, the doctor said nothing about Buddy's behavior in the steam room. Buddy thought that the doctor must think it inappropriate to talk about this outside of a therapy session. Instead of talking about sex, Dr. Kuttar was telling Buddy about the advantages of good genetics and bodybuilding. "You've got a good, long look," the doctor said. "You'll have to try harder to bulk up, but when you do, you'll have some terrific proportions." Buddy was not certain if this was a compliment.

When they arrived at the halfway house, the doctor asked Buddy if he wanted to go to a restaurant for dinner the following day after Buddy's session; the doctor had an hour to kill on Thursday evening before seeing his last patient.

Buddy agreed and the next evening they went to a diner two blocks from the halfway house. Dr. Kuttar had a glass of wine at the restaurant, which did not loosen him up at all. Buddy decided he wanted to unravel the doctor's mysteries, but Dr. Kuttar would not answer any of Buddy's questions except in the vaguest of terms. "How old were you when you got that tattoo?" ("About your age.") "Did it hurt?" ("I don't remember much of it because I passed out.") "Did you ever have sex in the barracks?" ("I was an officer.") "Does all that stuff in the steam room bother you?" ("I try not to be judgmental.")

They kept this up for close to two months. Therapy, gym, restaurant, pointed questions and vague answers. In therapy, the doctor asked questions about sex and Buddy answered them candidly and watched the doctor squirm. The doctor grew more and more agitated, especially when he realized how much sexual activity Buddy was having in the steam room of his health club, and his questions grew sharper. "Are you being careful? Are you using condoms?" Buddy knew he had tapped a soft spot. At dinner, Buddy tried to get the doctor to talk about his own sex life. Buddy began to ask the doctor about a boyfriend, or girlfriend, or an ex-wife or any kids. The doctor seldom provided any details, except to say he had been involved in an abusive relationship. "With a girl or a guy?" Buddy had asked, though the doctor's response had been to sip his wine. Buddy wondered if the doctor was a latent homosexual, had been closeted in a long-term relationship or marriage, or had some legal problems in the service or previously with another patient. Once Buddy suggested that they could go to a gay bar after their dinner, but the doctor said it was not a good idea; he still had another patient to see.

Buddy's path of self-improvement continued to advance. He held down his job and his body began to develop; he confessed that he had strayed from his drug-free regimen and smoked a joint with a trick he had met on Market Street but he had not wanted to take anything else in the following days. Dr. Kuttar said he was recommending Buddy for a discharge from the halfway house and he would help him get a subsidized apartment. Buddy would only need to see a social worker once a month for a progress report. Buddy was not happy with this news. He realized he was addicted to the doctor's presence and his weekly trips to the health club and the diner. He wondered if the doctor had planned it this way. "But what about us?" Buddy said.

"I'll help you settle in," Dr. Kuttar said. "And if you get in a bind, I'll help you out."

"Can we still do the gym?" Buddy asked. "And dinner on Thursdays?"

"If you'd like," Dr. Kuttar answered. "But you will no longer be my patient."

Buddy found an apartment in the Haight on the top floor of a large remodeled Victorian house. On a Friday evening, when Dr. Kuttar did not have any scheduled patients, the doctor helped Buddy buy an inexpensive futon bed, which they carried themselves up the narrow, winding staircase of the building. Buddy's belongings looked meager and untidy in the bare apartment and for a second he was worried about surviving. Dr. Kuttar stood with his hands on his hips and reiterated that he would help Buddy out, then looked embarrassed to still be in the apartment. The doctor was nicely dressed in an expensive shirt, slacks, and polished leather shoes. Buddy offered the doctor a beer and they sat on the edge of Buddy's bed and drank from the cans since Buddy did not have any glasses.

"I might have some kitchen stuff I don't use that I can give you," Dr. Kuttar said.

Buddy nodded and said, "Thanks. I'll pay you back."

The doctor said he didn't have to. Buddy should consider them a housewarming gift.

Suddenly Buddy felt small and poor, like the welfare case he realized he had become. "We can work out some kind of arrangement," Buddy said. "I can find a way to pay you back."

The doctor did not respond except to place his beer can on the floor. Buddy took this as a sign that the rules between them might now be different since they were no longer doctor and patient. Buddy placed a hand against the doctor's pants, just at his upper thigh. The doctor did not flinch or try to move away from Buddy's touch. Buddy kept his hand there for a few more seconds, then inched it farther up the doctor's leg until his fingers were dangling at the edge of the doctor's crotch. The doctor still did not give any indication that Buddy should take away his hand, though the doctor looked out at the room and not at Buddy. When Buddy's hand inched farther up and rested in the warmth of the doctor's crotch, he clutched the fabric and found the doctor's cock already hardening. The doctor slipped his legs open wider and Buddy moved in closer. He unzipped the doctor's pants and reached his hand in and began stroking the doctor's cock. Soon he had the doctor's pants halfway down and the doctor's cock in his mouth. Dr. Kuttar leaned back onto the mattress, closed his eyes and began making soft, chesty moans. Just when Buddy thought he was about to bring the doctor to an orgasm, the doctor sat up and said, "Wait."

Their eyes met and the doctor reached down with his hand and gripped Buddy's crotch. The doctor made Buddy stand and remove his clothing while the doctor took off the rest of his—his dress shirt and T-shirt. Soon, the doctor had Buddy's cock in his mouth and his hands groping Buddy's butt until Buddy could wedge himself free and bury his face again in the doctor's crotch. They kept this up for as long as they could, back and forth, till the doctor let out an exasperated moan, pulled his cock out of Buddy's throat and came on his chest. As the doctor hovered over him, Buddy easily finished himself off.

They began to see each other several times a week for sex. The doctor would take Buddy to dinner or to the gym and then they would go back to Buddy's apartment for sex. The doctor brought Buddy drinking glasses and silverware and a rug for the bathroom floor. Buddy rimmed the doctor, tied him up and pissed on him. Their past seemed no longer to be a concern, only the next moment they would be together and trying something new in bed.

Buddy's body continued to improve; his biceps now had small peaks, his abdominal muscles showed a six-pack, and he could flex the muscles of his thighs so that the striations were detectable. He studied himself in the mirror of his bathroom and in the mirrors at the gym. He thought about shaving his body hair and getting some tattoos. The doctor wanted to try more new things in bed—poppers and coke and sex on X. Soon the doctor began calling Buddy during the day, asking him if he could meet him at the hospital for a quickie in his office or for an afternoon tryst at Buddy's apartment. Buddy usually obliged, though he no longer did the drugs that the doctor was experimenting with, waving them aside to take the doctor's cock in his mouth or wet his fist up with lubricant. Whenever the doctor could not track Buddy down, the doctor was full of questions when Buddy reappeared. "Where did you go?" "Who were you with?" "What did he want from you?" and "Were you trying to lead him on?"

Buddy adopted a "don't tell" policy. The doctor was possessive, asking Buddy why he needed to see other men if they were seeing so much of each other. The doctor's complexion turned pale and he looked like he had lost weight. His eyes were always streaked with red. Whenever he was with Buddy, the doctor was always checking the money in his wallet, asking Buddy if he had taken anything from it because there was always less money there than he thought he had and Buddy always seemed to be wearing a new outfit. The doctor began stealing drugs from the hospital pharmacy and the nurse's station, sometimes selling them to other members of the hospital staff. He offered to sell drugs to Buddy, though Buddy always declined; he wanted no kind of arrangement like this with the doctor.

They went on this way for a couple of months. One night the doctor said he was in love with Buddy. Buddy answered that it was mutual. The doctor got Buddy a sanitation job at the hospital which paid twice as much as he made at the grocery store. They met each other for lunch and sex in the stockroom. Buddy got a tattoo that circled his biceps, which infuriated the doctor. The doctor accused him of baiting other men. "You think you're hot stuff, don't you?" Dr. Kuttar yelled. "You think this can get you a better boyfriend."

The doctor moved more things into Buddy's apartment—a dresser for the doctor's clothes, a shaving kit for overnight stays. Buddy got a flaming tattoo around his navel, and told the doctor he didn't want to have sex until the swelling went down. The doctor made Buddy stay up late with him and watch porn movies. When Dr. Kuttar could not get an erection, he blamed Buddy. "You've been seeing someone else, haven't you? You're doing this to get rid of me."

Buddy began going to the gym alone; the doctor no longer had the enthusiasm and Buddy could afford his own membership. Buddy met guys in the steam room, went out on dates with other men, and tried not to feel like he was cheating on Dr. Kuttar because he was enjoying having sex with another man. Back at Buddy's apartment, the doctor would be stoned or high or drunk and waiting for Buddy to return. He would follow Buddy around the rooms, saying, "You can't give up on me. The hospital is watching me." Buddy reassured the doctor that he would never expose the missing drugs or tell anyone of their affair.

One day Buddy changed the lock on his apartment and arranged to have himself assigned to another ward of the hospital where he worked the evening shift. When Dr. Kuttar finally found him, the doctor yelled, "You're ruining me," and pushed him into an empty room on the ward. They stood glaring at each other. Over the doctor's shoulder, Buddy noticed his reflection in the glass pane of the window. He understood exactly what would happen though he could not do anything to escape the scene.

The doctor closed and locked the door and told Buddy to take off his clothes. Buddy complied because he was still in love with the doctor; he took off everything except the black thong he was wearing as underwear. Dr. Kuttar told Buddy to lie face down on the empty bed, he wanted to give Buddy a massage.

Buddy lay down with his face against the bed and felt the doctor's hands kneading his shoulders. "You're body's really terrific," Dr. Kuttar said. "I bet everyone wants you now."

Buddy thought about protesting but held the thought in his mind. He felt a sharp sting beneath his shoulder blade and then another one about an inch away. It took him a few more seconds to realize that Dr. Kuttar was stabbing him with a surgeon's knife.

Buddy pushed himself off the bed and twisted around to face Dr. Kuttar. Dr. Kuttar's knife landed in Buddy's stomach. Buddy felt his abdomen tear and saw blood bubble up. He yelled at the doctor to stop and reached his hands up to strangle Dr. Kuttar.

The retaliation startled the doctor and he stood up, his lab coat covered with blood, and the knife fell on the bed. Buddy found the doctor's neck again and they both fell struggling to the floor. Buddy felt the doctor's hands at his throat, his breath trapped in his chest. He struggled to stay conscious, to get up, but the doctor had his arms pinned against his chest.

Buddy wanted to say he loved the doctor but he could not get any words out, and worse, he heard himself moaning, and was frightened because he could not control the strange sounds coming from his throat. Suddenly,

Buddy's body was lifted from the floor and he thought that he had fainted, or maybe died. The room brightened. Dr. Kuttar stood over him with his bloody knife. In the windowpane Buddy saw the fangs of his own smile and his spidery hair. He couldn't speak but his mind was filled with thoughts and a vision of himself watching the reflection of his murder in a dark glass pane of a window.

◈

Buddy was told he was unconscious for almost two days. He had been stabbed fifteen times. The doctor was arrested, made bail, and skipped town. Buddy was in the hospital for close to three months and required six surgeries to repair his stomach, liver, and lungs. He would not agree to see another therapist. Instead, he consulted a lawyer and sued the doctor and his employers but settled out of court for an undisclosed sum. The doctor won a series of continuances before his arrest in Santa Barbara for writing bad checks. He was charged with fifteen counts, including attempted murder, though thirteen of the counts were dropped because the district attorney did not believe that he could convince a jury that the doctor had intended to kill Buddy, even though Buddy had legally been considered dead for ninety-eight seconds.

Dr. Kuttar was sent to jail for five years for assault with a deadly weapon and a sentence enhancement for great bodily injury. Buddy did not attend the sentencing, but he did have an affair with his lawyer, who told Buddy every detail of what happened in court, including that the judge had ordered Dr. Kuttar to "be put to good use counseling other prisoners." Buddy felt that this was an unfit sentence, not so much for the doctor, but for the prisoners who would be forced to see him.

Buddy required eight more surgeries and periods of recovery before he was able to return to the gym and work his way up to the same workout he had done before the attack. The surgeries required him to take a lot of pain medication. In nineteen months or so Buddy's arms and back and neck were thick again with muscles. His desire for sex grew less and less as more and more guys felt possessive toward him. For a while Buddy thought about becoming a personal trainer, but he decided he could make more money if he worked in the medical field. Later that year he began his first semester of college, his tuition paid for by the hospital he had sued. In another year, he decided to work toward entering medical school: he could see himself being a good psychiatrist, the kind of doctor he never had.

A TOUCH OF DARKNESS

The first disturbance was minor. The framed photograph in the upper hallway fell to the ground. It was an original print of the Mapplethorpe self-portrait with a whip coming out of his butt that Gabe had found at a garage sale in Sag Harbor. I had never really liked it, but had learned to tolerate it because a) its value seemed to increase exponentially every year, and b) guests who took the steps to the upstairs bathroom never failed to comment on it. It had been hanging above the antique Shaker table where Gabe had placed the velvet-lined jewelry box we had purchased that morning at a flea market in East Hampton. The Mapplethorpe picture landed with a heavy thump-de-thump the next afternoon when I was taking a nap. It had been expertly framed, and the glossy black wood frame and the glass covering were intact after the fall and I rehung it, only to hear the same thump-de-thump hours later while I was in the kitchen on the ground floor. Gabe was outside tinkering in the garden he thought he could make flourish and didn't hear either crash. I went up the stairs and leaned the photo against the wall, behind the Shaker table, thinking I would need to find a stronger hook or longer nail, but forgot about it because other things began happening. That evening Gabe was suddenly struck by a rattling noise in his head that ended up as an upset stomach and he went upstairs to sleep early.

I dismissed the rattling-brain-tumor-causing-ulcer phenomenon and chalked up Gabe's malaise to the weather and the heavy pollen floating around and the fact that he was always the first one of us to get something or another, especially when he was outside working in only a T-shirt and shorts and getting sweaty and chilled. Then Chester, our two-year-old collie-shepherd mix, began acting restless and disoriented and threw up on the carpet while I was checking my e-mail. After I had cleaned up the mess and let him out into the backyard to do his business, probably on Gabe's freshly planted garden, I lay down on the couch and started to watch one of those PBS mysteries and drifted off to sleep. I woke about an hour later drenched in sweat, my forehead burning as if I were feverish and vibrating, vaguely remembering pieces of a dream about being nauseous and angry.

We'd lived in the house for four years after spending three seasons in summer shares in Southampton, Water Mill, and Sag Harbor. We looked at several houses before we settled on this one—an A-frame in the Northwest Woods built in the 1950s with an enormous stone fireplace as its centerpiece, situated on a wooded lot at the rise of a hill that sloped down to a small inlet of Gardiners Bay. It was not exactly the sort of house we wanted. We had our hearts set on living in a cottage in East Hampton near the village and the stores and the beach, but neither Gabe nor I generated that kind of an income, so we settled on "Far Hampton" as I liked to tell our guests from the city, since just when you thought you were almost at the house, there was always another mile or two left to travel. Gabe and I gave up the city too, subletting our individual apartments in Brooklyn Heights and the East Village to live together year-round in the South End of Long Island and telecommute to our corporate jobs, making cameo appearances when required to do face time with our less fortunate colleagues.

Over the following days there were more mishaps at the house—the fire alarm went off on its own accord, requiring me to make a pleading phone call to our security company not to send anyone out to the house and follow up with an exorbitant bill for the unnecessary service, then the pilot light went out in our water heater and our phone lines went dead for about three hours. When everything had been restored our laptops suddenly ceased working for another hour and then rebooted themselves without our help. I might have overlooked these things if two other events had not triggered my suspicion that something "otherworldly" was at work on our property. One morning there was an infestation of flies in the guest bedroom that seemed to be beating themselves to death against the window screen and Chester began snarling at something unseen and then broke into fits of barking. I tried to calm him down, pushing him into another room, but like the good companion and guard dog we had expected him to be, he continued to snarl and bark until whatever ominous thing it was that frightened him had disappeared.

But those things were also forgotten because our jobs required this or that, we had to leave the house to go to the grocery store and get gas for the car and take Chester to the groomers, and Gabe's instant brain tumor and peptic ulcer drifted into an occasional headache, which was not something out of the ordinary. But a few nights later when I was turning off the television in the living room on my way upstairs I heard a scratching noise within the wall beside the fireplace. I called up to Gabe in the bedroom to come down and listen to the sound, but when he walked into the room the scratching stopped.

"It could be bees," he said. Gabe was always practical. I was more suspicious.

"Bees?"

"Burrowing into the wood."

"At night?"

"Or squirrels."

"Squirrels?"

"Storing their food."

"In May?"

"Well, then getting at last year's haul."

"Wouldn't we have heard them before?"

"What do you think it is?"

"I don't know—that's why I called you to listen to it. It didn't sound like bees. Or squirrels."

"What did it sound like?"

I refused to say the g-word and spook us both. We both stood in the middle of the room quietly, listening, waiting for the scratching sound that didn't return.

"I'll call an exterminator in the morning," Gabe said, before going back upstairs.

◈

The exterminator arrived and found nothing. No squirrels or bees or termites or bats, though he did make an offhand comment about our gutters being clogged with leaves and that we should have had them cleaned out the prior fall. "You've got a lot of trees, you know," he said before he handed me his overpriced bill, "that's a lot of leaves." I hated having to be at the mercy of these beefy know-it-all service men who arrived in their logo-bearing customized vans with quotes of expertise painted on the sides. I was a city boy who fell in love with the country when I should have known better, always a little bit out of sync, like Oliver Douglas in the satirical universe of Hooterville.

I didn't know anything about cleaning gutters, nor did I want to if I could avoid it, so I called Jerry, our neighbor's son who helped out with our yard work. Since becoming homeowners, Gabe and I had attempted to divvy up our responsibilities for keeping up the house and yard. Gabe oversaw everything about the lawn and the exterior of the house, hence his garden, which usually yielded strangely shaped tomatoes and squash, because the land he had cleared was almost always shaded by one of our enormous trees. I managed the washing machine and the phone and the cable and anything that required indoor servicing, which on some days could mean ruined clothing and endlessly running toilets. It never seemed an even split to either of us, particularly when the car broke down and we both grumbled about being overwhelmed by something else outside of our usual domain. Poor Chester was sometimes caught in the middle—there was always some kind of bargaining going on where he was concerned over who would feed him, bathe him, walk him, or take him to the vet and the groomers (though he never lacked for love).

Hours later, Jerry showed up with a ladder and cleaned the gutters and helped Gabe restock firewood that we had chipped away at during the winter log by log. Gabe always imagines himself as more of a guy's guy, capable of brandishing hammers and saws and shovels and lifting heavy objects, but most of his projects end up incomplete and at the mercy of other experts and in no time that afternoon his back began to hurt, which made the brain tumor and the ulcer resurface, and Gabe left Jerry to finish the project, and went to lie on the couch with a heating pad and an ice pack. Chester and I were smart enough to stay out of the way while the work was going on outside, and then dote on the lord and master of the house once he became an invalid.

But that night, the pounding began.

We were in bed reading our books and magazines, the late news on the TV, and Chester on the floor gnawing at a bone. The pounding seemed to begin inside the bedroom wall, travel to the hallway and then down the stairs into the main living room. I was so shocked it was like someone had crawled inside my body and started punching at my ribs. Once Gabe and I had gotten over our initial fright and disorientation, we tried to follow the sound as it traveled around the house, watching the walls rattle and shake and our books and pictures and *tchochtkes* fall to the floor. It was as if an earthquake had happened at an isolated point and decided not to stay put, but the accompanying sound was more disconcerting, hollow and deep and mournful, as if something alive had been trapped inside the walls and was on its last breath. Chester reacted with barking and then fled beneath our bed upstairs, where he stayed until Gabe and I coaxed him out when the shaking had stopped, after a good ten minutes or so. We waited for more rumbling and pounding, but it didn't arrive, as if a message had been properly sent and it was now our turn to interpret the alien signals sent from another universe. Gabe began to search out practical causes and similar occurrences—going to the Internet first to see if there was any news of earthquakes or explosions in the Long Island area. I took Chester along and walked outside and around the house, looking for damages that wouldn't be covered by our homeowners' insurance but worrying I might discover something more startling like a leering giant green ogre, but I found nothing. There was no answer to our growing questions.

That night, we all slept fitfully, arising at the slightest creak in the house.

In the morning, we were dulled with faux hangovers, grumpy and cranky and pretending we didn't know each other until Gabe called Jerry's parents and asked if there was any kind of disturbance in the neighborhood. (Nope, not a thing, they told us.) When Magda arrived to clean the house—we used her once a week and relied on her and her son Domi to look after Chester if Gabe and I both had to be in the city at the same time—I asked her if she had experienced any kind of disturbance. Her eyes widened and I knew she was uneasy and already spooked. Magda was suspicious of a clogged drain, believing that every house had "things we don't want to know about inside them," and she traveled with her own set of prayers, potions, Voodoo charms, and crosses to get her through the day. I thought about asking her to look for anything unusual while she was working around the house that morning, but didn't want to alarm her or cause her to quit and leave the house a mess. We needed her as much as we did Jerry, and once she started on the kitchen, I spent the day in our upstairs office moving from one teleconference to the next with marketing plans, statistics, and graphs, and emerged bleary-eyed and raspy-voiced in time to catch the evening news.

That evening, the prior night's disturbances seemed years away, and we fell deeply asleep as if caught in a magical spell. I had a dream that I could not wake up from a heavy sleep. Each time I tried to rise into consciousness, I found myself in another layer of slumber. I dreamed that I tried to wake Gabe, only to find that I was still asleep myself and involved in a dream where I was trying to rouse Gabe.

In the morning I pulled myself awake, sluggish and hardly conscious, with my heart pounding in my chest as if I were frightened and my blood pressure out of control. Gabe was still asleep and I went downstairs to make coffee. I noticed that Chester was not in his spot on the floor beside the bed and I expected him to appear at any moment, wagging his tail and full of need and hunger or ready to go outside and squirt on Gabe's vegetable garden. I found him in the kitchen, lying on the floor. He didn't rise when I entered the room. He appeared to be dead and I stooped down and touched him. His fur was warm, and there was light breathing through his nose. But he wouldn't wake when I tried to shake him and my heart seemed to split in two, one part falling into my stomach and another part getting stuck in my throat.

I called up the stairs to Gabe, but got no answer. I began searching for many things all at once—my car keys, my shoes, my cellphone, a jacket, and a cap. Gabe wasn't answering my repeated (and increasingly urgent) calls up the stairs, and I finally raced into the bedroom and found him still sleeping. I tugged and shook and prodded and pulled at him and his old, ragged blue T-shirt that he liked to sleep in, but it was like he was drugged. He finally stirred and I screamed, "Something's wrong with Chester. I'm taking him to the vet!"

He didn't understand me, so I said it again, and he mumbled something about going back to sleep. I began my routine all over again, and finally, when he was sitting up at the side of the bed, I yelled at him to call our veterinarian and I ran down the stairs and lifted Chester off the floor.

Chester was a big, heavy, furry dog. It would have been easier to get him to the car with Gabe's help, but my adrenaline-fueled sense of purpose was strong and intense. Chester was like a child to us, an important, vital, and necessary part of our family, and I was out the door and out of the driveway by the time Gabe registered what was happening. When I reached the end of the block my cellphone was ringing and I saw it was Gabe calling, but I didn't answer because I was too focused on my mission. I hoped that he would have the good sense to call the vet like I had asked him to.

Chester seemed to come more and more alive the farther we got from the house. The receptionist was waiting at the door when I arrived and she led me into an examination room. Chester was panting now, able to sit up, and he lapped at a dish of water that was placed before him and looked at us with his most worried expression. I explained what had happened to Sheila, the receptionist, then explained it to the doctor when she came in to the examining room.

Chester was fine. The vet could find nothing wrong with him. I called Gabe on my cellphone but he didn't answer his, or the house landline. I knew he was being passive-aggressive because I had failed to answer his call, and I left a message on both answering services that Chester was okay and I was headed home after making a few stops in the village for coffee and groceries.

It was a beautiful morning, warm and sunny and lazy-feeling, and since it was early in the week Main Street in East Hampton wasn't crowded. I made a few stops, making sure Chester was calm and his usual self, then headed home after I had picked up the few groceries we needed.

Chester began whining when I turned the car onto our block, pacing back and forth on the backseat where I had placed him, his nails scratching against the upholstery and making me as anxious as he was. By the time I had parked the car in the driveway he was moaning and agitated. He barked at me and wouldn't leave the car, yelping when I tried to lead him outside. I reached into the car and lifted him into my arms, but he began squirming and squealing and snapping at my fingers. I had managed to make it a few steps carrying him toward the house when I realized that Gabe was standing in front of us.

Chester's squirming turned violent. I could feel his toenails scratching through my sweatshirt and jacket. I thought I heard Gabe yelling, "Let him go, let him go!" but I was trying at the same time to calm Chester. Gabe twisted my arm so that Chester jumped to the ground, and as I pivoted my body so that the dog could land smoothly, Gabe slugged me in the side of my face.

I stumbled back a few steps, lost my balance, and sat down hard on the driveway. My face burned and I let out a string of expletives at Gabe. Gabe glared at me and then turned away without saying another word. There was something dark and fierce in his eyes that had never been there before.

It was Gabe, but it wasn't him. In retrospect, it's clear that something had taken hold of him, but at the time I was stunned and in pain from his punch. We had never had this kind of altercation. Gabe had never hit me before, nor I him. Such behavior wasn't even part of our consciousness. My nose and lower lip were bleeding and I could taste the blood as I used the sleeve of my sweatshirt to stopper my nose. I shouted another obscenity at Gabe as he headed back to the house and picked myself off the ground, turning away and calling out to Chester, who was running down the street. I finally caught him near the path that led down the hill to the bay and called Domi, Magda's son, on my cellphone, explaining that there was some trouble at our house and I needed a place to keep Chester safe until things had calmed down. Domi and his wife and two daughters lived in a small house in Springs. Vira, Magda's daughter-in-law and Domi's wife, who weekdays cleaned some of the big empty houses in East Hampton south of the Highway, was at the bay a few minutes later to retrieve Chester.

"What kind of trouble you have?" she asked. Vira was from the

Dominican Republic, and she had developed a stern, detached manner to deal with her wealthy and eccentric clients in town, which was how she was treating me now, though I only had a moderate income and an overcompensating wit.

"You wouldn't believe me if I told you," I said. "I don't believe it myself."

Vira was dark and short and thick and more suspicious than her mother-in-law Magda. She looked at my face and started to ask another question, then found her manners.

"It was an accident," I said. "Chester got spooked."

"Spooked?"

"I took him to the vet," I tried to explain. "I thought he was dying."

"Ah," she breathed. "He spooked you? He a sick puppy?"

"He doesn't want to go back to the house."

"He see something?" she asked and we both looked down at my dog.

"I don't know."

"Doggie see something?" she asked.

When I didn't answer her, she broke her composure and touched my hand and said, "I say prayer. That will help."

I muttered that we were beyond the hope of a prayer.

"I know someone to help," Vira said. "You leave puppy with me. We get you good help."

◆

After Vira took Chester away, I walked back to the house and put the groceries away in the kitchen cabinets. Gabe was asleep on the couch. I went upstairs to the office and locked the door, knowing that it wouldn't keep anyone out who urgently or angrily wanted to come in, but that it made an unforgiving statement and protected my sanity. I knew at some point Gabe and I would have to confront what had happened, but right then, I wanted and needed for us to remain enemies. I had always been prone to harboring grudges too long, grudges that I was continually talking myself out of. I studied my nose and lip in the mirror. Gabe didn't have the strength to do too much damage, but whatever force had taken hold of him had caused a small bit of swelling and a tender pinch of pain and a lot of bruised pride. I said a little prayer then, though neither Gabe nor I were what you could call religious, that this too should pass, leaving us unharmed, and that maybe, just maybe, our mutual passive-aggressiveness could make us forget that it had even happened and I could learn to live without complaints and resentment.

But there were times I worried that something like this would be the catalyst to end our relationship. Gabe and I had been together for so many years, we'd lost the passion and romance of being a couple. We'd become two men with habits and routines who inhabited the same space and occasionally looked to each other for companionship and wondered if this was what we had been expecting the night eleven years before when we met in a bar. We'd never been monogamous, but we'd never cheated or lied to the other either. We were just two guys, flawed and sluggish, trying to consider the other as someone special and close and necessary. Still, I couldn't imagine my life without Gabe. He was the center of my universe because I had willingly shrunk my orbit to accommodate his lack of gravity.

I worked on a spreadsheet at my desk until the numbers were making me exhausted and sleepy, and I leaned back and dozed off into a deep nap—until I was awakened by a pounding at the door.

It was Gabe, yelling, "Kirk, what's going on? Why is the door locked? Is Chester in there with you?"

When I opened the door he asked, "What the hell happened to your lip? And nose?"

"You don't remember?"

"Remember what?"

"Slugging me."

"What?"

"I was trying to calm Chester down and you decided to punch me instead."

He looked at me and said, "But that was a dream."

"I don't think so."

"I had a dream that it happened. It didn't really happen."

"Tell that to my face."

"Where's Chester?"

"With Domi and Vira."

He looked again at my face. "Does it hurt?"

"What do you think?"

"I didn't do that, did I?"

"You think I just walked right up to you and *asked* you to hit me?"

"Are you starting a fight?"

"*Starting?*"

He looked at me squarely, and I saw in his expression that his dream had become a fact to him. "I'm going to go get Chester," he said and left.

They both returned about an hour later. I refused to come down for dinner because I was annoyed, frightened, and trying to concentrate on putting together a coherent marketing analysis for a client. And it was my turn to be the passive-aggressive spouse. When I finally made my way downstairs later Gabe and Chester were both in front of the television asleep. I turned off the set and left them there, though I was conscious when they both arrived later in the bedroom and settled into their usual places.

◆

I might have forgotten everything (or harbored a grudge for a while, then forgotten everything), if I hadn't seen Magda and Gabe the next morning leading a thin woman in heels awkwardly around the yard. Chester followed them, wagging his tail and leaping in the air as if they were walking to the next ride at Disneyland.

The woman was bony, with veiny arms and hands. She was taller than Magda and wore something on her head that resembled a brightly colored babushka and made her almost as tall as Gabe. She held her wrist at her chest, the way I've seen a lot of drag performers do, the metal bracelets as far down her forearm as they could go. Her long fingers were covered with lots of knobby rings. When I stumbled out of the house and caught up with them in the back yard, Magda introduced her to me as "Sammie."

"Short for Samantha," Magda said. "Like the show."

"What show?" I asked. I had not even had a cup of coffee yet and was trying to catch my breath.

"The one about the witch," Gabe said.

"Are you a good witch or a bad witch?" I asked Samantha instinctively, trying to make my line reading honest and not the high-pitched imitation I heard laughing through my mind. It was too early in the morning for me to be serious about anything.

Sammie didn't laugh. In fact, she didn't respond, and I supposed she'd taken my calling her a witch as an insult. She walked a few steps, her spiked heels digging into the damp ground, then stopped and turned to me and said, "He's not happy he is in your house."

"Who?" Gabe and I both responded at the same time.

"I don't like to do the ghosts," she said. Her accent was different from Magda, Domi, and Vira's, a tinge of the Caribbean to it. "Very dangerous. This one very dangerous. He is unhappy. And evil. Be careful of this man."

"Who?"

She folded her arms across her chest and said sternly, "I see house now."

We entered through the back door into the kitchen. Sammie stood for a moment, her head bowed toward the speckled tile that a previous owner had liked more than we did, and said, "No, not here."

In the living room she stood in the same way in front of the couch and the fireplace and said, "Something here, but not evil. Something unhappy. In pain. Very, very sad."

She turned and walked to the stairs that led to upstairs bedrooms, looked up the steps and began to take them slowly one at a time. I dreaded what she would see because our bedroom was mess—the bed was unmade, Chester's toys and bones were scattered on the floor, and Gabe had a nasty habit of tossing his underwear in a corner where we had once kept a hamper. I was filled with such suspense over what Sammie would say about the state of the room or the look she would try to suppress that I expected the walls to shake and roar at any second. But at the top of the staircase Sammie stopped in front of the Shaker table and the Mapplethorpe photograph, still on the floor and leaning against the wall.

I could tell she was studying the picture, maybe trying to decide whether the whip was supposed to be a tail or something more obscene, and we waited for a condescending remark. But instead, she ran her hand over the top of the carved wooden box on top of the table. "His name is Jacob. A man of the Good Book. A minister. Maybe judge or policeman. Very important. But very evil. He hurt many people. Boys. Young men. That is all I want to know. I must go now."

She turned and clomped down the stairs, without even gazing into our messy bedroom. At the bottom, she looked up at us and said, "He is here. The devil is here."

Gabe moved quicker than I could, thumping down the stairs and stopping Sammie at our front door. "How do we get rid of him?" he asked.

Sammie looked up at Magda and said something in Spanish. "She will call you," Sammie said. "She will bless this house."

◈

Gabe's first response was to get rid of the jewelry box. "I'll just throw it out," he said.

"Are you crazy?" I stopped him. "Why don't you put it up on eBay?"

"You want me to sell someone a haunted box?"

"Maybe we can give it to a museum or something."

"So you believe this crazy woman?"

"Don't you?"

"I can't believe we're having this conversation," he said. "And I can't believe this is happening in our house."

Suddenly we were detectives. Sherlock Holmes, Miss Marple, and Hercule Poirot all rolled into two frustrated middle-aged gay men with only a handful of clues of who—or what—was disturbing their home. An evil man named Jacob who might have owned a velvet-lined carved wooden jewelry box and who might have been a minister or a judge or a sheriff or a policeman. And now we were afraid of getting rid of the box because we might offend our evil guest.

Gabe went upstairs to his desk, where he found the receipt from the flea market in East Hampton where we had purchased the box. An hour or so later he found me in front of my laptop in the kitchen. "It isn't a jewelry box," he announced.

"The receipt said it was."

"The woman I spoke to said it was a lady's velvet-lined jewelry box. That's what it was used for, but that's not what it was. Is, I mean. That's not what another woman I spoke to said it was. *Is*."

"What do you mean?"

"It's a Bible box."

"What?"

"Circa 1755. It was part of Allan Schneider's collection. He gave it to one of his caterers—Eva Wheeler—and her son gave it to the flea market. She was only using it as a jewelry box."

Allan Schneider had been a wealthy Hamptons realtor with a passion for collecting antiques. He had died a few years before we began our own Hamptons summers. Eva Wheeler had been one of the premiere caterers in the area but her company had gone out of business shortly after her death the previous year. Her son had donated several items for the flea market to benefit the village historical society, and he had only told the volunteer that it was a gift to his mother from the realtor. Gabe had called a town librarian who catalogued many of the antique items that had gone in and out of the homes Schneider had lived in and sold. He knew immediately that the jewelry box had been a Bible box.

"Okay Sherlock, where did Allan Schneider get the box?" I asked Gabe.

"From the estate of Joanna Hammond."

"Did she have any preachers in her family?"

"Get to it, Watson. That's your mystery to solve. I'll fix dinner tonight."

◆

A Bible box, like the name implies, was originally meant to store a Bible. In Colonial America, it was used to safely transport what was then a very costly book. Ours—or Mrs. Wheeler's jewelry box—had a flat top, so it was safe to assume it was not the kind used for writing or as a lectern or a podium. The wood was oak and the outside carvings were repeating patterns of vines and flowers. The brass lock on the front of the box was added at a later date, probably in the late 1980s when Mrs. Wheeler began using it as a jewelry box, since it had a simple deco look to it and was decidedly newer than the iron hinges that kept the lid in place when the box was opened. My detective work on the Internet revealed that many antique Bible boxes could also hold hidden compartments on the bottom and sides. I ripped out the velvet lining that had been stapled and glued into place, probably at the same time the brass lock had been added, and found no secret parts. Only a *V* inscribed on the bottom of the box, done in the same style by the person who had carved the outside panels, which I assumed must be the initial of the surname of the box's original owner, perhaps one of Joanna Hammond's ancestors.

As for Joanna Hammond—her family history was easy to untangle since I found her obituary in the on-line archives of the newspaper from when she had died in the early 1980s. She had been born Joanna Josephs in 1898, and her mother was Elizabeth Whitten Josephs, a descendant of the early settlers of the village. Joanna had met her husband, Jefferson Hammond, at the Maidstone Country Club in East Hampton. They were married in 1927 and honeymooned in Maine. Jefferson Hammond was a banker and from a long line of bankers. Joanna's father, Thomas Whitten, had been a village trustee and a founding member of the Maidstone Club. Thomas Whitten's father had been a farmer, but his older brother and Thomas' uncle had been a judge and his maternal great-grandfather was Joshua Veales, one of a long line of stern Calvinist ministers who had presided over congregations in East Hampton.

My guess was that the Bible box, dated by the appraiser around the mid-eighteenth century because of its design and iron hinges, might have belonged to one of the branches of the Veales with its carved *V* in the base. Joshua could be someone related to Jacob, the "devil" Samantha encountered when she stood in front of the Shaker table.

But this was all speculation and I did not have a chance to do any more investigation. That night, after dinner, the pounding returned while I was upstairs at the computer. Chester went into hiding and Gabe went over to the dark side.

The knocking was soft and tentative at first, as if it were questioning its right to be in the house, but then it increased in volume with an angry, demanding assertion. Gabe was downstairs and wasn't answering my shouts as the pounding increased. I went out into the hall and stood by the Bible box, expecting it to become a burning red color and burst into flames. It didn't. I looked down to the bottom of the stairs and saw Gabe standing there stiffly. Only it wasn't Gabe. It was whatever horrible and insensitive demon had decided to possess him.

I went into the bedroom and locked the door. I opened our bedroom window and popped out the screen and climbed out onto the ledge of the roof, just as I heard the pounding at the bedroom door. It was Gabe, wanting to come in and do some kind of damage to me or our dirty laundry. I slid down the side of the roof till I reached the gutter (not failing to notice it was bare of any leaves), grasped my fingers around the lip of it and edged myself onto the front yard as it groaned under my weight. I ran to the back of the house and opened the kitchen door and called for Chester. He ran out immediately and I followed him out into the street.

This time I didn't have a cellphone or car keys or even a wallet, but I was thankful that at least I hadn't yet taken off my sneakers after dinner. The cool wind rippled through my T-shirt and sweatpants as I glanced back at the house and ran away from it.

The easiest thing would have been to crash at Jerry's house, but it would have also required an embarrassing confession and hysterical sounding explanations and Jerry's parents would have wanted to involve the police, something that I didn't want on anyone's record. Instead, I decided to walk to Domi and Vira's house, a good eight-mile trek in the dark. I also thought it would be the safest way for Gabe to find us if he wanted to once he had shape-shifted back to himself; maybe he'd drive up beside us on the darkened road and beg us to return home.

But Gabe didn't show up and I walked slowly on the shoulder of the road, looking at the plastic bottles and beer cans that had been tossed in the drainage ditch. I was worried more about Chester being hit than myself—he was always ahead of me, sniffing and squirting everything as he darted in and out of the brush—and I expected to be confronted at any moment by a drunken *artiste* in a convertible swerving out of control and pinning us all to a giant tree. Wouldn't that be a tragic and fitting end to the night and our life in the Hamptons? I stopped and took the laces out of my sneakers and tied them together to make a longer strand and looped it through Chester's collar to make a leash. His expensive obedience training paid off. He stayed close to my side, eying me to keep his pace slower than he preferred and ready to bolt whenever I gave him the pleasure.

It took us a couple of hours to make the trip. At Domi's I struggled through an explanation as I gulped down a glass of water and Chester played with Leah and Heather, who were glad to see him. I was broaching the subject of Samantha and the house blessing with Vira when the phone rang. It was Gabe. Vira handed me the phone.

"It's over," he said.

My stomach turned and I struggled for breath. "What's over?" I asked him.

"I burned it."

I didn't answer because I was struggling to hear him over the thunderous sound of my heart. My first thought was that he had burned down the house.

"First I smashed it. Then I burned it. In the fireplace."

The box. He was referring to the Bible box. "You think that will stop it?" I asked.

"The noise is gone," he said, then added. "The noise in my head is gone too."

"Magda will drive us home in the morning," I said.

"I'll come pick you up in a few minutes."

"Gabe, we should stay here tonight. Domi said I can sleep on the couch. Leah and Heather are playing with Chester. Vira is going to get her friend to bless the house tomorrow. Maybe you should get out of the house, too. Go over to Magda's and stay the night."

Now it was his turn to remain silent. Just before he disconnected, I thought I heard him start to cry.

◈

The next morning we arrived en masse at the house: Magda, Samantha, Vira, and Danielle, a heavy woman with skin darker than Samantha's, who seemed to move by shifting her large hips up and down one at a time like pistons of a giant machine.

Gabe was silent and contrite when we showed up, but Chester was needy and intent on being the center of attention as all of us began "the blessing" by walking the property line.

There was a lot of stuff said in French between Samantha and Danielle, and it made me wonder if our demon was multilingual and if he would understand any of this better than I did, which wasn't much at all. I tried to keep an open mind about everything, even as perpetually cynical as I was, but the gibberish made me smile too widely and roll my eyes in disbelief. I was also concerned that I had not worn the proper outfit for the exorcism—I was still in my jeans and the T-shirt—and the women had shown up in their Sunday finest—bright and smartly tailored ensembles.

When we reached the front door Danielle placed on the ground what looked like an ashtray full of weeds. There was some struggle to set them aflame because of the morning breeze and a faulty lighter she was using, and I went inside the house and found the long matches we used to light fires in the fireplace. They worked and the weeds, which I was told were sage and other herbs, began to smoke and create a bitter stench.

There were more words in French and Spanish, the foul smoke was waved one way and then another, I coughed to suppress my giggling, and Danielle turned to Gabe and asked him for his Bible.

"My Bible?" he answered, startled, and looked over at me. "Do we have a Bible?"

I had a Bible from my boyhood somewhere in the house, the one I had been given by my parents' Methodist church when I had completed my confirmation classes in Georgia. Where in the house it was I had no idea, possibly in the attic, but I remembered there was a children's book of Bible stories in our office that Gabe's sister had left at the house two years before and neither of us had remembered to mail back to her.

I went back inside the house and found the children's book, and when I handed it to Danielle, there was all sorts of startled conversation in French and Spanish between the women. Finally, Vira decided that the book would do and Danielle placed her hand over it and said something that I took this time to be Latin.

When she was done, she turned to me and said, "He gone."

"Just now?" I asked, somewhat shocked that it could be over so quickly. I was almost disappointed we had not even been able to hug him goodbye and thank him for giving our relationship a little bit of excitement.

"He gone up the street now," she said. "He not bother you no more."

Samantha unfolded her arms from her chest, though she kept her fingers at her throat, and added, "Your Guardian Angel will protect you."

I flickered my gaze to Gabe, who caught my expression and deflected it back to Samantha. "Guardian Angel?" he asked.

"Light a candle and pray to her," Magda said.

"*Her?*" I answered.

"She will protect you."

I wanted to explore this a little more; why wasn't our Guardian Angel around to help us when all the pounding and possession started? And since she was now supposed to be our new best friend I thought I deserved to know her name and style; was she pre-Raphaelite or Goth? But before I could do this, I saw Vira whispering something to Gabe and I knew instinctively it was about money. Gabe disappeared inside the house, probably to check his bank balance before he turned over our life savings to these women, and I took the opportunity to ask Samantha where her evil spirit friend Jacob might have gone.

"The devil is everywhere," she answered. "He a sneaky fellow. He go where he want to go."

◈

The next few days passed without problems. Comfort and sanity were restored, animosities and bruises were forgotten. On Friday we had another gay couple from the Woods over for dinner, Ty and Charlie, who weekly traversed the one-way three-hour drive from Manhattan. They talked about the renovations they were making to their saltbox cottage a few miles away, the problems with their contractor, and the permits and perils that lay ahead as they tried to put a small pool in their backyard before next summer. Our ghost story seemed quaint and provincial when we told it, but as I was cleaning up in the kitchen with Charlie he told me he thought spousal abuse was not a joking matter. "You should report it to the police, file a complaint," he said.

"Against Gabe?" I asked shocked.

Charlie nodded.

"But it wasn't Gabe who hit me," I answered, shocked to realize that Charlie had seized on the altercation as a relationship crisis. "It wasn't *him*. It was somebody else."

"You don't know that for sure," he said. "You might not think that the next time. *If* you live through it."

"It's over," I reassured him. "A freaky phenomenon. We've banished all the unwanted demons from our Little House on the Bay. We haven't had any problems since Gabe burned the Bible box and our immigrant fairy godmothers broke the curse."

"Do you realize how absurd that sounds?" Charlie persisted.

"Of course," I answered. "My life as a fairy tale, just as I've always imagined it to be. Prince Charming is no longer a nasty toad."

After our guests had left, Gabe went upstairs to work in the office and Chester followed him. I was worried about the perception others had of our relationship—Gabe and I were not a volatile couple, but we had spent the evening arguing in front of Charlie and Ty over the details of the haunting—I had found them silly. Gabe had found them annoying and expensive. Just when I had dismissed my concerns and sat down to relax and watch TV, I discovered that I had overlooked the glasses and appetizer trays in the living room on the coffee table in front of the fireplace. While I was collecting the items to carry into the kitchen, something caught my eye in the ashes beneath the fireplace grate. It was the old metal hinges from the Bible box. I went to the kitchen, washed up the remaining plates and glasses, and found a paper bag I could use to dispose of the hinges and the ashes. As I entered the living room I heard a light scratching sound within the walls. I thought I was hallucinating, so I stopped to listen to make sure I had heard the sound correctly. The scratching became bolder and louder and wasn't coming from the walls, but from the fireplace. And then it stopped.

The quiet was more frightening than the scratching. My blood pressure rose and my heart started its rib dance, anticipating the next thing that would happen. I knelt on the hearth and scooped up the ashes and the hinges with the small trowel and dumped them into the bag. I waited for the scratching to resume, but it didn't, and I remembered Samantha's advice to pray to our Guardian Angel. I didn't pray or ask for a blessing. Instead, I muttered a mental thanks. *Thank you for watching over us.* That was when I noticed something deeper within the fireplace. A brick near the bottom of the back wall was slightly askew, as if it had been forced out of place from the outside of the house. The mortar around it had fallen away. I reached into the fireplace and tugged at the brick and it gave way. I sat it on top of the grate. I expected a squirrel or a bat to come exploding out of the dark space and frighten me. Instead, I had a bigger shock. At the corner of the hollow space was something that resembled a long, light-colored stick, bent at the tip. When I reached in to touch it I realized that it wasn't a stick at all, but a bone, and the tip was a toe. A big, bony toe.

◆

The police arrived. A forensics team dismantled our fireplace over the next three and a half weeks. The media stood outside our house and reported on the skeleton found inside our chimney. The bones were almost three hundred years old. How they got into our chimney was the cause of much speculation and many theories that would take months to understand and probably never be fully solved—how a fifty year-old house contained three-hundred year-old bones. Suddenly we were the topic of conversation, Long Island's newest *Amityville Horror.*

While Gabe and I waited for all this to unfold, a change began in our relationship. I had a comfort with the outsiders and professionals who arrived to our house that Gabe did not. I found it amusing and interesting to be caught up in history and a ghost story, listening to town historians and firemen and inspectors talk about other houses they had investigated, and the crap and garbage they uncovered in other people's basements. I offered our visitors and guests coffee and cake and doughnuts and iced tea, exactly as my mother would have done if this had happened in her Southern home. Gabe could not shed his darkening moods. He resented the intrusions, felt abused in his own house, hated his work being interrupted by one question after another, and scowled through the window at policemen and reporters. The stain that had arrived with the ghost of "Jacob" had not been washed away. Gabe began drinking too much, arguing with whomever he could and asking those he couldn't to leave. I felt he was displaying his unhappiness with other aspects of his life—his family, his job, our relationship. Gabe had always been the one of us who was reluctant to settle down. I remembered how early on when we had first started dating he'd told me he didn't love me and probably never would. It had upset me because I had loved Gabe immediately and my frustration with him had caused him to soften. He had never wanted the kind of home life his parents had in suburban Connecticut and I had often wondered if I had trapped him into having one, though once he had accepted the idea that we could be a couple, he was the one who plowed ahead with keeping us together. And now that tenacity was gone.

When the East Hampton weekly published an account of the haunting it was picked up by one national news service and then another and another. We were contacted by a variety of scholars and eccentrics wanting another piece of our lives—an archeologist who wanted to see if there was an Indian burial ground in our backyard, a team of professional paranormal investigators from Illinois who were willing to fly in to give our home a discounted state-of-the-art spectral sweeping, a movie producer wanting to send out a writer to flesh out a plot he had outlined, several teenaged ghost hunters too eager to be the next Buffy, and a Baptist minister from North Carolina who told us our sins had uncovered the portal to Hell. One local reporter speculated that we were living on land where Elizabeth Garlick had once practiced black magic during the seventeenth century. "Goody" Garlick had lived on nearby Gardiners Island and had been tried and acquitted of witchcraft.

I began to joke with Gabe that I had asked our Guardian Angel for guidance and protection from all of these zealous intruders, and that if we could prove we were heathens and pagans then we had no worry about whether we were currently experiencing Hell. Gabe was not amused. He wanted to sell the house and start over someplace new. But I didn't want to give up our home, and I thought we could eventually return to our normal routines, even though our visitors were becoming increasingly disturbing. One afternoon a man arrived with his prepubescent daughter who writhed on the floor and spoke in tongues, even as I tried to explain that our ghosts had already been relocated and there was no possibility that she could have been "suddenly" possessed by them. The next morning Gabe stood in front of me in the kitchen with his head bowed and his eyes pinned to the speckled tiles of the floor and said he was moving out. He'd found a rental in Manhattan via the Internet.

"That's it, just like that?" I asked him. I was shocked, and yet I had sensed it coming. In fact, for years I had prepared myself for this moment. I knew that Gabe and I were perfect for each other, but I also knew that Gabe did not always hold the same belief.

"We've had eleven good years," he said. "We could use a change. Both of us."

Gabe kept his investment in the house. The plan was for me to either sell the house or slowly assume the entire ownership with a loan, a process that was more difficult than it sounded on paper because every loan officer I spoke to in East Hampton knew I was asking for money for a haunted house, a property that would now never "recoup its original value."

But I had no desire to sell and move to a new home, so I soldiered on without Gabe, using my best virtues and the Guardian Angel Gabe had left behind as allies. I gave tours. I e-mailed pictures and tried to let everyone know the case was closed. The ghosts were gone, even though the mystery wasn't solved, there were no more bones to be found in the house. I wasn't invading sacred ground. Indian spirits were not seeking retribution. But I was haunted and heartbroken by Gabe's leaving, fighting daily through layers of denial, anger, and grief. His absence hit Chester as hard. At night he would roam through the rooms of the house, his toenails clicking against the wood floor or the stairs, looking for Gabe. He slept with his ears cocked, waiting to hear the sound of the car in the driveway or the lock turning and Gabe walking into the house. Winter arrived and the crazies forgot about the haunting when the temperatures dipped below freezing. Loneliness hit me hardest in January, after Gabe and I had spent the entire holidays apart.

◆

About a year from the day we had first bought the jewelry box at the East Hampton flea market, a professor at Southampton College published the most plausible theory of the bones found in our chimney. I had spoken to him only a handful of times—to confirm our lot number on a map, the date of purchase of the house, and a few other inspection and town records that I was aware of.

To summarize, his theory was this: Forensics had determined that the bones had belonged to a young man of about twenty. Professor Abrams believed the young man was one Simon Parker.

The first farm was not established on the wooded Northwest area where we lived until 1757. The Coast Surveys of 1838 and 1846 show fourteen farms scattered throughout Northwest, but no home is noted in the location of our house on these maps. These farms were either adjacent to the meadows found at inlets or at areas of more fertile soil in the wooded interior. The original structure that might have contained the chimney that had been incorporated into our home might have belonged to a man who was a laborer on one of the farms or on nearby Gardiners Island, which was accessible by ferry or boats. Professor Abrams suggested that the original house on our property might have been built by a fisherman or a whaler, since our hilltop view provided easy access and a view of the inlet of water that led out to Gardiners Bay. The house might have later been abandoned after the original owner had been lost at sea.

Professor Abrams, who was a firm believer in the supernatural and who had previously written about the intersecting spirit and real worlds in India for his doctorate, explained that in modern ghost lore there are several reasons why the dead return. Sometimes ghosts appear to recreate something that was normal about their lives or to reenact their deaths. Sometimes a ghost will return to complete unfinished business, such as pointing out a missing will or a hidden treasure or to request a proper burial. Some spirits are vengeful, seeking to punish the living. Others arrive to warn or reward or offer comfort.

Simon Parker was the second son of a family of laborers on Gardiners Island. One of the East Hampton village elders at the time of Simon's youth was Jacob Veales. At that time the colony had strict sodomy laws. In 1765 Simon Parker was arrested and tried on sodomy charges before Jacob Veales' younger brother, Judge Henry Veales. He was acquitted, it is believed, because Jacob's son, Jeremiah, had been charged with the same crime. Jacob is said to have delivered a scathing sermon against sodomy, masturbation, and other moral iniquities following the trial, and Simon Parker was run out of town, disappearing without a trace.

Dr. Abrams proposed that Simon Parker might never have left town, because Simon was in love with someone who was still in the village: Jeremiah Veales. Abrams reasoned that Jacob Veales was so incensed by Simon's acquittal and the fear that he would continue to morally corrupt the youth of village, including his son, that he kidnapped the young boy and imprisoned "the tempter" within the stones of the large hearth of the sea captain's abandoned house originally occupying our property. Veales tied up the young man and added a layer of stones in front of the original hearth. A 1913 map of the Northwest Woods shows a house on our plot of land in the same location as our house stands today. That house burned down in 1944 and a new house was not built until 1955, when the new homeowners incorporated the original hearth; hence Simon Parker had remained sealed up for almost three centuries. Abrams also believed that the Bible box, which might have belonged to Jacob Veales or his father or a member of his family, in the guise of a velvet-lined jewelry box, had disturbed the sacred resting ground of the imprisoned Simon Parker and awakened the fear that more harm was to follow him or others. The ghost had contacted the current residents of the house, a contemporary gay male couple (Gabe and myself) to warn them of the presence of something it considered evil. In essence, a demon had awakened Simon Parker's ghost and our hasty and impromptu exorcism had restored the balance by awakening our Guardian Angel to calm the spirit world. After I had finished reading the article it was suddenly clear to me that this alternate universe might be as large and interconnected as the physical world it related to—ghosts and guardian angels and devils and even fairies and witches and goblins and ghouls seemed more credible and plausible, as silly as it sounded, even though my personal experiences had left me less than expert on the phenomena. I was skeptical, but I was also a believer.

And Professor Abrams' explanation was not without flaws; he failed to raise the issue of doubt when dealing with supernatural events or to even consider more mundane explanations. I also thought he had failed to consider that the crime was unlikely to have been undertaken solo; Jacob Veales must have drawn in other conspirators—those who held the body of Simon Parker in place as the chimney was bricked over, those who carried the bricks, fixed the mortar and assisted in the continuing deception throughout the village that a young man had simply disappeared one day. Maybe it had involved an entire community.

I mailed a copy of the professor's article to Gabe in New York at the address he had given me the day he walked out, but he didn't respond, nor did I expect him to. I had heard through Charlie that he was dating a guy regularly, and the painful thought of it, the jealousy and anger and hurt and disappointment were too much for me to bear. The summer passed by and the garden yielded its usual strangely shaped vegetables, which I cooked and simmered for guests from the city, many of whom were eager to set me up with someone or someone's friend. The house and the haunting were no longer a news item, but I could not shake the story of Simon Parker and Jeremiah Veales. In a way, Jacob Veales had had the same kind of impact on my relationship with Gabe as he had on the male lovers centuries before.

In August, Jerry finally left home—to go to college in upstate New York—and I began using a handyman, laid off from his corporate job in the city, who was living with his girlfriend in Montauk and had all of the husbandry skills our house required. Hank liked hanging out at the house, especially after he had broken up with his girlfriend and I no longer had any chores for him to do. I found his company pleasant and Hank liked reading through our small collection of first edition British novels that Gabe had started collecting the year we began dating. That was until he met one of Chester's groomers when he accompanied us to the village one afternoon. After Hank was introduced to Beth, I seldom saw him unless I needed him to repair something at the house.

In November, Jerry returned from school for the holidays and one afternoon, Chester, in his excitement at seeing his old friend again, darted under the wheels of his car as he was leaving the house. At first, we thought it was just a broken leg, but a day later it was clear that a severed nerve was causing Chester pain and incontinence and I had no choice but to put him down. An operation was not even a viable alternative. It all happened so swiftly and I had no one to make the decision for me and so I had to make it myself.

I hesitated about reaching out to Gabe. Instead, I invoked Simon Parker as my patron martyr and asked him to adopt Chester in his otherworld, and this seemed to calm me and lift my depression, imagining Chester with a place and a purpose and a new friend. One morning not long thereafter I got up and wrote Gabe an e-mail to tell him about Chester.

The following night he called. "I've been praying to our Guardian Angel," he said. "Asking her for a reason to call you."

I was surprised by this. Gabe had never been religious—or superstitious—or spiritual. But if a haunting had torn us apart, I supposed a Guardian Angel might bring us back together. "You don't need a reason to call me," I said. "You can call me anytime you want."

"I know," he answered. "I figured that out on my own."

We spent the rest of the conversation catching up on things we hadn't talked about in a long time: mortgage payments, the professor's article, dirty gutters, and the broken-down toilet. Gabe mentioned that he had done a lot of thinking since he moved out of the house, which in my mind meant that he had been through enough bad dates and bounced checks to feel nostalgic for the compromises of a relationship. He was sad about Chester and I tried to keep from crying, though my voice was often shaky and uncertain. The mind is a strange mechanism, but the heart is far stranger, and I found both of them yearning a bit too much for a return to the way things had been between us, and I said a quiet prayer of thanks that Gabe had passed safely through the darkness that had come between us. I invited Gabe out to spend the holidays at the house—it was still partially his, after all, and he was welcome to bring out a guest and they could come and go as they pleased. I knew it was time to move on and bring him back into my life in some way.

A week later, Gabe arrived by himself and he stayed longer than he expected. In fact, he didn't return to city again, except to pack up his belongings and return to the country. I had not seen him since the day he had moved out of the house and I could tell he had changed. Something was different; he had worked his way through the dark spell that had been cast over him. And us. Gabe acknowledged the change himself, in fact, crediting it to praying and talking with our Guardian Angel.

Gabe also explained that our Guardian Angel had led him to look for a present to give me. I laughed because the whole idea of ghosts and guardian angels was nonsense. *And wasn't.*

"I don't require a present," I said. "I'm just glad you're here."

"I know," he answered. "But I require having to give you something, to make up for being away too long."

I am hesitant to close our ghost story with a sentimental ending. But the gift was unexpected and too perfect, a small, velvet-lined box, the kind a man presents to someone he loves when he wants to make that sort of statement. Inside were a set of silver rings, one for each of us. "For better or for worse," Gabe said when he handed it to me, "this is where I want to be."

THE MAN IN THE MIRROR

Adrian Chase walked into his dressing room and stood in front of the air conditioner. It was over ninety degrees on the lot and not even noon. He was sixty-nine years old and out of breath from the walk from the soundstage and the three short stairs up to the door of his trailer. He sat in the chair in front of the makeup mirror and was surprised to see a clear tumbler filled with ice and an amber liquor. He did not remember pouring himself a drink and certainly would have thought twice about starting a cocktail so early in the day. He usually waited till four o'clock before reaching for a drink, unless he was particularly rattled.

He *was* particularly rattled. The baby-faced assistant director had brought him new pages for the pilot moments after they had finished the first table reading the day before. But he had been pleased by that, not rattled. He had gone from a mute grandfather who sat in front of his television ignoring his family to a crotchety character with a line and, he hoped, a laugh from the audience. That certainly wouldn't have provoked pouring himself a drink so early in the morning. No, he had even taken it in stride when the AD had flagged him down as soon as he had arrived on the soundstage and handed him *another* set of new pages. On his way to his trailer he had stopped and chatted with Lissa, the stage manager, before flipping through the new script and seeing his line.

Yes, that could do it. The *newer* pages. That could have caused him to pour himself a glass of whiskey. But he couldn't have done that himself because he had just stepped inside the trailer. Some kind soul must have done it for him, knowing what his reaction would be. Now, he deliberated on whether to drink it or toss it out. Years and years of analysis had taught him what he already knew: he was a nasty drunk. This, this glass of whiskey, would be sure to set him on that path the moment the fire hit his belly. No, he needed to remain calm and focused. This *was* a job. Just as he reached for the glass to toss it down the sink, he noticed a man standing behind him, reflected in the mirror. Startled, Adrian spilt some of the drink on the counter as he tried to put the glass back down.

The man in the mirror was himself. He was smiling and Adrian was not.

"Go ahead, have it," the man in the mirror said with a wicked, leering grin. "You deserve it. After all you've put up with."

Adrian, anxious and intimidated by his own image, lifted the glass as steadily as he could and then stopped. *What the hell was going on here?* He turned around and looked out at the room and no one was there. He looked in the mirror again and there he was. The same fellow. *Himself,* standing over his shoulder, wearing the same outfit he was wearing now, dark slacks and a white shirt. Adrian didn't think he was hallucinating. He certainly wasn't overworked, not with *this* job. He hadn't worked in close to a month. And he wasn't sick—or at least he certainly didn't think he was ill, only momentarily winded from the heat and old age. Last week he had been to see a doctor because of the episode of vertigo he had experienced after taking an antihistamine. The doctor had said there was nothing wrong with him; his hearing and vision had all tested fine and the doctor suggested he might be stressed and overworked. *Stressed and overworked?* Of course he wasn't stressed and overworked. He had flown to the West Coast so he *could* be stressed and overworked, stressed over a fabulous part and worked to death, but nothing had come his way. Bored and depressed was more like it. First, the movie he had been cast in was canceled when the star dropped out to take another project, and then the advertising agency decided the national commercial Adrian had been cast for was the wrong approach for the client. Now, he was testing for a role in a sitcom. *A pilot. Not even a sure thing.* Adrian was certain this lousy script would never make it to prime time. It was a waste of his time. If anything was going on then it was most certainly *not* because he was overworked. No, he was a professional who had showed up to do his job, no matter how lousy the finished product was to be in the end.

Adrian studied the man standing over his shoulder. He looked exactly as Adrian looked now—graying hair turning white, bags beneath the eyes, fleshy jowls framing his cheeks, and pale, colorless eyes. "If you've come to scare me," Adrian said. "You could at least be younger. I was a rather dashing fellow once upon a time."

He had been a handsome boy on the stage. Perfect posture, perfect teeth, thick curly hair. A signature baritone voice that belied breeding and class. And his career as a lover was as notable as his acting résumé. The man standing behind him was the lecherous kind of fool Adrian had spent years avoiding in dressing rooms, an old troll who lusted after nothing else but youth.

In the mirror, Adrian watched the figure pick up the glass and offer it to him first.

"Go ahead," Adrian said to his image. "Drink yourself miserable. I don't need a crutch. I can do this crappy role in my sleep."

Adrian cast his eyes away from the mirror and down to the script. He found his line, read it, and tried to imagine himself saying the words. Then, he said the words out loud to the man in the mirror: "Gotta run and blow some gas!"

"Pretty lousy, if you ask me," the man in the mirror said. "Fifty years' worth of top-notch acting experience and you're reduced to doing lines about flatulence."

Adrian tried to ignore the comment, which was like ignoring his conscience, only more tangible, like someone was standing over his shoulder and admonishing him, which was exactly what was happening. Or was it? Maybe he was just talking to himself. He looked up from his script and there he still was, standing over himself with his arms crossed and resting on his paunch. The glass of whiskey was still on the counter.

"Not your proudest moment, eh?" the man in the mirror said.

"I've no regrets," Adrian answered himself. "I've had a terrific career."

"Career?" His image smiled back at him. "What about the rest of your life?"

"What 'rest' are you referring to?" Adrian answered. "My career *is* my life."

"Precisely," his image replied. "It's all made up. Nothing real to it, is there?"

◈

"I'll junk up the sweatshirt a little," Candy said. "Put a soda stain on it at the chest. Maybe ketchup at the hem."

Candy was the assistant wardrobe consultant. Adrian had never met the wardrobe consultant or costume designer for the pilot, *if* there was a costume designer. He was standing in front of a mirror in a curtained-off area of the wardrobe department wearing the oversized sweatshirt and pants that his grandfatherly character would wear. Candy's interpretation was that the grandfather would be a slob.

"Perhaps Grandpa is a neatnik," Adrian said.

"Neatnik?"

"Conscientious."

"The guy stinks up the house!" Candy said and laughed.

Adrian wasn't sure if the laugh was directed at him or his character. "*Un-knowing-ly*," Adrian enunciated slowly.

"That's why it's so funny," Candy said. "In his mind he's a *neatnik* but in reality he's an old man who spills things. Maybe I'll add a mustard stain too."

"Mustard?"

"I hope it won't make you hungry!" Candy said and laughed again.

It was a harmless sort of laugh which Adrian did not appreciate because he found it irritating. He found everything about the woman irritating. Her silly oversized jewelry. Her smelly perfume. Her name. *Candy*. Candy should be a hooker's name, not that of an assistant wardrobe consultant.

"Take them off and leave them on the hook and I'll dirty them up before the taping," she said and left the curtained area.

Adrian was alone in front of the mirror. His throat was dry and a wave of nausea made him dizzy. *Mustard!* He was about to take off the sweatshirt when he saw an image of a young man reflected in the mirror and standing behind him. He was dressed in a dark suit with a thin tie. His curly hair was longish and wild, like the rock stars of the early sixties. The Beatle bob.

"I'll be right out," Adrian said to the fellow.

"Don't hurry on my account," the young man said.

The young man didn't leave. He folded his arms across his chest. One hand held a drink: a tumbler of ice with an amber liquor. He rattled the glass so the ice gave out a light tinkly sound. Adrian knew immediately who it was. He didn't have to turn around and find that he was still there. Or not. It was a vision of himself at twenty-five. "Nice and neat," Adrian nodded to his younger self in the mirror.

"Sharp," his younger image replied and held the tumbler out as a toast. "Don't you think?"

He'd landed on the London stage as a brash young man from Dorset. He was fearless, no role was unapproachable, nor out of his grasp. He played the game and played it well. He allowed himself to be fondled and always provided an extra "service" when an audition required one. His future was promising. He had played Hamlet by the time he was twenty-one. *Twenty-one*. And garnered laudable reviews for it. His career skyrocketed. He was willing to tackle any role. Including Eddie Lord, the nasty young lover in a new play bound for the West End. A nasty young lover—*to another man*. A role he could do in his sleep because it mirrored his own life so closely. His life with Jon. Jon, the stocky working class stiff from Glasgow who wanted to be an actor, too, with a barrel chest full of dark hair and a bag of accents he could change on cue. They had met at the Academy. Jon was rugged and handsome, like he had spent seasons roaming the moors. He was serious and committed to everything. He unleashed something in Adrian that otherwise might have taken years for him to accept as more than something he only did to get ahead. They moved in together while still studying and doing workshops. It was a good arrangement. Two bachelors sharing a flat. No one suspected. Even when fame arrived it was never a topic of conversation in the press. Until he became Eddie Lord.

Adrian's performance as Eddie Lord was so credible it started critics' tongues wagging about his private life. Did he or didn't he like guys? Jon thought they both should be out and open about their relationship, public about everything, including their other lovers, tricks, and affairs. Adrian balked and resisted. His opposition created arguments and nasty scenes. He moved out of the flat and got a bigger place in Soho by himself. Jon protested. It made what was invisible now highly suspect when one of them stayed over too late with the other. It didn't help that Adrian had also filmed a small part in an American film that made a big impact. Another nasty young man. A nasty young *homosexual*. It was one of his smallest roles, but his most bitter performance on record. And then Jon was arrested in a public toilet. He had no choice but to stop seeing Jon and start being seen with Izzie. And it helped that he liked Izzie. Elizabeth Rippen, the American heiress and would-be actress. Izzie was outrageous. She liked drinking and partying and creating a scene in public. With Jon out of the picture and Izzie as a decoy Adrian could be as hedonistic as he wanted because everyone wrote about *her*. Or him and *her*. He asked Izzie to marry him. To squelch what rumors remained about his homosexuality. Even though his colleagues, his peers in the theater and in film, those other gay actors in London and New York and Hollywood, knew all about him and the guys he slept with—many of these same fellows, in fact, he *had* slept with himself.

They were engaged until she met another man she liked better. A man who *would* sleep with her. And their spats became *more* public, more *visible*. The media adored the sparring couple so much that they had to remain apart.

"You couldn't escape it, could you?" the man in the mirror said. "It was always a part of your résumé."

"I wasn't Eddie Lord."

"But you were. You broke Jon's heart."

"We were young. What did we know?"

"He knew he loved you."

"I found him a decent barrister," Adrian said. "I kept it out of court."

"For which he was grateful," his image replied. "And after which he expected you would return."

"We couldn't go back to the way things were," Adrian said. "He knew that."

"He was willing to risk what you wouldn't," the man in the mirror said.

"I got him that part, didn't I?" Adrian said. "The part he begged me to help him get."

"But he died before he could do it. *Suicide.*"

"It was an accident."

"An accidental overdose."

"Why bring this up after all these years?"

"Why haven't you forgotten it, if you don't feel some form of guilt?"

"Guilt?" Adrian replied. "It was different then. It was a different time."

"Always a bit ashamed, aren't we?"

"He knew how I felt about him."

"Which was why you know it was no accident."

◆

He wasn't ready to return to his dressing room and face another image of himself. Instead, he spotted Glenn, the production stylist, at the crew table, mulling over the spread of bagels and doughnuts. Glenn was an openly gay guy, a fellow with a shaved scalp, tattoos, piercings, and big arms.

"Go ahead," Adrian said to him. "I doubt if a few carbs would do you any harm."

"Why can't they do something healthier?" Glenn moaned. "How about crudités and low-fat dip for a change?"

"I doubt that would attract anyone to the table," Adrian answered and reached for a pastry. He followed Glenn to a row of chairs against the soundstage wall and balanced a paper cup of hot coffee and the pastry on his lap. They made chitchat about the weather ("It should break on the weekend.") and the lot. ("Everyone's buzzing about the reality show being taped next door.") Adrian eyed the beefy fellow—he must be in his early thirties—from his peripheral vision—the way Glenn's bicep flexed as he ate the bagel he had smeared with cream cheese, the size of his lips and the width of his jaw, the stubble of hair on his scalp. Youth, he thought, wasted on the youth. He wanted to strip the fellow, ask him to prance around nude so he could admire his physique, then suggest they get down to the real business at hand. *Sex.* Ah, *if only his heart could stand such delicious torture.*

Instead, Adrian asked if the pilot taping was still on schedule for the afternoon.

"Yep," Glenn said between mouthfuls. "When you flying out? Tonight? Tomorrow?"

"No, no," Adrian said. "I'm here for a while."

"Where you crashing?" Glenn asked.

"A friend's place in the Hills."

"Cool."

There was a lull in the conversation, as they both finished their food. Glenn shifted in his chair as if to leave, then stopped and said to Adrian, "Do you mind if I ask you a personal question?"

"Of course not. My personal life is rather public these days."

"My lover would kill me if I let the chance pass."

"Hmmm... Well then, go ahead."

"Was it true about Sir Harry?"

"Harry?"

"The myth?"

"Ah, the endowment?"

Glenn nodded and widened his eyes. Sometimes Adrian resented these questions, the perverse curiosity of the voyeur of fame, but he liked this young fellow and didn't mind sharing and perpetuating The Myth of Harrold Harcourt.

"Whatever you've heard," Adrian said. "It was all true."

Yes, it *was* true. Sir Harrold Harcourt was a perpetual cad. A rogue. A louse. He could drink Adrian under the table and out whore him on every level. But he was the great love of Adrian's life. They were together for sixteen years—not all of them brilliant and not all of them lousy, but every one of them full of drama. Best friends, to the public. Partners to the industry crowd. Lovers in the eyes of the community. The dinner parties that they gave in Kensington and Bel Air were notorious. Guests always brought guests. The police always seemed to hear of them.

"How could you ever let him out of your sight?" Glenn asked.

"Dear boy, I had it so many times it wasn't new anymore. And the novelty wore off early on. Harry's cock was such an inelegant thing. You couldn't quite get your lips around it, and it took forever for it to get hard."

The salacious detail delighted the young man. "Be still my heart," he said and smiled, then feigned swooning by lifting his fist to his forehead in a showy fashion.

The gesture provoked a loud laugh from Adrian. "But when it was hard," he added. "Harry certainly knew what to do with it."

◆

Adrian watched the rehearsal until it was time for his scene. On the set, he sat in the old armchair, pretending to watch a television. He delivered his line effortlessly. When the director called it a wrap, Lissa mentioned that sound effects would be added for the taping.

"Sound effects?" Adrian asked.

"The gas," Lissa said and laughed. Adrian disliked her laugh as much as he did Candy's, though this one had a little too much intelligence behind it, as if Lissa were laughing down at him.

Adrian walked back to his trailer dejected, his stomach grumbly from the pastry and the acidity of the coffee. His agent had been able to negotiate two things properly for this fiasco—a private dressing room and featured billing. Adrian stepped inside the trailer and saw the glass of whiskey on his counter. He had forgotten all about the man in the mirror.

"Go ahead," a voice said. "Have it."

The man in the mirror was younger than the one he had seen in his trailer before, but considerably older than the youth he had been with in the costume room. He was The Widower. The Man Who Was Left Behind.

"It was Harry's choice not to tell anyone he was sick," Adrian said. "I was only honoring what he wanted."

"So you concocted an elaborate rouse," the man said. "A liver disease. How convenient. In front of the world with your lover dying of AIDS, you went before the cameras and said it was a *liver* problem and you were stepping in to save the day. No one trusted you after that. Not even your *own* community."

Harry's star turn as a gadabout in a BBC miniseries had brought him a lot of notoriety. And the rumors started. Especially when he decided not to act anymore. He didn't like the way he was aging, wasting away daily before his eyes because of a virus in his blood. His retirement was a way to gracefully step aside and get better. Only he didn't. Didn't get *better*.

"We were great friends," Adrian said. He felt a weakness in his chest and voice.

"That's what you told the press," the man in the mirror said. "He was furious with you. Taking his part before he was cold in the grave."

Adrian lucked out when Harry turned down a role and it was offered to him instead. Adrian took the part and it was end of things between them. When Adrian left to film the movie, Harrold died.

"He turned it down."

"And you stepped over him to take it. With him on his deathbed."

"But I made up for it, didn't I? After he died," Adrian said to the man in the mirror. "I did all that campaigning against Clause 28. It was a big change for me."

"Ah, yes," the man in the mirror said. "It was suddenly very fashionable to be gay and angry. It served you well." The man nodded at the glass. "Take a sip. You deserve it."

"Think I will," Adrian said. "Think I will."

He laughed or thought he laughed. He looked up at the mirror but the man was gone. Adrian turned around, but there was no one else in the room. No one in the mirror. And no drink waiting for him.

He felt suddenly tired. The heartburn from the pastry and the coffee was overwhelming. He went to the chair by the air conditioner and stretched out his feet and fell asleep.

He was woken a few hours later by a knock at the door. It was Candy dropping off his clothes for the taping. On the sweatshirt were a yellow stain and a red stain. She laughed when she handed them to him. That obnoxious, irritating giggle.

Adrian dressed in the sweatshirt and pants. In front of the mirror, he waited for his image to appear. He was glad when he realized he was finally alone.

A few minutes later, however, Glenn arrived with a makeup kit and Adrian sat in front of the mirror while the younger man added more years to his face.

"Gay men always have younger complexions," Glenn said. "Don't you think?"

The comment rattled Adrian, but he held his displeasure in the tightness of his cheeks. He didn't like being marginalized into a category. The *gay* category. Even after all these years, after all that had happened. He never denied that he was a homosexual when asked. That was the concession he had made in his life. But he was an actor first. Not a *gay* actor.

Adrian distracted himself from the rising bad mood by focusing again on the movement of Glenn's bicep as he brushed powder across his face. *What would I do if I could have another chance?* he thought. *Another man. Another lover. I would dote on him and make him happy.*

"My lover and I are having some friends over on Saturday," Glenn said. "We'd love it if you would come."

"Hmmmm... Saturday?" Adrian lifted his eyes and found Glenn's.

"We know you're busy, but it would be a lot of fun."

"Sounds lovely," Adrian answered. "I would love it."

Glenn wrote down his address on the front page of Adrian's script. Adrian nodded and smiled. *An invitation. An invitation to something fun.*

When Glenn left, Adrian stood and stretched through some yoga poses, trying to relieve the lingering indigestion that haunted him. He felt optimistic and desirable because of Glenn's invitation, though still pessimistic about the upcoming taping and his ridiculous line. He felt the warring moods in his mind, which was when the man in the mirror returned.

"Nothing will come of it," the man in the mirror said to Adrian. He was again the old fellow he had seen that morning. The old fellow who had arrived on set to tape a lousy television pilot. And the glass of whiskey was back on the counter.

"Why can't you be happy for once in your life?" Adrian asked his image.

"Oh, I've had pleasure," the man said. "Plenty of that."

"No, *happy*."

"Happy?"

"Happy."

"To happiness, then..." the man said. He lifted the glass of whiskey off the counter and took a sip. Adrian felt the fire burn in his stomach. The man in the mirror smiled and took another sip, rattled the ice in the glass and drank some more. As he swallowed, an ice cube stuck in the man's throat. Adrian saw the man's expression change in the mirror. That horror of disbelief that something like this could happen. In his own chest, Adrian felt a burning fire and clutched at it dramatically.

He fell to the floor and felt a tremor of terror. He let go of a large bubble of gas that had been trapped inside him all day. It rumbled and burst through him with an awful sound and a dreadful stench. This had all been a mistake, he thought, clutching his chest and gasping for air. *An awful mistake.* This was not how he had imagined his life would end. This was no way to end a brilliant career.

THE BLOOMSBURY NUDES

I had overlooked the article until Keith pointed it out to me. "Didn't you know him? Was this the same guy?"

The article was buried at the bottom of one of those inside pages of the *Times* devoted to international news. It was about a sixty-two-year-old man whose body had washed ashore on the Amalfi coast. The dead man was a "former dancer" named Jared Tremaine.

Keith recognized the name because I had told him about Tremaine's relationship with the artist Clive Elliott and the strange events surrounding Elliott's death in London in 1981. Keith was something of a crime and mystery buff and a would-be novelist, always on the lookout for something or someone to write about. I had once thought that the details of Clive's life would interest him. Keith, never one to take any route I suggested, was more interested in the ex-dancer than the forgotten artist (which, in my estimation, didn't set him apart from anyone else). Jared Tremaine was a notoriously pretty man and widely admired as much for his looks as his talent. I remember the first time I saw him I felt as if God had sent an angel to torment me; I couldn't take my eyes off of him, but there was also the fear that if I looked too long I would become blind from his beauty. When I read the newspaper article Keith had discovered I realized that I had not heard anything of Jared in more than a decade. Since 1981, when I had last seen him, I had learned Jared was in Barcelona, choreographing parts of the Opening Ceremonies for the Olympics, and then, later, in Japan, where he was said to be directing commercials and music videos starring American and British pop music stars. I had filed our friendship away as a memory, but something about Jared—and Elliott's death—had nonetheless clung to Keith's memory. Keith was something of a romantic; he could never think evil of anyone or of anyone as evil (perhaps another reason why his "true crime" stories lean more toward tragedy than horror).

Keith and I live in Somerset, not far from the Burnham seafront. I'm fifty-two now and run a gift shop, a favorite of the locals in search of a special present for one of their more peculiar (or flamboyantly queer) friends. There is an array of unusual souvenirs on the shelves—cheap, locally made snow globes, shot glasses, and ash trays in case a tourist stumbles out of one of the arcades or pleasure parks and happens to find his way into our store. Keith, my business partner and lover (who is also in his early fifties), does most of the selling and dealing with customers; I tend to spend my time flipping through catalogs and brochures and visiting wholesale markets in search of the right items for our store or a special customer, sometimes bringing back an inexpensive antique that Keith will greet with a sigh and a roll of his eyes and an exasperated remark that the item will be unlikely to find a potential buyer. We're both collectors, and we've amassed quite an assortment of books, albums, movies, and *tchotchkes* that forever need dusting. We've done our best to keep abreast of the rapidly changing technology of camera cellphones, plasma screens, and iPods; we've even installed broadband at the store so we can swiftly cruise the 'Net when customers are scarce. We're the essence of the aging, queer British couple—suburban, bickering, and devoted to each other.

Twenty-seven years ago, however, I was single and in my twenties and determined to live and work in London as an openly gay artist. It was 1980 and I knew a few things about art history—I was appreciative of the Impressionists, frustrated by the Cubists, disliked most of the Modernists, and fell in love with the simplicity of the Pop artists. And I knew a few things about gay history—artists such as Michelangelo, da Vinci, Caravaggio, and Dürer were already part of the queer pantheon and scholars were hotly contesting the sexuality of John Singer Sargent and Thomas Eakins. And by 1980 Gilbert and George had successfully morphed from cheeky performance artists to being seriously considered *artistes* with *Dirty Word Pictures* and *The Penis*, Francis Bacon was drawing John Edwards, Andy Warhol was already an international legend, and David Hockney was experimenting with Polaroid pictures. But true art to me that year was the unmasking of the beauty of the male body via the Bruce Weber photographs in the American monthly magazine *GQ* and the hyperbutch illustrations of Tom of Finland that were reprinted in the London bar rags and imported porn slicks I could find in an underground specialty shop in Charring Cross. Clones ruled my imagination and libido and a male nude could suspend time for me, freeze me in place as I examined every nook and crack, yearning to understand both sex and love with another man. And even though I hadn't abandoned my desire to be a serious artist, I was sidelined by having to make a living as an assistant graphic designer at an advertising firm in Soho. This was long before Adobe and Quark and Photoshop made everything a lot easier and a little bit more fun, so most of my days were spent hunched over a mat with an X-Acto knife or a razor blade trying to make everything even and line up. I seldom got to draw anything at that miserable job. But every week I had a little more money in my pocket and on the weekends I went out dancing at whatever gay club was fashionable, be it drag or disco—Embassy, Regine's, Prince Albert's, Euston Tavern, The Bell, or Heaven.

I had known Clive Elliott as a teacher when I studied drawing with him in 1976 in Paris during a summer break from my college studies at Furness. At the time, my parents had wanted me to be anywhere but London, and I had ended up going to the university close to our home in Lancaster and working part-time at my father's lighting shop, mostly delivering lamps or helping install fixtures. My parents had acquiesced to my French sojourn, in part, because I had doodled a graphic of a winged foot for an ad contest sponsored by a local shoe company, which had been awarded first prize and printed in the newspaper, and I had expressed an interest in pursuing this artistic side of myself; and, in larger measure, to keep me from traveling to the raucous Liverpool clubs with my mates and their rock band and getting into all sorts of trouble. Drawing, as it were, was the lesser evil of the arts, and Paris, my parents believed, would be an educational experience for me.

Clive Elliott had made a splash at the beginning of the Pop Art phenomenon in Britain with a series of stark silhouettes of everyday items, such as familiar brand-name Coke bottles and Kleenex boxes, deceptively simple-looking paintings that were quickly snapped up by the Tate and the Modern in New York, though over the years they have been relegated to basement storerooms. The deep impression they made on the other artists of the movement has long been forgotten, particularly their impact on Americans such as Andy Warhol and Roy Lichtenstein, who seized on the notion of illustrating everyday items and took it to the next level. By the 1970s, Elliott had settled into being a respected and requested illustrator and designer—sometimes at work on a children's book, other times on the set design for an opera company—leaving behind the limelight and the large canvases unless something like a hefty commission determinedly yanked him back into it.

In Paris, in Clive's drawing class, we drew silhouettes of objects, learning how to form lines and shapes. I had had little artistic training other than a few school classes and a limited experimentation with my self-taught doodling.

I felt that Clive knew I was one of the least talented pupils of the class. And the truth of the matter was I only wanted to be in Paris in order to explore its nightlife and get away from the prying eyes of my parents. Clive was fifty-six that year and had long before shed his own lithe silhouette. He was arrogant and conceited, like most great artists become when exposed to fame, but warm and insecure as a puppy once he felt comfortable with you and the bitter façade was dropped. In the classroom he could be condescending to his students. "I agree it is pretty, dear, but is it art?" was his favorite way of judging a drawing. As an art instructor he felt that a line should be seamless, even when it was shadowed, and there was always something about my work that was not straight enough for his liking—it was all too bent and disconnected to please him. "You seem to have lost control of your hand somewhere," he would say to me, leaning into my sketch. "Right about here. And here. And here. And *here.*"

Clive would have disregarded my drawing talent entirely had I not caught Jared's attention.

Clive had met Jared in 1973 when Jared was twenty-nine and dancing with a Paris ballet troupe and already something of a legendary beauty, more breathtaking in person than he was onstage. Jared's parents had met in the Dutch Resistance and he had been born shortly after the end of World War II. He did not begin studying dance until he was sixteen, when he accompanied his younger sister Sabine to a dance class and was offered a small fee by the instructor to stay and help spot and lift the girls. Jared knew right away that he had no desire to "augment a ballerina" and he embarked on his own journey of pirouettes, jetés, and leaps into the history books. He trained with Roland Petit and the Paris Opera Ballet and made his debut at nineteen as the *Nutcracker* Prince. He might have gone overlooked were it not for the fact that the troupe had announced an "international exchange program" that would send Jared and three other dancers to Russia for a year in order to study with Pushkin and perform at the Kirov Ballet. That plan never materialized because of concerns over defections of the Russian dancers being sent to France, and Jared went to Vienna instead, where his Romeo in a production of the Berlioz ballet created a sensation and he caught the attention of film director Franco Zeffirelli. Zeffirelli flew Jared to Rome and screen tested him for a film version he was preparing of the Shakespeare play, but Jared's English was abysmal and the director found him "too distractingly beautiful." While in Italy Jared made a small film for Alberto Maresca, one of the lesser known Italian New Wave auteurs, and he returned to Paris where he danced *Swan Lake* to great acclaim and became a star attraction. Five years later, a motorbike accident in Cannes while he was the guest of a wealthy financier—Jared was riding down a slope in a chilly rain when the bike slid out from under him—caused a fracture in his ankle and sidelined him for months because the injury proved difficult to heal. Out of the limelight, he soon found his celebrity eclipsed by the Russian dancer Mikhail Baryshnikov, four years his junior.

That summer I spent in Paris, 1976, Jared was dancing less and less because of a reinjury to his ankle the season before. He was thirty-two and, in between physical therapy sessions, he was doing what most aging male ballet dancers do, looking for ways to expand his performance career with acting classes and modeling. Jared showed up in our drawing class one day to be drawn. He slipped out of his jeans and T-shirt and Clive, admiringly, told the seven of us, to depict Jared as a silhouette. "Dear ones, take this magnificent specimen of *Homo sapiens* in front of you and attempt to have your line and shape contain all his beauty," Clive instructed the class. Like many male ballet stars Jared was tall and slender and athletic, with full, deeply muscled buttocks and a generous crotch. He was a good head taller than myself and Clive—slightly over six feet—and he had the smoothest skin imaginable, which would have made him feminine and ghostlike were it not for his extraordinary physique and the black coloration of his hair and eyes.

I didn't know anything of Jared except that he was extraordinary looking. I understood little about gay relationships then—I was twenty and had only had a handful of sexual encounters with men, and I could get an erection at the mere hint of another man's flesh. An "open relationship" between two gay men was simply a foreign and mystical concept to me—I had never even had a boyfriend. I remember I stood in front of my easel that day shifting from one leg to the other as I tried to see Jared's body as one continuous line, hoping to hide my sexual ache and avoid revealing too much about my own tortured interior. I wanted to know Jared, know what it was like to be with him and to *be* him, the envy of other men, to float easily through life and unabashedly shed my clothes for a roomful of strangers and be admired, and here I was instead, a frustrated young man with a charcoal pencil in my hand, nervously sweating, flustered and dizzy from the nearness of Jared's body.

Jared must have detected my squirming because I honestly don't believe my silhouette of him was striking enough to get his notice. But there was also something strange and restless about him—as if he were about to bolt at any moment and the only way he could remain in place was to find something curiously interesting about someone and detect the adoration reflected back at him. At the end of class we started a conversation while Clive was being monopolized by one of the more aggressive and less gifted female students, a petite Franco-Asian woman named Chloe who had made it clear she did not want to spend her class time drawing silhouettes.

"I will hear of that later," Jared said to me. His English was heavily accented and the tone of his voice, like many Europeans', emanated as much from his nose as his throat.

"He complains about us?" I asked, trying not to look at Jared dressing but unable to look elsewhere.

"To draw more attention to him," Jared answered and smiled. It was a gorgeous smile, the kind that deserved to be painted for all its mysterious complexity, not as a line but as a sharply detailed portrait like the *Mona Lisa,* "Involved with only him, you know?" he added. "What artist is not, yes? We are creatures of our design and not flattering, no?"

We began an awkward conversation in French—my vocabulary was minimal, even after years of classes. He asked me where I was staying in Paris and I launched into a flustered description of our neighborhood and the austere qualities of the dormitory where the students were housed. I was breathing heavily, trying to concentrate on my French and trying not to swoon like a girlish fool.

"There is a pleasant café near you," he said. "Café Florizelle. Meet me there. We have espresso and a long talk, yes?"

Outside the classroom Jared flirted and brazenly held my hand at the table, flattering me as *"la vraie beauté,"* and *"prachtige kunstenaar."* He thought my sketch was the best in the class. He asked me about my family and *"Angleterre"* and he spoke fondly of his sister Sabine, who was teaching history at a school in Ghent. He followed me back to the dormitory and we began an affair that lasted until the end of the summer came and I returned to Lancaster. I call it affair because I also had no understanding then of what a sex buddy was—I could not emotionally disconnect myself from my partner during sex as Jared so easily did. And his body soon became more familiar to me than my own, capturing my desires and imagination more than any masterpiece on display at the Louvre. I ached to hear the sound of his voice, watch his lips move and his struggle for words as he criticized something he had recently seen—a soprano's aria or an actor's performance, watch the way he used his hands and wrists to express himself, smell the sweet-sour pulse of his breath as he leaned in closer to me to make his point clearer. My notebooks from those days are full of sketches of him. I had tried to capture the full beauty of his body as he lay stretched out or curled up on my bed, but I soon settled for smaller, more detailed portraits of his face and hands and legs. There is even a sequence of portraits of his face as I tried to render his expressions during the moments before, during, and after his orgasm—that rush of painful pleasure as it soared from his chest to his eyes. I can look at them today and still weep from the sheer beauty of his body and find myself amazed that I had been so close to it. I was ready to give up everything for him—to be with him in whatever way he wanted—a slave, an errand boy, the adoring fan, and yes, even his fuck buddy—anything as long as he did not leave me. "I am with Clive, you see," he would say gently when I protested every time he made an effort to leave my dorm room. "You break my heart when you depart me. You will leave me for another lover."

I leave *him*? I doubted that and sulked in his absence, trying to reconstruct his day away from me, obsessively wondering where he was and who else he was meeting and why. I often overlooked Jared's moodiness and depression because I was so overwhelmed by my own, and when it did surface in him and demand to be accounted for—that black despair of misunderstanding—I played the clown, or the fool, or the seducer, anything so he would not want to leave me. Jared's depression often had as much to do with Clive as it did with dancing—or not dancing—"He does not understand," Jared would moan and press his beautiful face into his hands while we were at a café and pretend to weep in a dramatic, theatrical fashion. "He does not *get it*," he would whisper as he pressed his lips against my chest if we were in my narrow little bed. "What it feels like to fly—*om te vliegen*—to have a control over the body—*ascenseur à un fantôme*—to be, how do you say it? Possessed by a spirit."

It was clear to me that Jared loved Clive and that Clive reciprocated that love, and it often left me feeling like an outsider. I ceased to exist when I was with both of them, because they were a couple and I was their friend, or student, or secret amour. My last weeks in Paris, Clive must have learned about my affair with Jared because I began to receive little invitations from him, sometimes during class—"Dennis, there's an exhibit I want to see in the Marais, can you walk with me after class to find the gallery?"—other times through a phone message scrawled on a piece of paper and shoved underneath my door—"Mr. Elliott called and asked if you can go to the opera tonight." Clive was always a gentleman, never trying to put a move on me or ask me of my feelings for Jared, and we became good friends. He'd grown up not far from Lancaster, in the Lake District, so we also had that in common. "My father used to deliver packages from the train station to Beatrix Potter," he told me. "She was quite old then and had given up publishing her stories and drawings because she was helping the farms and determined to save the land from developers. But if I accompanied my father in his van, she would always draw a little animal on a piece of paper for me to travel back home with—a small rabbit, perhaps, or a duck. She was my introduction into the world of art."

Two years later, in 1978, after spending agonizing time in classes in marketing and economics at Lancaster, I moved to London with a roommate, despite my parents' disappointment that I would not stay closer to them and eventually take over my father's shop. I was following a college mate I had become obsessively infatuated with after my summer fling with Jared, but after six weeks of our living together in the city in a tiny flat near Russell Square, Geoffrey announced that he was moving into a bigger place with his new boyfriend. I was both heartbroken and relieved and determined to make it on my own. My experience with Jared had left me wiser and stronger.

But I was thrilled when Jared's letter arrived at the beginning of 1980 to say that he and Clive were moving back to London. Clive was planning to design the sets for a West End play that was to star Jared. Whether Jared got the part in the play on his own talent or charisma, or through the aid of Clive's intervention or participation, I don't know, but Clive had promised the producer and director that he would create a bold, minimalist look for the play, designing the sets and costumes and any related merchandising materials.

It wasn't long, however, before the play's production budget had escalated out of control and a major investor had fallen through and the production was cancelled, but Clive and Jared still thought that living in London for a while would reinvigorate their careers, and Clive secured a teaching position at the University of London. Jared was also going to give choreography a try, working with a small avant-garde dance company and offering "master classes" for promising students.

Clive and Jared should have become as famous a gay couple as Benjamin and Peter or Gertrude and Alice, but too many personal setbacks and tragedies intervened and prevented this from happening and the public seldom got a chance to witness the full beauty of their relationship. I had no idea what part I was going to play for Jared when he arrived in London—resurrected lover or an ex-fling turned friend. I was still in love with him—I'm still in love with him today. Jared was my first love, which was why the painful news of his death in Italy unnerved me when Keith had presented the newspaper article to me, but by the time Jared and Clive arrived in London that fall I had progressed from wanting to make love to Jared's body to wanting to help him love himself and be happy. Jared did not exactly push me away, but he remained aloof and detached and there was no hint of wanting to resume our affair, and I began to have a closer friendship with Clive, introducing him to the better Indian restaurants in Bloomsbury and the art supply store on Tottenham Street. Occasionally, I would hear secondhand of Jared's depression through one of Clive's accounts, but I knew it was not from any regret over our affair or our diminishing friendship and more from the fact that Jared's career as a performer seemed to be drawing to an end whether he tried to pursue it or not.

◆

I'd love to blame the events of what happened that year on the townhouse Clive and Jared settled into on Gordon Square, not far from the British Museum. It was clearly too large and well beyond their means, one of the last buildings erected on the west side by Thomas Cubitt sometime in the mid-1850s. Their staff consisted of a housekeeper and a cook who showed up on sporadic days I could never figure out, their salaries paid for by the university, who had leased the house to Clive. At first glance the interior might have seemed like that of any grand, upper-crust quarters—not quite as extravagant as Apsley or Leighton or Spencer House, but certainly filled with antiques, curios, and relics of the Empire. But there was also something deeply troubling about its interior and furnishings. The entrance foyer was laid out with a swirl of black stones that swept up into a dark circular staircase and looked like the sprawling limbs of a giant tree. Above was a mock-domed ceiling flamboyantly painted in a Renaissance style with a battle scene between angels and demons. At one point the house had belonged to a colleague of Aliester Crowley and a member of the Hermetic Order of the Golden Dawn. Small touches of the dark arts popped out of nowhere—a sepia portrait of a frightened woman in a tarnished frame sealed with a ringlet of hair and pressed flowers, a large gilt mirror in the shape of a hexagram, an obelisk at the center of a paneled levitation box being used as a side table. The parlor was filled with gorgeously illustrated books on religion, mysticism, magic, and the occult, leather-bound volumes of *The Book of the Law, The Equinox, The Secrets of Conjuring, Deceptive Conceptions, Malleus Maleficarium, Clavis Salomonis, Pseudomonarchia Daemonum,* and early issues of *The Magic Circular, The Criterion,* and *The Tatler.* The lamps were shaded and fringed so that shadows of sickly colors filled most of the rooms.

There was medieval armor and shields and swords and mounted antlers and tusks and animal-skin rugs. A bayonet hung on a wall that Clive had been told was used in the American Revolution. The previous renters had been a succession of scholars and professors and explorers, each leaving behind his own bizarre touches: exotic daggers and snuffboxes and tapestries and lanterns. One resident had been a noted collector of magician's ephemera— there were small chests full of disappearing coins and scarves and gilded cages that had once been used on stages around the world and where now perched an assortment of stuffed doves and canaries. In every room there was a sense that someone was watching you and you were never alone—eyes stared out from grim photographs and gray marble sculptures and mounted animal heads, from behind wrought iron spokes or inside engravings and inlaid patterns on the sides and lids of wooden boxes, as if you were constantly in the presence of distressed and imprisoned spirits. The upper-floor rooms were equally ornate and disturbing, but Clive had cleared out a guest room and turned it into a study where his drawing desk, shipped from his Paris apartment, was placed, and Jared had achieved a similar effect in a large third-story room to create a space to exercise and dance.

"Everything in this place has a distinct history," Clive said to me the first time I came by for dinner. "This, for instance," he said, touching a chipped clay fragment of the face of the Buddha, whose chiseled-out eyes made it look soulless, "is from Afghanistan. Discovered by a French Catholic archeologist digging in a Muslim country."

"This belonged to Herr Wingard, the royal conjurer, almost a century ago," Jared added, reaching for an antique cane that rested inside an urn beside several black umbrellas. He tapped it on the ground and the cane changed colors—from a brown wood to a deep blue. He tapped it again and tossed it in the air and it changed into a bouquet of silk flowers, certainly one of the brighter, and less ominous artifacts within the house.

"And I particularly like this curio," Clive said, lifting a block of stone that was carved on the underside with a map to make a print. "The Seal of Solomon. Rumored to summon demons. It would be rare to find this as a woodcut—but carved in stone, it is priceless."

"We could retire if we found the right buyer for it," Jared explained.

"And face the wrath of God in the process," Clive added with a light laugh.

I'd love to lay blame for what happened on one of those relics, or even on one of those *objets d'art* Clive and Jared brought back to the house on their own. I had not known they were collectors of dark curiosities and when I asked Jared when it had started, he answered that it had only begun recently, since they had arrived in London. In that time, they had found a marble chess set with carved gargoyles as pawns in South Kensington and at the flea market in Notting Hill they had purchased a bronze figure of Osiris, holding the crook and flail and wearing a braided beard with a curled tip and the atef crown. But the truth of it is, I was partly to blame because I was the one who brought Bart Pearson to the house for dinner, and Bart was dark and curious and about as handsome a man as you could find anywhere.

I had met Bart at a pub in Islington and we'd had sex three or four times, but I was smart enough by then to know that I couldn't fall in love with him because he was the kind of man who wasn't interested in a commitment to a guy like me. But I loved showing Bart off to whomever I could and he loved being on display. Bart was tall, dark, broad-shouldered, and chiseled with muscles and furred with black hair—sideburned and goateed on his face and spread-eagled across his chest. A Tom of Finland clone breathed into life. I had tried to get him an interview as a model for a designer jean ad but the account executive on the team took one look at the Polaroid photo I had taken of Bart and proclaimed him "too bloody sexy" (and then asked for his phone number).

Bart wasn't conscious of the power of his looks, though he did like getting compliments; he also wasn't interested in going out with less appealing guys—no fats, femmes, or geezers need apply, no matter how much money was waved in his direction. He wasn't conceited or vain, just young and choosy like many gay men his age. I wouldn't say he was dim-witted, more easy going and unconcerned; much of the conversation you figured might be going over his head—stuff like politics and stock prices and theater trivia—was really being consciously tuned out and considered inconsequential. He was self-focused and a creature of habit, not roaming far from his flat, even when he was cruising—he liked spending time at the gym, playing football on Saturday mornings with his mates, helping his mum out during the week, and hanging out at the local pub at night. He liked to be around people who liked to be around him and in that regard he was no different than Clive or Jared.

Clive and Jared took an immediate liking to him, in large part because of his unspoiled simplicity. Jared more so, I knew. I soon learned from Bart, of course, what was happening between him and Jared. They would meet up at Bart's flat at night—Jared telling Clive he was going to the park, or for a walk to Russell Square where he might stop in to say hello to me, but actually hopping on his motorbike and cruising over to Islington to have sex with Bart in his tiny flat above a fish and chips takeaway. Other times, Bart would finish work—he did an early morning delivery route for convenience stores—and he'd park his van in front of the house on Gordon Square and pop in for a quick visit with Jared if Clive was away at the office. Since I knew what both he and Jared were like in bed—Jared passive and encasing, Bart eager and assertive, it wasn't difficult for me to summon up images of them together—Jared's long beautiful legs thrown up over Bart's wide shoulders, his buttocks swelling and rising off the bed as Bart's grip tightened and lifted to find a deeper or more pleasurable position. I could see the sheen of sweat gathering in the hollow of Jared's neck, smell the rank woodsy cologne Bart had a preference for when he thought he needed to make a special impression, and I knew how Jared would grasp for Bart's meaty arms just before he reached an orgasm.

Since Clive and Jared were so open about their "openness" I did not expect any problems would arise because of Jared's newfound infatuation with Bart, and I thought that, like his other affairs, this one would play itself out with time. I did suspect that something darker and more sinister was at work when I met Clive for dinner one night at a new Spanish restaurant that had opened on Charlotte Street and I asked him about the progress of his new drawings.

"I'm afraid this is all I've been able to do the last month," Clive said and reached for a briefcase he had carried from his office at the university. He slipped out a few sketches. He looked older and tired—worried semicircles had appeared beneath his eyes—and his hand trembled slightly as he handed me the drawings.

On top was a pencil sketch of a nude young man reclining on a bed. I was amazed that the body was so familiar to me—the dark hairy legs, the hirsute chest, the muttonchop sideburns, and goatee.

"I didn't know Bart posed for you," I said.

"He hasn't," Clive answered dryly.

The technique was different from the flat, stationary, and cartoonish style Clive normally used. The lines were broken and the effect gave the drawings more animation and passion. I flipped through the other sketches. There were of the same man, in a variety of sexual positions with another young man—long-legged and slenderly athletic, with the same balding pattern on his head as Jared. There was an inherent motion of desire that was seldom apparent in Clive's finished drawings. The final sketch was of Jared alone, seated on a bed with a look of despair. It was exactly as I had imagined Bart and Jared together in their tryst.

"Is this all imagined?" I asked. "Or were you a polite voyeur?"

"Hardly," Clive answered. "It's copied."

I gave him a quizzical look to show I didn't understand. He took one of the sketches out of my hand and pointed to the leggy young man. "That's me, not Jared. And this fellow is not Bart. His name was Theodore Rushton."

I wasn't following his logic. "What do you mean?"

"Did you know I once posed for Duncan Grant?"

"The Bloomsbury artist?"

Clive nodded. "I was eighteen. He picked me up on the train. He had a studio not far from here, at the back of Fitzroy Street, that had once been Whistler's studio. It was around 1938 and we had a friendly little romp and then he asked to draw me." He laughed and added, "It was all very illegal and pornographic and I was delighted that someone took a fancy to me. Duncan used to pass his nude sketches along to friends like party treats. I posed for him several times, alone and with a fellow named Theodore Rushton, who was an acquaintance of Edward le Bas. I think I've still got one or two of those drawings in the Paris flat."

"I don't understand."

"Neither do I exactly. It looks like Bart and Jared, but it's not."

"Are you sure you're not projecting something here?"

"Not at all. Teddy and I became involved with each other outside of Duncan's studio. I was living in a room above a store on Parker Street and spending my time shuttling between the Museum and the National Portrait Gallery, sketching. My father thought it was silly that I wanted to be a painter, but since I had told him I was coming to London to learn cartography he felt that I was entering an admirable field and would have a necessary talent if we went to war. Teddy was one of the most beautiful men in London. He was the son of one of Roger Sage's groomsmen at Marbleton Place."

"I don't know the name. Sage?"

Clive nodded. "Sage was from a wealthy Devonshire family. His great-grandfather had invented some kind of piston that everyone needed and the family was extremely well off. Roger Sage had been one of Duncan Grant's first lovers, caught up in that whole Strachey-Keynes melodrama. Sage and Strachey had a thing, too, if I'm not mistaken. Sage only dabbled in painting, which was why no one has ever really heard of him—he wasn't a part of the Bloomsbury set. In fact, they abhorred him—though not publicly. Only privately. But it was Sage, in fact, who had sketched Duncan nude first when he was eighteen and passed it on to his cousin Lytton, who wasn't amused by it at all. In fact, he was infuriated by it—as liberal as he was, Lytton was still something of a prude now and then—particularly when it came to one of his favorites, such as Duncan. And Lytton hated Sage because he was a great champion of anything having to do with the occult. Lytton was cynical of everything. Duncan escaped falling under Sage's spell—or being cursed by it—by remaining friends with him.

"Sage became more malevolent as he aged—he was notorious for instigating all sorts of sexual rituals under the influence of one drug or another. He taught Crowley a few things, too, if I'm not mistaken. Sage and Crowley passed around lovers the same way Duncan passed around his naughty little drawings. But Sage was very possessive of Teddy, more so than of any other man he was ever involved with. He was more than thirty years older than Teddy and had such a dark influence over him. He had created everything about Teddy, from paying for his education to fashioning his appearance. Teddy was like a beautiful wild beast, moody one moment, amiable the next. Sage refused to let Edward le Bas—another artist and collector—draw Teddy because he thought the fellow had no talent, so Edward suggested Duncan do a private drawing of Teddy for Sage. Sage thought it was the most delightful and wicked thing he had ever heard of—taunting an aging, old lover by sending him his newer, much younger one. But Duncan was a lot smarter than Sage. Sage hadn't expected that I would be thrown into the mix.

"When we met at Duncan's studio for that first portrait session, Teddy was desperate to leave Sage—and he would, for days at a time, holed up in my little room or at Edward's studio in Chelsea. He finally became so distraught that he confessed everything about our affair to Sage and said he was leaving him to live with me. He wanted us to go to Ireland together, or America— any where to get away from Sage—and the War—the Continent was going through such dramas because of Hitler and the Nazis. Then Parliament introduced the National Service Act and he registered for service. We were suddenly in the War and Teddy was gone. One day he just upped and left to fight. It devastated Sage. And it devastated him when Teddy was one of the casualties of Dunkirk. Sage blamed me for Teddy leaving. For Teddy's death. I think he would have blamed me for the War, if he could have. He had no idea how devastated *I* was. Sage had always been a heavy user of whatever was at hand. Opium. Heroin. Cocaine. He died during the last days of the blitz. May 10, 1941. It was never established if it was due to the shock of his house being bombed or from an overdose. His body was found unscathed in the rubble of his home."

"Why draw this now? After all these years?"

"Something's triggered it, I'm sure. Something about being back in London, walking through the same streets again. Maybe something in that house where we're staying. All those eyes looking at me all the time—you were so right about that—very unnerving once you realize it. And something familiar about Bart probably resurrected even more memories, because he does look so much like Teddy."

"You should try to work on something different," I suggested. "Inanimate. Without feeling. Go back to the silhouettes. It's what you do best."

"Perhaps," Clive answered. "Though there is some joy within this tug of memories."

◆

I had another taste of suspicion that all was not well when about ten days later I arranged to meet Clive and Jared at Sotheby's. One of Clive's early silhouette paintings—*The Wine Bottle with Glass*—was up for sale and Clive was curious to see how it had held up. Clive had telephoned me at the office and thought the outing would be good for him; he had taken my suggestion to heart and thought a new round of silhouettes might make an admirable new project. "And if I'm going to be so damned melancholy," he said, "I might as well mope about how damn brilliant I used to be."

On Saturday afternoon at our appointed time, only Jared appeared. "Migraine," he explained about Clive's absence. "*Terrible*," he added in French. "He is becoming *impossible*."

We viewed the auction items and discussed the condition of Clive's painting so we could relay our impressions to him later, then shopped along Bond Street. Jared wanted a new wallet, something thin and sleek that didn't leave a "line" showing against his rear pants pocket. Bart's name only came up once during our outing, when we had strayed into a recessed alcove of a leather store where there were some vests and chaps and some more sexual attire and toys for sale. Jared picked up a small leather band—a cock ring—and said, "I bet Bart would like this."

I agreed—it was dark and simple, and something Bart would appreciate being given.

We had drinks at a pub, but Jared did not elaborate on his relationship with Bart (nor did I want to hear of it) and we avoided discussing Clive. Instead I listened to Jared describe the pupils in his master class, all talentless "*jeune filles avec grandes chaussures*," and sounding more like the critical Clive than the sensitive Jared I had fallen in love with. Then I followed Jared back to Gordon Square, thinking I would visit awhile with Clive, cheer him up with some recaps of a few movies I had seen. Almost at once when we were inside the house Jared made excuses about having to leave because he had forgotten to find a birthday item for one of his new pupils. I knew it was an excuse to meet up with Bart—Bart, at about that time, had finished his soccer game and his visit to his mum, and was probably coming out of the shower, clean and ready for a hook-up with Jared.

As soon as Jared left, I wandered upstairs to look for Clive. I found him in his second floor study, lying on a sofa. His shirt was unbuttoned and untucked, the sleeves rolled up to his elbows. He appeared to be ill and uncomfortable—his eyes were glassy and unfocused—I thought he must have been working and become exhausted because there were scattered pages of drawing paper around the room. I only had a few seconds to detect that they were more sketches of nude men coupling—Bart and Jared or Teddy and Clive—and a few other different-looking men as well.

"Leave," he waved to me, annoyed that I had found and disturbed him. "I cannot see a bloody thing today. *Leave.*"

"Do you need a doctor?" I asked him. "Should I take you to a hospital?"

"*Out,*" Clive ordered. "I can sleep—*or drink*—my way through it."

Unnerved by Clive's anger, I retreated to the hallway, where I had the impression of something holding me in place and observing me. I don't know exactly what feeling it was that drew me to enter upon an exploration of the house; normally, I would have hurried away, particularly since Clive had left me so agitated.

I peered into a bedroom—it was tidy but cluttered with the kind of *tchotchkes* years later Keith and I would find so fascinating—crystal balls, black candlesticks, wicker baskets, dragon-shaped lamps, and a beautiful handmade quilt of five-pointed stars draped across the bed. There was another bedroom equally cluttered, with a large bronze gong suspended between a pair of demon-faced swordsmen. To the side of the room was a stark, large, black-tiled bathroom that felt to me like stepping into a vacuum. I confess that the house displeased me strangely. I was conscious of something powerful and controlling, and for a moment I was lightheaded, as if something had been pulled out of my body. I soon realized I was sweating, my forehead was burning as if I had a fever, and I was suddenly ready to leave but felt like I was pinned in place. In the hallway where I stood hung a series of grim and faded portraits of Edwardian and Victorian aristocrats looking locked up and trapped within their clothes, and I had an imagined flash of unhappy quarrels between the posers, conversations of spiteful jealousies. As

I tugged myself away from them and down the swirling black stone staircase, I spotted a small, carved wooden table on the ground floor near the entry to the parlor, guarding the door like a crouching beast. Sitting on the table beside a vase of dried flowers was a stack of cards, and as I moved closer to it, I noticed the artwork—an elaborate and stylized illustration, like those done by monks centuries before in a medieval monastery. It was only when I lifted the top card and turned it over that I realized it was a tarot deck. On the backside of the card in my hand were a winged, horned devil and an inverted pentagram. The Devil's card. I knew enough of mysticism and the occult to know that a tarot card is never interpreted at face value. But I also knew that I wanted to be out of the house—and that I should warn Clive and Jared that they should leave it, too.

◈

I did my best to counsel them without alarming them. I left messages on their answering machines at the house on Gordon Square saying that I felt there was something seriously odd about it, and that they should move elsewhere because it felt like such an unhealthy and unhappy place. I went to Clive's office and Jared's dance studio to discuss it with them, but they were never there or would not see me—out on an errand, or with a pupil, or not feeling well and holed up "at home and not wanting to be disturbed." I went to the house, clapped that ominous-looking gargoyle knocker over and over against the door and banged with my fists, but no one ever answered it. I sat in the park so I could see the comings and goings in front of the house or at its windows, but no one ever arrived or departed while I waited, not the housekeeper, the cook, nor Bart. Sooner or later I would give up my surveillance, done in by the cold or the rain or my need to return to work. It was as if the house knew it could easily defeat me, and I would arrive back at my flat or my office and make another round of warning calls till one day I realized that I sounded like a madman and I should back off and not bother Clive and Jared any longer.

As it happened, I ran into Bart about a week later coming out of a pub as I was going inside. He looked thin and restless, his eyes darting back and forth as he stood in front of me. "You didn't warn me about the deep mess I would fall into," he said and added a laugh that sounded part observational and part nervous.

"What's been happening? I've been trying to reach Clive or Jared for weeks and I'm not getting anywhere. They seem to be avoiding me."

"Your mates are falling over to the dark side. Setting up little parties for all sorts of kinky fellas. Bondage. Candle wax. Body paint. You name it, they're trying it."

"I don't know what you mean."

"Yeah?" he asked and stubbed his cigarette out with the tip of his boot. I noticed that they were new ones. Black with engraved silver tips and oddly reminding me of the wicked curios on display at the house on Gordon Square.

"Your dancing fella likes to tie me up and taunt me with a few of his toys," he laughed. "Good thing is, I don't mind it—I know how to keep it all fun. But his old man is into some deep shit. I don't want to have to keep waving away the drugs, you get me? Come to think of it, I should tell 'em to add you to the guest list as referee, so nobody steps over the line."

"Are you sure?"

"We could have a lot of fun together again, if you like."

"I mean, are you sure about Clive? And Jared?"

"It's a dark world," he said. "Full of dirty secrets. Guess you just learned a few about your mates."

Even after he had left me, I was sure Bart was mistaken, and I put whatever worry I had about Clive and Jared out of my head because I was upset that I had been clearly dropped from their list of close friends (and I fell into bed with an Indian fellow named Rajan, who lived in a tiny flat behind Euston Station). But the next day, once I was back on my own home turf—my flat—Bart's conversation continued to bother me and I began obsessing again about Clive and Jared because I knew they were pushing me away. I tried reaching them at their various haunts, this time to confront them on their drug use, though rehearsing what I might say, not wanting to sound like a prude—after all, I had gladly shared a joint with both of them more than once.

Toward the end of the week, I took a long lunch and walked by the house and hit the knocker several times, but no one was home, so I walked over to the university and found Clive in a small office napping while pretending to read a book.

"Not sleeping well," he said, when I startled him with a light knock and he recognized me. "That house is like being in a dream factory. All sorts of things haunt me. I'm finding it more relaxing to be here."

"Perhaps you should move," I suggested.

"It's a terrific space," he answered. "And the university is subsidizing most of it. I doubt that I could get that elsewhere."

I offered to take him to lunch and we walked a few blocks to a pub he was fond of. Again, he brought along his briefcase and again he showed me his latest work. Even though I was somewhat prepared for what I would see this time, it was nonetheless startling. The two nude figures were now in a struggle for domination. The first sketch was a basic wrestling scenario, flat and uninspired, like something that could have been found on a Greek vase, but the following ones developed a stronger narrative, the dark-haired fellow submitting to the taller, fairer one, first on his knees, then bound to a chair and gagged. Any hint of romance and seduction was now replaced by the depiction of torture.

"Did this happen?" I asked him.

He gave me a vague look, as if he hadn't realized what he had drawn. "It started with a few wrestling poses for Duncan," he said. "But later on, it grew different. Teddy wanted me to tie him up so that he couldn't leave, but then he'd be begging me to let him go back to Sage. It was hard for me to separate what was real and what was fantasy with him. He wore me out. I finally told him that I couldn't go on. That we had to end it. That was his breaking point. He threatened to kill me. Then kill Sage. Then kill himself. I never saw him after that."

"Does Jared know of these?"

"Jared?" he asked, as if he had forgotten him. "No."

"Has he said he was leaving you?"

"Jared?"

"Has he threatened you? Or Bart?"

"Bart? No. Not that I am aware."

"Has he hinted he's unhappy?"

A flicker of Clive's former personality resumed. "Dear boy, Jared's *always* been unhappy. I've never provided him the self-confidence that dancing—or his fans—have given him. He's taken this whole injury thing rather hard, I must say."

"You should tear these up," I said, handing him back the sketches. That moment I realized that I wanted to save him because I loved him. I loved his talent, his wit, his friendship, his inspiration. And I loved him because I still loved Jared. I couldn't bear to accept what was happening and I owed it to Clive and Jared—and myself—to help Clive get through it. "I can find you a program," I said next. "A clinic, if you need one."

He looked at me with his big brown eyes and said, "I'll pretend I didn't hear that."

"Roll up your sleeve. Show me your arm."

He narrowed his eyes and shifted away from me. "Young man," he said sternly. "I think it's time we part."

◆

I tried to keep up with them, but I also had to work—I wasn't subsidized by a trust fund or a university grant or even by the credit cards of a sugar daddy. But I had no intention of letting Clive simply discard me because he was insulted by my offer of help. I waited a few days after my blowup with Clive and phoned Jared and made dinner plans with both of them for Saturday night, so they knew that I was thinking of them and that I wanted to stay in touch, no matter how they felt about me now. But on a cold, cloudy Friday afternoon, just as I was trying to get everything pending off my desk, I got a call at work. "Dennis?" the caller began in a faint voice. "Dennis? ...Is that you?"

"What is it? ...Clive?"

"Dennis? ...Help?"

I rushed out of my office. A gray mist had settled over the city and I arrived at the house on Gordon Square damp, chilled, and panicked. The front door was locked, and I knocked and pounded but no one answered. I finally jimmied the lock on the servants' entrance below ground and made my way up the workday roots of the grand black staircase.

Clive was not in any of the first-floor rooms. There was a smell of stale cigarettes and booze, as if a party had recently ended, though all of the rooms were neat and tidy as I made a quick check of them. I bounded up the massive, swirling black-stone staircase two steps at a time. I found all three of them in Clive's bedroom. Clive and Jared were in bed, syringes and needles nearby. They were barely conscious. And in a corner of the room, facing the bed, was Bart. Nude, tied to a chair and gagged, his eyes fluttering to stay alive. Scattered on the floor were sketches, mirroring the events that had led up to the present scene.

I untied Bart and called for emergency assistance, waiting for the police and medics to arrive by stretching Bart out on the floor and stroking his hair. I tried not to notice that his body was in the exact position Clive had drawn in that first sketch he had shown me more than seven months before. "Baby, hold on," I said. "Help will be here soon."

There was more explaining needed than I could do on my own. I tried to be as clear as I could to all the authorities and officials who were canvassing the rooms for clues and details. Something in the house had possessed them, driven them all to this evil craziness. The interrogating officer looked at me as though I was the one who was loony.

Clive did not survive, but Bart recovered quickly, echoing my testimony to the officials that it had all been a bit too weird to believe. I stayed with Jared at the hospital until he was released, but Jared never attempted to explain or apologize for anything that had happened, and it was as if I were babysitting a corpse; neither of us had anything to say to the other and whatever emotional thread I felt was still attached to him he had purposely snipped. I couldn't blame him for what had happened so I loved him and hated him, hated what had become of all of us—Clive, Bart, him, and myself.

I was tugged through the next weeks by despair. The newspapers and television programs reported on Clive's death as though it were a scandal. Drugs were seized, more officers arrived with more questions. An inquest was held. Bart's and my account of the strange doings inside the house on Gordon Square were ridiculed by reporters. I skipped the funeral and memorials. Instead, I wandered around London crazed with grief and sorrow. I tried to remember what a decent man Clive had been with me, especially when he discovered how deeply I loved Jared, but there was a sense that my sadness was deserved because I was at fault. I was ashamed that I had been unable to save Clive. I had robbed the world of an immense talent. I had prevented masterpieces and great leaps of insight and the training of future talent. I missed days and days of work to the point of losing my job. I drank too much. I overslept. I couldn't see Bart without breaking into sobs. I finally began to let go one afternoon when my boss told me to "straighten up, or else."

Clive Elliott is probably best remembered today as the promising artist of such iconic art as *The Soda Bottle* or *The Tissue Box*. Jared Tremaine became the executor of Elliott's estate, which is the primary reason why Clive's work has lapsed into obscurity. Jared never danced on stage again and, in part, I believe he blamed this on Clive, though I also believe that whatever artistic spirit had possessed him before—his ethereal yearning to dance—had been robbed from him by an unseen power while he lived in the house on Gordon Square. Bart Pearson did not live beyond the first decade of the AIDS epidemic and his illness and death six years later was the reason why I finally decided it was time to leave London behind. I went through every doctor's appointment and disappointment with him. We'd been best mates since Jared disappeared. I moved away in 1988, after having met Keith on a holiday in Brighton.

A decade later, sometime in 1998, as the power of the Internet was surfacing, I began to roam away from the chat rooms I had become so immediately fond of and into other areas of the Web. I stumbled onto a site that generated free tarot card readings, and learned that the fifteenth card—the Devil—can symbolize temptation and addiction. This triggered a memory and I began researching the Bloomsbury townhouse in Gordon Square that Clive and Jared had briefly rented that awful time in London and learned that the university had torn it down to make way for a new building, though no specific reasons were given for the destruction or what had happened to its contents. I searched for more details on Teddy Rushton and Roger Sage. I did not turn up much more than I already knew, though a few details surfaced, including a photograph of the two men, taken in "the foyer of a house of a friend." In the photograph, behind the two men, was the swirling, ominous black staircase of the house on Gordon Square. And yes, Theodore Rushton looked shockingly handsome and too similar to Bart Pearson for comfort.

After Clive's death and before Jared left town for wherever it was he was headed to—I can't remember the destination, nor did I want to hear about it at that moment—he came round to my flat with Clive's briefcase. "Some day, yes? *Bon art. Richesse,*" he said flatly, when he handed the sketches over to me. *"Peut-être. Une nouvelle simple."* Jared refused to ever see Bart again. When Bart died, I wrote Jared a letter that went unanswered.

My lover Keith still professes more interest in Jared's "true inner beauty" than in any of Clive's lurid sketches that I've buried at the bottom of one of our bedroom drawers. For years he has held on to this romantic vision of Bart and Jared roaming through London by motorbike, so much so, that I have also adopted it as one of my own and I have to remind myself that Clive was always there, too.

"Do you think it was an accident?" I asked Keith over breakfast as I folded up the newspaper to toss into the recycling bin. "Or did he jump to his death?" Jared's abandoned motorbike had been found the day before on the cliffs above Positano. The article had not elaborated on his fame or infamy. His dancing achievements were overlooked; his life with Clive invisible; the scandal in Gordon Square forgotten.

"Amalfi is such a gorgeous area," Keith answered. "One of the most beautiful places I've ever been to. The cliffs are very dramatic the way they hang over the Mediterranean. Like they are leaping out of the sea and into the sky. Rather inspiring and beautiful, I think, not at all depressing and suicidal. I can't imagine why anyone would be unhappy there, dear. Can you?"

ABOUT THE STORIES

THE WOMAN IN THE WINDOW

A few years ago I had noticed a submissions call posted on the Internet for an anthology of short fiction revolving around items that could be found in a curiosity shop. It occurred to me that this might be a good idea for a ghost story about a haunted object. I immediately seized upon the idea of someone finding one of those large, beautiful, glass-domed snow globes in such a store, because I collect them myself. (Most of my snow globes are not of the expensive glass variety, however, but the inexpensive plastic souvenirs found in airport gift shops.) I never submitted the story to the anthology because I did not finish it in time for the editor's deadline—the reading and consideration period comes and goes so quickly for a lot of these speculative fiction markets—and the story languished more in my mind than in words. It wasn't until I read two stories by M.R. James—"The Mezzotint" and "The Haunted Dolls' House"—that I understood what kind of haunting the snow globe could play in the story. I had also recently re-read Truman Capote's *In Cold Blood* for background research for another story I was writing and I wondered if the Clutter's house where the murders took place still existed and if it was ever reported to be haunted. I specifically wanted to write a gay-themed ghost story and it made sense to me to fashion the back story of the haunted house inside the snow globe to have been lived in by two women who had come together to raise their children after abusive relationships with men. It did not occur to me to make the present day couple in the story a gay male couple until my final draft, just before I work-shopped the story with my writing group (as I do all of my fiction), when I realized that the story could make some kind of statement about homophobia in suburbia and the rising influx of alternative families into those neighborhoods.

The village that I had in mind in the story where Tom goes to purchase the snow globe is based on Lahaska, Pennsylvania, in Bucks County, about a ten minute drive from New Hope and the Delaware River. There is a large cluster of specialty shops there that cater to tourists, and I knew there was a children's store, a variety emporium, and across the street an inn. (My parents had stayed there during a period when I was renting a small cottage nearby.) As I recall, that inn is not as architecturally elaborate as the one I envisioned for the story; it is a small farmhouse near the edge of the road which has been made into a nice guesthouse.

The name of the story was originally "The Snow Globe" and was changed to "The Woman in the Window" when it was accepted by the magazine *All Hallows*. A story with the same name had recently been accepted for publication by the magazine and the editor suggested that I rename my story. Steve Berman also gave the story a second life in 2008 by including it in his first edition of *Wilde Stories: The Best of the Year's Gay Speculative Fiction*.

THE INCIDENT AT THE HIGHLANDS INN

The true story behind this tale has haunted me for years since I first heard of it—an ex-boyfriend gunning down a young waiter outside the restaurant where he worked. Originally, I had conceived this incident as part of a larger story that occurred many years after the event had happened, but after rediscovering and re-reading Ambrose Bierce's "An Occurrence at Owl Creek Bridge," about a man's last moments during a hanging that occurred during the Civil War, I decided that the emotional moments of this incident could be used in the same way to reveal these characters' transformations from living beings into ghosts. The images and sounds—light, colors, and gun shots—are specifically heightened in the story—since they will be what is noted by guests in future hauntings at the inn. This story, begun in its earlier form in 2003, was completed in the spring of 2008.

THE COUNTRY HOUSE

For a period of almost two years I lived in a cottage which was on the property of my friends' country house in New Hope, Pennsylvania. The house, set near Aquetong Road, was originally a small stone cottage which had been renovated and expanded several times. The back story of the haunting derives, in part, from my relatives who fought in the Civil War and who lived in the nearby Easton area. I am indebted to the historians who uncovered the gay history embedded in the Civil War, particularly the research and writings of Jonathan Ned Katz. This story was begun in 2006, and revised and published in *Best Gay Romance 2008*, edited by Richard Labonté.

THE AFTER PARTY

One of the spookiest and unsettling elements of a ghost story can be the unexpected impact on a character after he has listened to a ghostly tale. One of my favorite stories is Somerset Maugham's "The Man from Glasgow," about a haunting told by one man to another one night in a bar and its ramifications in the ensuing hours. I wanted to include a gay-themed story that had the same effect on a reader and the haunted hotel-circuit party setting offered a logical and surreal backdrop to accomplish this. This story was one of the last stories I wrote for this collection, the idea crashing around in my head for a long while before I put in into words in the summer of 2008.

THE HAUNTED HEART

For many years I had wanted to write the story of an acquaintance of mine, whose first lover was a composer, and how he became involved with another man after his first lover's death. I hesitated writing this story for several reasons—one of which was the way commercial gay fiction was shifting away from AIDS-themed stories.

I must have read several hundred ghost stories as I tried to formulate a few guidelines for writing my own ghost story (and which, as I have discovered by writing additional ones, can change). For "The Haunted Heart" I wanted a ghost that did not speak (as opposed to the ghosts in Dickens's "A Christmas Carol," where they are all thoughtful chatterers). One of the first stumbling blocks to writing the story was also grappling with the issue of my own belief in ghosts. (For example, who can believe that there is such a thing as a chattering Marley.) Reading Fay Weldon's "Watching Me, Watching You," in which a ghost follows a couple through its divorce and several homes was instrumental in how I shaped the ghost of Raymond Hennegar. The story of my friend and his composer boyfriend began to surface, and Boston and Provincetown seemed logical settings because of their large gay communities, as well as their rich history (and tragedy).

The working title of the story was "The Peerless Troubador," in part, because early in my writing career, I had been told never to use the words "heart" or "love" in a story title, but in the end, I went with the title I felt was more accurate and evocative and always my instinctual first choice for the title.

I work-shopped the story with my writing group—they were instrumental in helping me figure out the final scenes—but the story was longer than many literary journals accepted for publication—so I held on to it before sending it to David Tullis to consider for his on-line literary journal *CreamDrops* (hoping its length might not be a deterrent—and it wasn't).

THE THEATER BUG

Having been a part of several summer houses shared by gay men, I decided to use this as a setting. Since many summer shares revolve around gay men working in similar professions, I decided to go with a theatrical house, in part because it was a familiar milieu to me, having worked and acted in the theater myself. I've always been in awe of how stories are elaborately told by gay men over the course of a dinner party and an old, hammy English actor seemed the perfect narrator to monopolize this re-telling of a murder and its impact on the narrator. The genesis for this story began with my reading M.R. James's "An Evening's Entertainment," which is a ghost story being told by a grandmother to her grandchildren around a fire at wintertime— and part of the gruesomeness of her tale—the swarm of flies congregating around old blood—made their imaginary flight into this story. I began writing this story in 2003 and returned to it in 2005, when I decided to heighten the individuality of the characters sharing the dinner together. The story was originally accepted by *Blithe House Quarterly*, and was to appear in the e-zine's final issue, but the journal folded before its last issue could be completed.

WAIT!

After reading several ghost story anthologies and encyclopedias, I decided that I wanted to write a gay version of "the phantom hitchhiker" legend and I began writing this story in 2002. I was never satisfied with the original ending I had created—I had the story end after Clay's first visit to Lisa Braden's house after his accident—and I let the story sit unfinished for several years. Then, in 2006, I realized that the story did not end with the initial scene at Lisa's house and that Clay's search should continue for many years, and that the phantoms Clay witnesses are not a random encounter or his own haunting, but belonged to Mack, the guy he had originally tried to pick up at the club. The story was finally polished and finished in the fall of 2008 and published in *Velvet Mafia*.

DEATH IN AMSTERDAM

This was another story that sat in my notebook unfinished for many years because I saw Brian's chase through Amsterdam in my mind but could never detail the back story. After the news of a gay editor's mugging in the city, the story began to take more shape, and while I was visiting Amsterdam in 2007, an encounter while walking through the Red- Light district propelled the story forward and into words.

THE VISION

This story was written in 2003 and was based on an article which I had read a few years before in the *Bay Area Reporter*, which detailed an obsessive and destructive relationship between a doctor and his patient. I had never intended to write this story as a "ghost story," but after reading the foreshadowing opening of Agatha Christie's story, "In A Glass Darkly," the conceit of Buddy witnessing his future took shape.

A TOUCH OF DARKNESS

This story stems from several inspirations: a love of haunted house stories, a desire to write a ghost story set in the Hamptons, where I had spent many summers since 1981 as a guest of friends or with ex-boyfriends, the history of the sodomy laws that were in existence in the area during the time of the early colonists, and the combative stance of organized religion against homosexuality. The means of bringing all these elements together arrived when I read an account of a haunting in *Haunted Cape Cod & The Islands* by Mark Jasper, a book of true ghost stories, about a woman who buys a Bible Box and an antique doll and how the resulting phantoms disrupted her home. This story was begun in the summer of 2008 and polished in early 2009.

THE MAN IN THE MIRROR

This story sat in my notebook unfinished for many years because it was always one of those stories I had finished "writing in my head" and did not find the time to "put it down on paper." Adrian Chase's doppelganger is the herald of his death. As I was putting together the stories that I would include in this collection, I knew it would offer a variety and distinction to the collection, and I finished writing it "on paper" in the summer of 2008. The story appeared in the inaugural issue of *Icarus*, Summer 2009, a new magazine devoted to gay speculative fiction and edited by Steve Berman.

THE BLOOMSBURY NUDES

In 1988, on the death of a close friend, I came into possession of several Bloomsbury artifacts—correspondence of Lytton Strachey, a sketch by Dora Carrington, and a drawing by Duncan Grant. I knew more of Virginia Woolf than I did of these other Bloomsbury folks, but over the course of many years more knowledge seeped in and my appreciation for these artists deepened. I had always been intrigued by Duncan Grant, an openly gay artist, and was particularly impressed by his nude sketches that I had seen in a catalog published by the Anthony d'Offay Gallery in London.

I learned more about these nude drawings through the writings of Douglas Blair Turnbaugh, particularly *Duncan Grant and the Bloomsbury Group*, published in 1987, as well as from the advent of the Internet and the exhibits and information on the artist available through the Leslie/Lohman Gallery in New York and Adonis Art of London. For years I had toyed with the idea of creating a fictional back story of the men who had posed for these sketches, and I researched quite a bit on who they might have been. When I sat down in 2007 to write this story, I was influenced by a lot of the horror anthologies I was reading at the time, and I decided it was apropos to have a young artist be one of Duncan Grant's nude models, and that's how I came to the character of Clive Elliot. It was during this writing process that I decided to overlap the influences of Aleister Crowley, another legendary British fellow whose life and career and writings had always intrigued me. In the story, Clive Elliott, Jared Tremaine, Bart Pearson, Roger Sage, and Teddy Rushton are all fictional characters and Crowley's link and association with the men of the Bloomsbury group is purely from my own speculation.

The story was originally included in the anthology *Unspeakable Horror: From the Shadows of the Closet*, edited by Vince A. Liaguno and Chad Helder, and published by Dark Scribe Press, which went on to win the Bram Stoker Award from the Horror Writers Association for Superior Achievement in an Anthology. Steve Berman also included the story in *Wilde Stories 2009: The Best of the Year's Gay Speculative Fiction.*

ACKNOWLEDGEMENTS

Once again, my special thanks and appreciation go to Anne H. Wood and Brian Keesling, who have continually read my work and offered me valuable advice on early drafts of these stories. For career support and guidance, thanks and gratitude also go to Arch Brown, Edward Iwanicki, Hermann Lademann, Kevin Bentley, Andrew McBeth, Steve Berman, and the New York Foundation for the Arts. Gratitude is also due Kevin Patterson and David Feinberg.

I am also grateful to the editors, publishers, readers, and fellow writers who helped shape these stories, particularly Barbara Roden, Christopher Roden, Steve Berman, David Olin Tullis, Richard Labonté, Sean Meriwether, Chip Livingston, Vince Liaguno, and Chad Helder. Special thanks are also due Lawrence Schimel, Greg Wharton, Ian Philips, Greg Herren, Paul Willis, Charles Flowers, Aldo Alvarez, David Groff, Michael Rowe, Jim Marks, Jonathan Harper, Tom Cardamone, Mark Sullivan, Wayne Hoffman, Toby Johnson, Tom Long, and Craig Gidney. I would also like to thank Richard Taddei for his painting which is used for the cover of this edition, and John Malloy for his graphic design assistance. And no thanks would be complete without those to my coworkers, among them Kathy Corey, Ellen Herb, and Edward Bohan, and to my friends Martin Gould, Larry Dumont, Jon Marans, Deborah Collins, John Maresca, Joel Byrd, Jonathan Miller, and Andrew Beierle.

ABOUT THE AUTHOR

Jameson Currier is the author of three novels: *Where the Rainbow Ends,* a Lambda Literary finalist, *The Wolf at the Door,* and *The Third Buddha;* and four collections of short fiction: *Dancing on the Moon;* *Desire, Lust, Passion, Sex; Still Dancing: New and Selected Stories;* and *The Haunted Heart and Other Tales,* which was awarded a Black Quill Award. His short fiction has appeared in many literary magazines and Web sites, including *Velvet Mafia, Blithe House Quarterly, Absinthe Literary Review, Rainbow Curve, Christopher Street, Harrington Gay Men's Fiction Quarterly,* and the anthologies *Best Gay Stories, Men on Men, Best American Gay Fiction, Rebel Yell, Mammoth Book of Gay Erotica, Best Gay Erotica, Best American Erotica, Circa 2000,* and *Making Literature Matter.* His ghost stories have also appeared in *Wilde Stories, Unspeakable Horror, Best Gay Romance, Best Gay Stories, Velvet Mafia, Icarus,* and *All Hallows: The Journal of the Ghost Story Society.* In 2010 he founded Chelsea Station Editions, an independent press devoted to gay literature, and the following year launched the literary journal *Chelsea Station.*

"Jameson Currier writes with venomous wit and a huge heart.
The Wolf at the Door is the tale everyone should be reading on the beach this year."
Lewis Whittington, *Edge*

The Wolf at the Door

a novel by Jameson Currier

When a death occurs at Le Petite Paradis, a guesthouse in the French Quarter of New Orleans, the spirit world becomes unsettled, or so Avery Greene Dalyrymple III, the co-owner believes. The son and grandson of Southern evangelists, Avery is also an overworked and overwrought middle-aged gay man, a cynical "big-time drinker and sinner" fairly certain he can maintain a family of "other deviants and delinquents stumbling along Bourbon Street" to keep him company. But Avery is also the only person in contact with the spirit world on his property—ghosts from the house's origins during the 1820s—and he must use the history left behind from another ghost—a gay man from the 1970s—to find a way to restore peace to his household and rejuvenate his faith.

"Currier is one of the few writers who can be equally literary, erotic, dramatic and damn funny, sometimes all in the same sentence."
Sean Meriwether, *The Silent Hustler*

"A delightfully spooky, often kooky, gay vision quest. Currier's Avery Dalyrymple is larger-than-life and intricately flawed, and the fact that he just can't seem to get out of his own way makes him primed for misadventure and gay mayhem. One of Currier's strengths has always been the ability to soak his narrative in a rich, authentic ambiance and *The Wolf at the Door* is no exception, with sentences that resonate with the decadent rhythms of the French Quarter and paragraphs that positively drip with Southern gothic moodiness. Genre fans will find plenty to appreciate in Currier's otherworldly version of *It's a Wonderful Life* fused with all the ensemble wit of *Tales of the City* and the regional gothic texture of Anne Rice's *Interview with the Vampire*. Savor this one like a bowlful of spicy jambalaya and a snifter of fine aged bourbon on a hot, humid night."
Vince Liaguno, *Dark Scribe Magazine*

"Marvelous! Currier's writing is up to his usually high standards, which means that he can make you smile and scare the crap out of you in the same paragraph. And I believe his work here to be his richest, most personal and heartfelt yet. More than being a good ghost story, *The Wolf at the Door* is one gay man's spiritual journey. Though he's been looking mostly in the bottom of bourbon bottles, Avery's search for spiritual belonging – finding God in ghosts – is as universal as it gets, and Currier brings it to life with both wit and wonderment. Blending philosophy with good old-fashioned scares, Currier makes the impossible look effortless. The ending, which I won't spoil for you, actually brought a catch to my throat and a tear to my eye."
Jerry Wheeler, *Out in Print*

"A masterful blend of genres that comes together like succulent literary gumbo. Currier's crew of querulous aging queens, offbeat beautiful boys and assorted oddball friends constitute an endearing found family of queers, while the author's historical flashbacks conjure the Big Easy's atmospheric past."
Richard Labonté, *Bookmarks*

2011 Gaylactic Spectrum Award:
Short List for Best Novel

ISBN: 978-0-9844707-0-9
282 pages, paperback, $16

www.chelseastationeditions.com
info@chelseastationeditions.com